On the Dock

A Tale of Grand Lake

Susan Vineyard

Printed in the United States of America
First Printing 2015
E-book: ISBN: 978-0-9864030-0-2
ISBN-13: 978-0692361542
ISBN-10: 0692361545

Westie Publishing
Http;//westiepublishing.com
info@westiepublishing.com
Tulsa, OK 74114

DEDICATION

To my husband, Dan and my son, Jon, who believe in me, and to all those who have read my manuscript and encouraged me to publish this book. I couldn't have done it without you all.

DISCLAIMER

TABLE OF CONTENTS

1 Abandoned

She wiped her sweaty palms on the seat of her shorts. The sliding door into the cabin of the abandoned boat was partly open. All she could see through the crack was darkness.

The wooden deck creaked beneath her feet. Goosebumps prickled her arms and a shiver raced down her spine, despite the oppressive heat.

Hadley sucked in her breath as she nudged the door of the cabin the rest of the way open with her foot and squinted into the gloom. She wondered what kinds of spiders and other disgusting creatures thrived in shadowy, deserted places like this.

But she could do it. She would do it. And she'd be OK. Because nothing else could possibly go wrong after this hell week. Surely, she'd used up her share of bad luck. OK. She sucked in her breath as she took a step into the shadows, feeling her way down the steps. One more step.

"Are you Hadley?" A deep voice echoed from the darkness.

Choking back a shriek, she scrambled backwards and upwards into the light.

What now? The muscles in her legs tightened. Her body wanted to run. She glanced over her shoulder, hoping someone was around who could help her. No. A quick look up and down the dock convinced her that she was on her own.

Merde. Run or stay? She gritted her teeth and calmed her breathing. She just didn't have time for this kind of nonsense. Whoever was in the boat had better have a damn good excuse for being in there!

"*Oui.* I am Hadley." She steadied her voice. "But who are you, *Monsieur*, and why are you on my boat?"

Heavy footsteps echoed inside the cabin. She stood as tall as she could for such a tiny person, crossed her arms, and lifted her chin.

Her mother would have been able to intimidate a trespasser, and Natalie hadn't been any bigger than her daughter. Hadley tapped her toe and stared narrowly at the man emerging from the darkness and mounting the steps toward her.

The golden streaks in his eyes, partly obscured by a strand of dark hair, glittered as the sunlight hit them. Smoldering tiger eyes, dangerous and angry, glared at her, before a deliberate blandness wiped the man's expression and a strained smile tightened his lips.

She didn't take her eyes off him, for more than one reason. Interesting. Not too bad.

The man stuffed a small flashlight into his rear jeans pocket and looked back at her, his demeanor now mildly friendly.

Dark stubble covered his square jaw and dark hair tumbled over the collar of his unbuttoned white shirt.

Humm... Tall, wide shoulders, a rather magnificent creature, exotic even.

She struggled not to let her thoughts show on her face. He might be a babe, but she would handle him carefully. After all, exotic animals often could not be entirely trusted.

"I'm Zane Bowman."

When he thrust his hand toward her, she offered her own, tensing her arm and fingers to give a firm handshake. What a waste of effort. Her tiny hand seemed lost in his big paw.

Her eyes traveled up his arm. His open shirt revealed an amber pendant dangling from a leather cord. Her senses spun for a moment before she jerked her mind back to her immediate problems.

Yesterday, her mother had been buried. What kind of daughter was she to be distracted by a man today? But Mère would have done the same. Beautiful men had been Hadley's mother's hobby. That woman had toyed with males the way a cat plays with a mouse. She would have been in her element in this situation.

And she had taught her daughter well. Yes, Hadley could handle this country boy. In fact, the idea of handling him brought a slight smile to her lips.

She shook her head, pushed her short dark curls out of her green eyes and scowled. Hot or not, why was he trespassing on her property?

"Again, you are here why, Monsieur?" She pointed to the open cabin door, held his gaze and waited for his explanation.

"Bob, up there at the marina office, told me you need help fixing up your boat to sell," the man drawled.

"You work here?" She tried not to sneer as she shot a glance down the length of the faded dock. He worked at this place? Then her eyes swept the dirty, spider-spotted windows of her boat. Who was she to judge?

3

Zane nodded, then ducked his head a little as he looked out at her from underneath his straight, dark brows. He took a breath that flared his nostrils, then arched one eyebrow. Ball in her court.

She had to think fast. He was offering to help her? Relief washed through her, but only for a second. She was not a woman who needed a man to help her!

But could she, realistically, do what needed to be done, to this dusty, shabby old wooden yacht herself? She took a deep breath. This guy, Zane, worked on boats. The manager at the marina had told him about her. He was sexy as hell. He wanted to help her. Why not?

She bit her lip. She had to do something with her stupid boat. And all she wanted was to just go home.

Maybe Zane could help her figure out how to sell this old albatross. Anything it took to get out of here. To never see Grand Lake, Oklahoma again. *Définitivement fini.*

Hum. She'd be hiring him. That wasn't exactly accepting help from a man, was it? OK. She smiled up at him.

"*Oui*, actually, I do need someone to work on this boat. So yes. Let's see if we can do business."

2 Spiders and Hummingbirds

"I've been making some notes here about things that need fixed." The small notebook he handed her was turned to a page of scribbles. Hadley scanned down it in dismay. The list wasn't very long, but she frankly didn't understand what most of it meant.

She rubbed her eyes. This boat belonged to her, but why would she ever want to know about all that stuff he had written down? She had never wanted to own a boat. She could craft a necklace better than anyone, but fix a boat? No thanks!

She handed the list back, peering up at him. "*Excusez-moi*, but I haven't been on this boat for years. Could you go over this list with me?"

"I'll tell you what." Zane pointed upwards. "Let's start up there on top. Haven't looked over the fly bridge yet."

He paused, looking from her to the upper fly deck. "Not sure how good that old ladder is. Let me go up first and you follow me, OK?" He started up.

Hadley eyed the rickety ladder. "OK. If you don't break it, I'll be right behind you."

She carefully placed her sandaled foot on the bottom wooden rung. Reaching up for the handrail, her eyes focused on what was right in front of her eyes. She didn't suppress her smile this time.

Oh Mère, I wish you were here with me! Zane's tight faded jeans molded to his firm derriere. Her mind was wandering again. *Down girl!*

Or not. Every day was a gift. This last week had slapped her in the face with that fact. And that she should make the most of each and every minute. Besides, Mère would have definitely appreciated the view if she'd been here. Her mother had been incorrigible, but also the most alive person Hadley had ever known.

She stepped up onto the fly deck and slowly turned around to survey the view. From down below, the top of the dock had seemed a long way up, but she could make out all the details of its corrugated metal underside now. Including the spider webs dangling down, just outside the fly bridge window.

A particularly large squishy specimen revolved on a tendril of web just on the other side of the window, repelling down toward the top of the boat in the next slip. She couldn't take her eyes off of it.

"Why, why are there so many spiders, Zane?" Shuddering, Hadley brushed at her arms as she watched the creepy crawler. Oh how she needed a shower. She hated this dirty, hot, stinking dock.

Zane reached around her to slide open the window, the only barrier between her and the spider. Hadley took a quick step backwards, and bumped into a solid hunk of flesh.

Spider or man? She froze, trying to decide. He chuckled and she chose the spider, stepping toward the open window, away from him.

"Always spiders around marinas. Lots for 'em to snack on here. And that's not a bad thing. If you get rid of the spiders, the mosquitoes and other bugs'll eat you alive. Anyway, the hummingbirds need spider webs to build their nests."

He was still so close to her that she could feel the heat of his body. He pointed upward, over her shoulder. "Look up there."

She squinted out the open back of the boat, searching in the direction he was pointing. All she saw was a chunk of dried mud with feathers sticking out here and there. The glob was molded around an electric wire, stung loosely from pole to pole, in the slip across the walkway.

"It's moving. No…" She leaned forward to see better. "Oh! A bird!" A little brown creature hopped out of the nest and flew away.

"A Hummingbird?" She turned to Zane. "My grandmother in Tulsa had a hummingbird feeder. But we don't have hummingbirds in France, you know."

"Huh. No Hummingbirds?"

"Before Mère and I moved to Paris, when I was really little, I thought they were fairies flying so fast that they were just blurs of color. But that one is just brown."

"The pretty ones are the males. Females are brown. True of most birds."

"Oh, of course. I should have known that. Poor little mama bird, all brown and plain, stuck home taking care of the babies. But why do they use spider webs to build their nests?"

She was babbling. She sounded like an idiot. Her brain was just not working, with all that had happened. And she needed a shower, air conditioning and a drink.

7

"The webs stretch. So when the babies get bigger, the nest stretches out and they'll all fit in. And trust me, she doesn't want the dad around now. Hummingbirds don't much like company. No love affairs for them, I'm afraid."

"No love affairs? I wouldn't want to be a hummingbird then." She laughed. "But at least they can take care of themselves and don't need any help. They're not just flitting fairies after all."

Zane shook his head and turned back to the gauges in the helm with a scowl. "But we need to figure out what needs to be done to your boat so we can get you back to Paris, Hadley." She watched Zane fiddle with some wires. What was wrong with him? She was trying to be nice.

"When old Bob heard that you were comin' down here today, he had the guys de-winterize the boat." He glanced over his shoulder at her, still frowning. "Seems your mother had this old thing pretty well taken care of for the last ten years."

This country handyman might not approve of her, but he seemed to know a lot about this boat. More than she did. Maybe he knew something about Mère's accident. The details she's been told were rather vague.

She needed to find out more. Besides deciding what to do with the boat, trying to get the bottom of what had happened to her mother was the real thing keeping Hadley here.

Zane patted the helm. "Bob said she started right up yesterday, but I need to check 'er out for m'self."

He pulled a key from his pocket. "He gave me your keys. Let's see what the motors sound like."

Well, it seemed he'd taken charge even before she'd arrived. A shiver ran down her spine as she remembered the anger in his eyes when she'd first discovered him on the boat. Was she right to trust him?

Settling himself in the captain's seat, Zane started pulling knobs and pushing levers. With a little cranking, he started one motor and then the other.

He thumped a gauge, and its needle sprang to life. He smiled the smug, satisfied smile of a man interacting with a well-behaved machine. Hadley leaned backwards against the rail, watching him.

"The instruments look to be in working order." He yelled to be heard over the roar of the twin diesels.

He adjusted a lever, reducing the roar to a purr, then reached out and caressed the helm tenderly. He treated the boat almost like a woman. Interesting.

So if he knew so much about this boat's history, how much did he know about her family? After all, they'd always owned it.

She had to start somewhere if she was going to get to the bottom of the story. Hadley took a couple steps over to where Zane sat. Standing close to him, she turned and looked out of the window.

"Daddy died ten years ago, so I guess this boat's just been sitting here all that time." She could feel his gaze on her. "I'm sorry I couldn't have given the marina more notice," she prompted.

She ran her finger through the dust on the windshield, leaving a streak. "I just found out that Mère still owned it yesterday, after her funeral." She pushed down the feeling of nausea that had plagued her ever since the doctor had called to inform her of her mother's death.

She wiped her dirty finger on her khaki shorts. Struggling to hold back her tears, she turned to Zane.

"I thought it'd been sold after Daddy was gone."

Was that pity in his eyes? He didn't say a word. Just sat there looking at her like that. Well, he wasn't going to tell her anything useful and now she was about to cry, thinking about it all.

Hadley abruptly turned away from him. Kneeling, she jerked open a cabinet door, hiding her face. She poked through the life jackets piled inside. He would not see the tear that escaped despite all her efforts to hold it back.

This old boat had only been a shadowy memory for so many years. But now it was real again. She could almost feel Mère and Daddy still here, and she felt eight years old.

Memories engulfed her, memories of lazy weekends, of a magical time when she'd still believed in true love and family. That time before her parents' marriage and her childhood had disintegrated.

But all that was over. Gone. Hadley knew the truth about love now. Mère had made sure she knew. And somebody here in Oklahoma was not telling her the truth about how her mother had died.

The hairs on the back of her neck prickled. She knew he was watching her.

3 French Women

Zane checked one last instrument before he shut down the motors and glanced back over at Hadley.

She'd been rummaging around in the cabinet, her eyes lowered under her dark bangs. Her eyelashes swept over her cheeks. A tear had left a streak in the dust on her face.

His jaw tightened. Women and crying. Geez.

Everyone lost a mother, sooner or later. Hadley would figure that out. He had.

He yanked the key out of the ignition, and stifled the stab of grief that tried to surface inside of him.

He didn't cry for his Mom. He hadn't then and he didn't now. Maybe he wished he'd done a few things differently when he was a kid, but she had known. He had made sure that she had known how much he loved her before she had died. *Shit.*

His eyes slid back to Hadley. Despite his determination, despite her tear, his body hummed in awareness of this girl.

No way. Just get that nonsense out of your damn head, Bowman.

He stuck his hands into his blue jean pockets, staring out across the lake. What was the fastest way he could get this chick out of his life, out of his father's life? She just needed to go.

He rolled his head on his shoulders, trying to relieve the tightness. Dad had promised her mother that Hadley would never know until the time was right. He glanced back down at her.

Sweetheart, I'm sorry, but the time will never be right now.

Barrington women were only trouble for him and his dad. Well, her mother wasn't any more, but he'd breathe easier when Hadley was gone too.

Damn foreign women. He pulled the notebook out of his pocket and checked the next item on his list. Dad'd gotten them into this mess it was up to Zane to get them out of it.

Hadley stood up and shut the cabinet door. No trace of tears now. She turned to gaze out the back of the boat. The mother hummingbird was returning to her nest.

It was really best that she never know the whole story. She'd sell the boat, her one link to this lake, and go back where she belonged. Everything would return to normal. His dad was convinced that was the best thing for everyone.

A rogue breeze blew Hadley's hair back, revealing her sculpted face and parted lips. Then her curls settled damply again as the breeze gave way to hot, humid calm.

Her eyes dropped as if she was avoiding his gaze as she turned toward him. As he stood there watching her, hands in pockets, she once again raised her sad eyes to his. His heart skipped a beat.

Yep. It was best for Zane and his dad, and best for Hadley too. Better that she get out of here quickly. She didn't want this boat and she didn't belong here. So it was time to get this thing done.

"All through up here!" He motioned for her to descend the ladder.

Back down on deck, Hadley lifted a canvas cover, and peeked down into what would have been her parents' bedroom when they'd stayed on the boat.

"This is the hatch to the master berth, isn't it?"

"Yeah." And her father's love nest after his wife and daughter had left, according to his Dad.

Zane rolled his eyes. All those Barringtons were alike. His father had told him the whole story after Hadley's mother had just showed up, disrupting their quiet lives.

Now here he stood, hands in his jeans pockets, shoulders hunched forward, watching the dead woman's daughter through narrowed eyes.

She looked just like Natalie, especially in the old pictures he'd seen of her. She was different though, softer, though she obviously tried not to be.

Oh Geez. He really had to watch himself. He knew better. She wasn't even an American anymore. She sounded like one of those foreigners, with her Euro-trash accent. Even worse than her mom.

Of course, Natalie had lived here a lot longer before going over there and getting all Frenchified.

Hadley sniffed, then smiled bravely, although he suspected the sparkle in her sad eyes was caused by unshed tears.

Standing up and walking over to the rail, she stared out at the water for a moment, where the light and shadow played across the surface of the lake. The fish created their own circular wakes, snapping at bugs skimming above them.

13

How different was this scene, so familiar to him, from what she was used to in her far-away world, her home?

Quit it! He scolded himself, turning and walking over to examine a discolored spot in the wood. He poked at it to see if it was soft or rotten. No. It seemed OK.

He felt Hadley's presence behind him through the hairs on his neck.

"I'm not sure what Mère would want me to do." Her voice was very soft. "I'll try to find someone who wants this boat. I guess I owe it, or her, that much. I don't know what else to do." She put her little hand on his shoulder and he froze.

"What would happen if I didn't fix it up, Zane? What if I just walked away from here and got on a plane back to Paris? What are my options?" She moved to lean against the cabin wall beside him, her eyes on his face.

He slowly turned toward her. Here was a test. She'd asked the question. How would she like the answer?

"You could always sell it to be parted out."

"Parted out? What does that mean?" She concentrated her gaze on him with a slight frown.

"It's got lots of stuff on it with some value, stuff that somebody could use to fix up another old boat. The motors are good. Somebody'd tear them out, then they'd probably burn the carcass."

"Burn it? Burn my BOAT?" She gasped, standing up straight, her hands on her hips. "I don't think so."

He shrugged, and turned back to examine another spot in the wood. She hadn't jumped at the easy way out. He gave her that.

Too bad. He'd never let this classic boat be burned, anyway, but she didn't know that.

Now just go away little girl and let me fix the damn boat. Go home, Hadley.

"So, do you think anyone would want to buy it, my boat?" She moved closer to see what he was doing. "Is it worth anything?"

He stared at the wood to avoid looking at her, sighing and rubbing his face.

"Maybe. You never know. I need to look at the condition of the wood of the hull down below now."

When he headed for the ladder to climb down to the dock, she followed him.

"I was turning your inside electricity on at the box when you showed up. The cabin lights should work now. While I'm down there, I'll fill up the water tank so there'll be running water while I'm working here, if you don't mind."

She climbed down after him. Kept following him around like a damn puppy. Down on the dock, he picked up a garden hose attached to a rusty faucet that stuck out of a rough hole cut in the wood planking, and dragged it back over to the boat.

Hadley was right behind him. Her scent clouded his mind. He needed to finish what he'd come to do and get out of here.

She was watching his every move, and he was trying to keep his eyes off of her. The June day was so friggin' hot. No breeze down here. He could barely breathe. Her shirt clung to her body where she was sweating.

Huh. Even fancy women from Paris sweat on an Oklahoma summer day.

Somehow that observation gave him a feeling of inner satisfaction as he thrust the hose into the empty water tank.

"Let me do it." Hadley reached for the hose.

She'd want to get her pretty hands dirty? Well, why not, if that's what she wanted? He had other matters to take care of anyway.

She wrapped her dainty hands around the hose next to his big tanned hand. The contrast was startling, and he stared at the two hands a second before he let her take charge of the gushing hose.

As he walked around the boat, he checked the angle of the sun to the horizon. He closed his eyes and rubbed his forehead as his thoughts strayed to his father.

It was almost the Fourth of July. That's when he'd light the amber fire for his mom. He and his dad hadn't been able to do it for her on St. John's Day.

They'd been in Tulsa with Natalie, and then she'd died. The first year his mom was gone and her son and husband hadn't done what they'd promised because of another woman. He would make it up to her and so would his Dad, now that that woman was dead.

He glanced over at Hadley. She peeped at him sideways through her bangs as she reached up and wiped moisture from her hairline.

Then she used one hand to splash water on her face. The water dripped down and soaked her white shirt and wet her short dark hair where it framed her face, turning her waves to ringlets.

"Ah, that feels better." Her eyes closed, and a sensuous smile softened her face. Zane, leaning against the dock pole, realized he was staring at her and stood straight. But before he could turn, Hadley held out the hose out to him.

"I think the tank's full." She smiled. Then she swung her wet head around, sending water droplets into the air.

Get a grip, Bowman! Why does she have to have dimples? He reached down to turn off the faucet. Clearly, it was time to leave. Do his damn job and get going.

"Wood down here looks OK. I need to finish up there." Zane nodded toward the deck above them and motioned for her to climb back up the ladder. Following her up, he instinctively reached out to boost her delicate body up the first step.

His big hands almost encircled her tiny waist. Her lightness surprised him, as she relaxed into his grip as if she had been expecting it.

She was clearly used to men touching her. And she liked it too. He could tell.

Well, little girl, I'm not one of those French men you and your mom twist around your fingers. I'm a Grand Lake, Oklahoma, USA guy and my plans don't have anything to do with you.

But telling himself that didn't quite work. His body reacted to the knowledge that she enjoyed his hands touching her. He stood there on the ladder, clutching the rail, gaining control.

From up on deck, Hadley glanced back at him with a quick grin as he paused there.

"I'll be inside." she informed him. "Waiting for you."

4 Breakdown

Hadley flipped on the lights as she entered the cabin. If any of the creepy crawly creatures in here were still alive, at least now she'd be able to see them before they slipped up on her. The furniture was covered in cracked, yellowed plastic and, of course, dead bugs and filth.

When she heard footsteps on the deck, she turned toward the open door. Zane stood there, paused in the doorway, casually leaning inward, his hands on the door frame.

"Yup. Needs some work." He grimaced, glancing around at the mess. When he ducked his head to enter, all expression left his eyes. He pushed up his sleeves and headed toward a closet in the hall, determination written all over his face.

He didn't look like he'd be easy to talk to right now. But Hadley had to know if that man knew anything about her mother's accident. She would get it out of him, she was sure, sooner or later.

But for now, she had a boat to clean. While Zane examined panels and batteries and the hot water heater, Hadley turned on the tap in the kitchen sink.

Foul smelling pink liquid squirted out, as a disgustingly sweet smell permeated the cabin. And that man was behind her. She could feel him there. He peered around her and snickered.

"Antifreeze." He threw the comment over his shoulder as he turned away. "Keeps the pipes from freezing when the boat's winterized. Let it run." The water gurgled as the air trapped in the pipes escaped with small noisy explosions, but the stream finally started to run clear.

Hadley wrinkled her nose as she looked around the galley. What a filthy place. Where to start?

She turned the tap to hot, but only cold water came out. She started rummaging through the cabinets.

Her favorite thing. Cleaning. Cleaning a boat she didn't want. On a summer day. At the lake.

A person had to make the best use of all of their time. After all, life didn't last forever. Mère had lived every day to its fullest and she had taught her daughter to do that too. How she would have laughed at Hadley in here cleaning this dirty boat. But it was her fault.

Nausea washed over Hadley again, and she leaned against the wall as it passed. Her mother's life was really over. Not fair. Not fair that a woman who had loved life so much had died so young. Not fair when her daughter still needed her.

Every minute counted. And spending time on this boat and in Oklahoma was not what Hadley wanted to be doing, now or ever. As she searched for cleaning supplies, she forced her emotions back. No time for that now. She'd deal with her grief when she got home.

Home sounded so good. She needed to get home. So why was she still here? Why shouldn't she just walk out the door, get in her car and drive to the airport right now?

Because she had to do something with the boat. Because she had to find out what really happened to Mère. What she knew now just didn't make sense. Something was missing in the story she'd been told. Someone was not telling everything they knew. Why?

Ah. A sponge, old, but still in its wrapper, in the drawer by the sink. And a half empty bottle of dish soap, almost dried up. She opened up the cap, added water from the tap and shook it up.

The cabinet top was filthy and gritty but she started scrubbing, determined to make a difference. Drops of sweat stung her eyes.

"It's stifling in here," she called out. "Does the air conditioner work?"

"I'll check that next. I turned the hot water heater on. Why don't you run water in the bathrooms to rinse out those pipes?"

Bossy asshole. But I guess it needs done. Sure enough, the facets and showers in both bathrooms spit out stinky pink water and air bursts.

Hadley emerged from the stateroom bath to see Zane, pushing the power button on the old air conditioner.

Please, please work, she silently begged the contraption. Gritty sweat rolled down her back.

The motor chugged to life, slowly at first. Then it seemed to gain strength. The noise emitting from the old system grew louder and somehow—crunchier.

But instead of clean, cold air, clouds of dust and bits of bug whooshed out, billowing through the cabin and engulfing Hadley. Coughing and gasping, eyes squeezed tight, she stumbled toward the open door, Zane, right behind her.

Blindly, she felt her way outside, then hurled herself sideways. She collapsed, sliding down the side of the wooden cabin, hacking the nasty mixture from her lungs and rubbing her running eyes.

"Sorry 'bout that." Zane coughed the words out, but Hadley couldn't answer. Her legs were splayed, her body slumped, her strength gone.

What a hell week. The tears streaming down her face may have been from grief or fatigue or just dust. She really didn't know.

What did she look like now, dirty and damp, bawling like a baby, flopped like a rag doll? No one from home would recognize her. And if they did, they'd pretend they didn't.

Almost hysterical laughter bubbled up to choke off her sobs. She wrapped her arms around her middle and laughed so hard her gut hurt.

"You OK?" Zane leaned against the wooden cabin, regaining his own composure and staring down at her. As he pushed his hair back out of his face, she nodded her head and stifled her laughter enough to sit up and wipe her eyes.

Zane reached down. She grabbed his hand, snuffling, as he pulled her to her feet. She struggled to gain her balance, looking up. Her awareness narrowed to those eyes and her hand still engulfed in his.

Yeah. This man, even as disheveled as he looked right now, was eye candy. But he was also strong and kind. She liked him, and was glad he'd showed up to help her. She was so alone and so far from home.

Zane dropped her hand. Reluctantly? He turned to peek into the salon.

"I think it's safe in there, now. Dust's settled enough to go back in." Was he suppressing a grin?

Inside, the air conditioner still ran. It seemed to have discharged everything it had gathered through the years, depositing even more nastiness on every exposed surface. But the air was no longer murky and was cooling off.

Hadley moved closer and turned her back to the machine, holding her short hair up from the nape of her neck. The cold air dried the sweat and made her feel cooler all over.

On the other side of the room, Zane pulled up a hatch that had been hidden under dirty carpet. As he directed his flashlight around the shadowy compartment, she could barely make out large pieces of equipment, motors or pumps or something, she supposed, crowded into the small space.

Leaving him to his mechanical exploration, Hadley headed back to the bathroom that opened into her childhood stateroom.

She quickly scrubbed the years of grime off the fixtures. Then, securely locking the door, she pulled off her grubby clothes and threw them into a pile.

The water should be at least warm by now. Yes, it felt perfect and was no longer pink, but she'd better make this fast. She stepped into the tiny shower. The clean spray washed away the grime and bug parts stuck to her sweaty skin.

She'd grabbed soap and shampoo from her bag, so she quickly soaped and turned to let the now cooling water hit every inch of her body as it rinsed the grit down the drain. The room was a cloud of wonderful girly smells.

She dried herself briskly with a towel she'd been smart enough to throw in, promising herself she'd take it back to that hotel when she passed through Tulsa again.

She pulled an oversized, filmy shirt on over a camisole and clean shorts, bent over from the waist to brush her hair upside down, then peeked into the mirror. She looked more like herself again.

Walking quietly back out onto the deck, she tiptoed around the gaping hole in the floor. She didn't want to disturb Zane down there. He must be fixing something with all those clanks and bangs.

Outside, Hadley unfolded an old metal and canvas deck chair, and shook it out over the side of the boat. She sat down carefully, making sure it wouldn't collapse, and looked around.

The cry of a gull faded away, leaving only quietness. A lot of boats must be out. Lots of slips were empty. Might get a little livelier tonight when everyone came back in.

Hadley leaned back with a sigh, just as Zane emerged from the salon, and stopped in front of her, scribbling something down on his list.

"Thank you for getting my water and lights working." Hadley circled her head with her arms in the high-backed chair. "As soon as I pick up some supplies in town, I'll be able to really start cleaning, and, as you can see, I've already used the shower!" She stretched out her arms to show off her clean self.

"You're going stay on the boat, and clean it yourself?" Zane's eyebrows shot up.

"I must leave as soon as possible, but it looks like I need to stay a few days. Inside definitely needs work, like you said. No one will want to buy a boat this dirty and uncared for, and no one is going to burn it."

She watched him carefully to see how he reacted to her next statement.

"And I need to find out how Mère was injured. I don't think I know the whole story about that yet."

A strange expression played across Zane's face before he shrugged and walked over to gather up some equipment piled on the deck.

Hadley sank father down into her chair. Was he surprised that she was staying on the boat? Or that she was looking for answers about Mère's injury? He was a local. Surely he'd heard something, but he sure wasn't telling her anything.

He seemed a little prickly, but she'd get more chances to see what he knew. She'd be here for a few days, at least, although she didn't want to be.

How could she have anticipated all of the things that had been neglected over the years? *Tant pis!* She hadn't even KNOWN she'd had this boat problem until yesterday. She pulled out her phone and checked her calendar.

How many emails did she have? Well, no time to answer them right now. She'd have to at least read the ones from her assistant later.

Hadley needed to get back to Paris in one week. Max. New gems she'd purchased at the show would be arriving any day, and she couldn't wait to get back to her studio. Her customers always anticipated her new line of jewelry. Even a week more spent away from home and her career was too long.

She needed to think. Her head hurt. When she'd checked her phone she'd noticed that Paris was 20 degrees cooler today. She already needed another shower, but she had a lot to do before she could rest.

5 No Wake Zone

Her legs were crossed and her elbows were propped on slender knees. Her chin rested on her hands. Her green eyes peered up at him through dark lashes.

Zane had just assumed that she'd hire someone to take care of all the dirty work. But there she sat, diamonds and gems gleaming from her bracelets. Even dressed in casual shorts, she was elegant. And she planned to stay on the boat and clean it herself. Huh.

"So, was the water hot yet?"

"Warmish, but it got me clean. Thanks for getting everything turned on."

That dimple again. This girl just didn't smell or act like the other girls he knew. She was different, somehow. Different, but not better he quickly reminded himself. And that darned little French accent got under his skin.

Zane didn't want anything from Hadley. Except to see her leave. But for now he had to work with her. That was part of the deal with his dad. He'd promised.

And that, he told himself firmly, was the one and only reason he was here. But before he could leave, he had one more thing to do. He had to close the deal. Shit.

"You know, with a little work, this old boat would be worth quite a bit of money." Zane cleared his throat. Next came the hard part.

"So I can get you an estimate tomorrow on how much the renovations would cost." He turned away from her and looked out over the water.

People usually begged him to work on their boats. He wasn't used to haggling about money. If he didn't love his dad so much he wouldn't even be here now.

Silence. He glanced over his shoulder at her. She just sat there, staring into the distance. He walked over to the rail and leaned over it, looking at the ripples in the water below. Must be a fish down there.

The silence stretched on. Why didn't she answer him? Just for his dad, he'd give her one more chance. Then he was out of here. He turned back to face her.

"OK. Should I come by tomorrow to give you an estimate?" As he brushed back his hair from his broad forehead, Hadley rose slowly from the chair.

"*Oui*, Zane. *Merci bien.* Tomorrow, then?"

He nodded curtly. *Deal done, Dad.*

Since Hadley needed to run into town, she grabbed her purse and her keys and tagged along as Zane walked down the dock toward where her rental car was parked.

He surprised her by stopping at the courtesy dock, where boats that didn't have a slip at the Marina could tie up temporarily. She expected him to continue up to the parking lot by the marina shop. She'd just assumed that he probably had an old work truck parked up there.

He turned to her.

"I'll be back in the morning."

She could swear that the look Zane gave her wasn't a result of thinking about boat repairs. As his gaze raked her body from head to toe, appraisingly, a warm sensation pulsed through her. He turned and headed down the dock.

She stood watching the muscles in his broad back flexing under his white shirt. His hair lifted slightly with each step. So he had obviously come in a boat, not in a truck.

She wondered idly what kind of boat he owned. Probably that old metal fishing boat tied up half way down the dock, where a Labrador Retriever patiently awaited his master. Sure enough, he stopped to pat the dog on the head.

Then Zane straightened, strode down to the end, and jumped into a classic wooden runabout, long and low, beautifully maintained, and sleek as a seal. An expensive boat if she'd ever seen one.

Casting off the ropes, he cranked the engines, sending sprays of water churning from the twin pipes in the wooden transom.

He idled past the no-wake zone. Then the boat lurched ahead like a wild creature, racing out into the lake. The tiny craft leapt out of the water as it crested a wave, and quickly disappeared around the headland.

Hadley stood there, staring at the place where the boat had disappeared. She wondered if whoever owned it knew the Zane was running around the lake in his boat.

6 Old Whiskey Road

Hadley's rented convertible roared down Old Whiskey Road toward the grubby lakeside town. If only she could just keep driving and never return to Grand Lake and that stupid boat. But she couldn't, and Zane would be by in the morning with an estimate.

She would set a plan in place before she headed back to Paris. She'd do that much for the boat, and for Mère. She'd see that her family's old boat found a good home, since it had meant enough to Mère to keep it all these years. At least she'd try her best.

And Zane. There was more to that man than met the eye. And the part that met the eye was *très tentant,* very tempting.

Her hair swept back as the wind cooled her face. Surely sunset would dispel some of the heat.

Hadley had traveled this road with her father years ago. What was that old story he'd told her about bootleggers who used to smuggle whiskey into Oklahoma? *No matter. Ancient history.*

The trees overhanging the road were silhouettes against the sun as she sped under them. Small houses sat scattered along either side of the patched blacktop road.

Cows grazed in the pastures, and tractors sat idle, only partially visible in the gloom of dilapidated sheds. Dogs slept wherever they could find shade.

Shadows stretched out. It had been a long day, but all Oklahoma days were long this time of the year.

Off to her left, she occasionally caught sight of another road. It ran along the cliff that bordered Grand Lake. Quick glimpses of cobalt water reflecting an equally cobalt sky flashed between the expensive houses.

Many of those homes had fantastic views of the old dam, she remembered. The biggest of its kind in the world, wasn't it? Kind of strange to think that the biggest of anything could be found out here in dusty eastern Oklahoma. Strange that she even remembered this stuff from her childhood.

In town, Hadley stocked up on food and a few cleaning supplies at the crowded chain store. At a hole-in-the-wall liquor shop down the street, she lingered over bottles from a local winery.

America made wine? Why, when there was French wine? And why did they only sell it in special stores here? In Paris, she could pick up a bottle in the corner market. Or a glass at McDonalds for that matter.

Well, she wouldn't be hanging around long enough for any of that to even matter. She had to concentrate on the boat, on what had really happened to Mère, and on how to get home quickly.

She pulled into the gravel parking lot back at the marina just as the sun was setting. She gathered all of the plunder she'd bought in town into her arms and started down the rustic walkway leading from the shore to the dock.

Ever moving reflections rippled across the edge of the lake and across the weathered boards beneath her feet. The water lapped lazily against the grassy shoreline, dragging a willow tree's long, leafy tendrils back and forth rhythmically, first toward the shore, then back out toward the dock and the bay.

Shadows and reflections of the setting sun intersected and interacted in almost hypnotizing patterns. Colored fire flashed from the gems in the bracelet on Hadley's bare arm.

She carefully navigated the worn boards of the dock, watching where she stepped. Through the thin soles of her sandals, a Caribbean beat throbbed. Where was that coming from?

Next to her slip, an opulent houseboat had pulled in while she was gone. On the deck, a tanned blonde-haired man, muscled as some wild cat, slouched in a deck chair, checking out her every move. Fascinated, Hadley watched the silvery hair on his sculptured chest blowing softly in the breeze.

The music blasted from large speakers behind him. Did the leopard man's heart pound to that beat as well? She couldn't help but wonder and smile at the thought.

A tanned, buxom woman in an animal print bikini emerged from the cabin of the sleek houseboat. Slinking forward, she casually placed a well-manicured hand possessively on the younger man's shoulder, her eyes on Hadley.

"Want another drink, Baby?" she purred into the man's ear through pouty lips, pushing back her red hair as she scrutinized Hadley with an experienced eye. Hadley flashed a bright smile at them both. They looked like people she could relate to.

"*Bonjour!* I'm Hadley Barrington. Looks like we're neighbors!" She pointed to her dusty, faded possession. "That's my boat!" The couple on the houseboat exchanged meaningful looks.

"Know anyone who'd like to buy her?" Hadley continued the friendly, one-sided conversation, wrinkling her nose in acknowledgement of the condition of her once beautiful vessel.

"I know some people who'd like to sink that old ghost ship," muttered the redhead. Hadley was pretty sure she wasn't supposed to have heard that comment, but she wasn't entirely certain.

She looked up at the deck of her boat, which stood about shoulder high. She'd have a hard time getting her packages up there. She turned back to the couple. All she saw was their backs, as they mixed fresh drinks at a plastic tiki bar on the houseboat deck.

"Don't have a stepladder I could use, do you?" The blond man turned to grin lopsidedly at her, in a feline, drunken way, then spoke to his companion.

"Darlin', do you have anything she could use? If not, I can give her a hand up." His mild, benignly lecherous laugh almost deteriorated into a giggle as his companion's hand tightened around his arm.

Hadley, not in the least intimidated by the scene on the houseboat, laughed at the skeptical look the woman shot her. The scenario was comfortingly familiar—the older woman and her handsome young cub.

Of course the woman was jealous of a younger, attractive woman invading her territory. That was the nature of Cougars.

Hadley managed to hoist the sacks she was carrying up and slide them under the rail and onto the deck, then padded around to the back of the boat.

"That's OK. I think I can make it.

She jumped onto the mahogany swim deck, and found herself facing the name on the transom, barely legible under many years' grime. Wrinkling her nose, she rubbed her hand over the painted letters, cleaning them enough to read *Black Gold*.

The name referred to the oil business where her family had made enough money to buy this boat. And support her dad's playboy lifestyle. And support Hadley's and her mother's lifestyle in France. The business of decorating boats had been more a hobby than a business for Mère.

Once again, memories washed over her. Memories of times better forgotten: her childhood; Mère and Daddy, motoring around the lake, stopping for a swim, meeting up with friends; picnics; fights between her parents; Daddy flirting with pretty young women; then Mère starting to flirt with handsome men to get back at him.

No. Too much to do to think about that now! Banishing unwelcome memories with a shake of her head, Hadley scrambled onboard. She made her way up to the starboard side of the boat, where she picked up her bags and waved down at the couple on the houseboat.

"Made it up," she yelled. "Guess I'll talk to you later!"

Time to face this mess of hers.

7 It's Good to Be Captain

Inside, Hadley looked around the galley then pushed open a sliding plastic door over the small stove. Old, rusty spice cans crowded the tiny space inside.

Her mom used to whip up some pretty amazing meals here for Hadley and her dad. Bet Dad had never cooked a single meal in here. Some other woman might have cooked a romantic meal for him, though.

Now all of it was headed to the dumpster. Good thing she'd stocked up on trash bags at the store.

Zut! She squeezed her eyes tight, grasping the edge of the counter top as she hunched over, head hung forward as the whole thing hit her again. Being here, on this boat, she wasn't going to be able to push those memories out of her mind. But confronting them was too hard. Harder than she could handle right now.

It wasn't that she was afraid of being alone. She was good with her own company. But being alone on this boat was different.

She had to just put one foot in front of the other. Keep moving. As she started unloading her groceries and cleaning supplies, Hadley could almost feel the ghosts of her past watching her. But she had to look forward, not backward. She had to think about cleaning the boat. Yuck. Getting everything done here so she could go home.

Was her stomach growling? Suddenly, her mouth was watering. What was that smell? The odor of cooking meat drifted through the open door of the cabin. She'd grabbed a sandwich in town, but something really smelled good.

She crammed the perishables into the old fridge, climbed the three steps up to the salon, and peeked out the open door. A cool wind fanned her face as she glanced toward the pale pink glow of the coming sunset. Escape called to her. Then she saw it.

A beautiful boat, smaller than hers, but in much better shape, emitted a warm glow through curtained windows, a few slips down. A grill on the deck was clearly the source of the tantalizing odors.

Hadley hated to disturb people at the dinner hour, unless she'd been invited, but she needed information and distraction. She closed the door of the boat behind her. Her nose led her down the dock toward the heavenly smell of roasting chicken and peppers.

A man, dressed in shorts and a tee-shirt, carefully flipped chicken breasts on the grill. A slim woman sat at a small table on the deck nursing an iced drink.

Her nose was slightly sunburned and freckled, and she looked a little overheated. Noticing Hadley walking toward them, she waved her over with a cheerful grin.

The man laid down his fork, wiped his hands on a paper towel, turned with a smile, and held out his hand to shake Hadley's.

She smiled her dimple smile. As a teen, she'd practiced it in front of her mirror until she had it down to an art. French women learned early what their best features were and how to enhance them. She knew the power of that smile, maybe not powerful enough to launch a thousand ships, but she'd bet it could sure help sell one old boat.

"Hi. I'm Hadley Barrington."

"I'm Gordon Kent." The man stroked his well-trimmed beard with a smile. His blue tee-shirt proclaimed, 'It's Good to Be Captain.'

Hadley turned to greet his wife, who introduced herself as Connie. Her short blonde hair curled around her face. Her tropical print sarong complemented a matching bathing suit.

As the two women shook hands, a little white terrier barked once as it peered over the rail of the boat. Its front paws balanced its small, sturdy body, its ears alert. Bright brown eyes reflected the lights from the Chinese lantern lights strung between dock poles.

"Toby wants to meet you too." Connie stood and kissed her dog on the nose. As Hadley reached to pat the pooch on the head, he gave her a quick lick.

"His name is really Sir Toby Belch, but for short, we just call him Toby. Or Tobbs. Or Dumbshit. Don't we, my handsome little man?"

The terrier's eyes twinkled at Hadley as she scratched behind his ears. She'd had a little dog once, before she'd left Oklahoma. She turned back to Connie and Gordon before the memories could come flooding in.

"I'm your neighbor, sort of. *Black Gold* is my mother's boat." The timeline of ownership flickered through her mind. "Well, it's mine now."

"We're very glad to meet you." Connie had such a warm smile. "Everyone's always wondered who owned that boat."

"I heard that some people want to sink it."

"Oh my! Who said that?" Connie's eyes widened.

"The red haired woman on the houseboat!" Connie and Gordon grinned at each other as they unfolded a third chair for Hadley to sit in.

"That's Margo. Don't worry. That's not a widely held opinion. In fact, I doubt even Margo really thinks it." Gordon winked. "*Black Gold* is a magnificent, classic boat. She just needs a little tender loving care. Can we get you a drink?"

"After this week, and this day, *Oui*."

Gordon's opinion of *Black Gold*, added to Zane's, raised her hopes that she'd be able to find a new owner for the old hulk.

"So, are you going to fix *Black Gold* up?" Connie peered at Hadley over the frosty rim of her glass as Gordon set off in search of refreshment for their guest.

The woman clearly intended to find out all she could about her, noted Hadley, amused. Just as she, herself, was here to find out information. These people might know someone looking for a boat to buy. Wonder if they knew Zane?

"*Oui*—fix it up enough to sell it, I think, if I can do it quickly. I just hired a man, Zane Bowman, to work on it for me."

Nope, Connie didn't know the handyman. Hadley could tell from the look in her eyes. Curious. Maybe he was new on this dock?

Hadley told Connie as much as she knew about how she had come to own the old Chris Craft. Gordon returned with frosty drinks and joined the women at the table.

"I should have come right away." Hadley played with the straw in her drink. "But Mère insisted she'd be OK."

Hadley explained how, when she'd been at the airport, on her way over to accompany her mother back to Paris, she'd received the terrible news that Natalie had unexpectedly died.

So, when she had arrived back in Tulsa for the first time in almost eighteen years, she had had to bury her mother rather than take her back home. And then she had found out that she owned a boat.

8 Counting Cows

"I'm headed home now, Dad." Zane punched the button to end the call and stuck his phone back into his jeans pocket. He leaned against the coolness of the metal wall of the studio in the back of his shop, and eyed a wooden sculpture standing in the middle of the room.

The wood flowed into the shape of a well-rounded woman, the kind he'd always liked. Today, though, something didn't work for him. The woman it portrayed seemed almost too voluptuous.

He'd found the figure in the piece of wood and set it free with his tools. The full, heavy breasts had been perfect. But now, as he squinted in the low light to take in the whole effect, he wondered.

Well, no time for that now. Both his boats and his art were on the back burner this week. That decision would have to wait for another day. He shut the door to the studio, walked through the shed, and climbed into his truck.

His boat, tied up at the little dock, caught his eye as he turned away from the lake. No storms expected tonight. It would alright there. He swung the truck away from the water, out onto the country road, where the blacktop surface shimmered in the heat.

They really needed a rain. He rested his arm on the open window and turned on the radio. Country music boomed out of the speakers. He relaxed into the worn leather seat as the wind blew back his hair and cooled his face.

Around a curve, a fat copperhead snake sprawled, partly flattened, across the right hand lane of the highway. Snake guts smeared across the rest of the road.

Well, the vultures would enjoy dinner tonight. Squinting into the setting sun, he could see them already, circling high above the truck. As he rounded another curve, he frowned at blinking lights in the distance.

Pulling into the parking lot of an abandoned gas station by a stop sign at the country intersection, he stepped out of the truck. A police car, a jeep with a broken back window and a van with two airbags billowing were parked at angles.

"Hey, everybody OK?" Good chance someone he knew was involved. Joe, a high school buddy, now a local policeman, talked to an unfamiliar man. The stranger gestured toward his damaged jeep. Joe turned to Zane.

"Old man was drunk. Rear ended him."

He nodded toward the broken window. "Old dude wasn't hurt bad, but we sent him to the hospital. He'll be OK, I think. Till I serve him with a DWI."

Just then a little convertible pulled up to the stop sign. A silver-haired couple looked over the accident before making a left-hand turn.

"Not locals. Must be from over on the oily side of the lake." Joe narrowed his eyes, watching the sports car zoom over the hill. "Don't think they belong over here."

Zane nodded. He understood what Joe meant. The two sides of Grand Lake were very different. Too many folks from his side of the lake were unemployed. And lots of those who did work weren't much better off.

Sure, some people had jobs on the other side of the lake at the marinas and restaurants. And some owned local businesses. Some had done quite well for themselves. But many subsisted, back here in the hills where their families had lived for generations. He understood. He'd grown up here.

And he knew his family was one of the lucky ones. He reached into a pocket for a rubber band and pulled back his hair into a ponytail before he crawled back into his truck and headed on home.

Actually the house wasn't that far from the shop, as the crow flies. But the main road wasn't a straight shot. He pulled up beside the impressive log cabin his dad had built for his mother. It stood tall on a bluff overlooking the lake.

His shoulders slumped. First he'd had to get used to his mother not being here when he got home, and now his dad wasn't even here. But Dad would be back soon, back in the house he and his wife had both loved. Back home with his son.

In the meantime, Zane was in charge of the ranch. His dad needed a chance to get better. Their old ranch hand would be back from vacation in a few days, thank goodness. But tonight, the chores were all Zane's. And even though the days were long this time of year, he'd better get a move on. The sky was already turning pink and yellow on the western horizon.

He climbed the back steps and pulled open the screen door. In the mud room, off the rustic kitchen, he kicked off his deck shoes and pulled on a pair of work boots.

He lingered, sitting a minute. He was tired. He hoped there was some beer left in the fridge. Ah! Cool air rushed out when he opened the door. And there sat a full carton of his favorite beer.

Yeah. Grabbing a cold bottle, he pushed the door shut with his butt. Grabbing a ball cap off the horns of the deer head by the back door, he walked outside into the fading light.

A long cold drink washed down his throat. Yes. That was the ticket. He mounted the ranch four-wheeler, parked by the back deck.

A tiny growl drew his attention to the opening under the deck. A black and white dog appeared. But the growl hadn't sounded like Missy. Oh. He chuckled. A puppy, a tiny clone of its mother peeked out at the world from the shadows.

Getting pretty brave, weren't they? He reached down with one big hand and scooped up the wiggly ball of fur. As Zane sat there on the four-wheeler, gulping down the last of the ice cold beer and snuggling the puppy, he stared at the fire pit on the deck.

He'd get it done. He'd promised.

When he had been a kid, his mother used to build a bonfire on St. John' Day and dance around it, while he and his dad watched. Thank goodness no one else had ever known.

She'd grown up in Latvia, behind the iron curtain, a part of the world that had maintained many of its old-world customs, including the midsummer fire. When Christianity finally took hold in her native land, the old pagan ritual had migrated forward in time to St. John's Day, but was still celebrated.

And she'd brought that tradition over here with her. It made her happy, his dad had said. She and her parents had been refugees. His dad had met her when he got back from 'Nam. And Sonny had fallen in love with the beautiful blonde girl with the European accent.

Zane grimaced. European accent. One of the things that had embarrassed him about his mother. Along with the fires. He hadn't wanted any of his friends to know about all that.

Over time, after the iron curtain fell, and his parents had gone back to visit the place of her birth, the bonfires had turned into amber fires. Burning amber flakes emitted a whitish smoke and a sweet and pleasant pine wood smell that meant something to his mother.

Well, he'd promised her and he'd would do it. He'd take care of the ceremony on the Fourth of July, next weekend. He touched the amber pendant, a gift from her, that hung from the thong around his neck.

I'll do it for you, Mom.

He set down the pup. Leaving the empty can on the edge of the deck to throw away later, he gazed out over the sparkling blue lake that reflected the fading wisps of the sunset.

After all these years, that view still amazed him. He loved Grand Lake. Especially the wild and beautiful hills that made up this side.

"Think you can leave those young'uns long enough to come help me, Missy?"

The mother dog perked up her ears and swished her tail. He smiled down into her sparkling eyes.

"You love this shit, don't you girl?" He gunned the motor of the 4-wheeler, watching Missy bound out toward the pasture. She slid to a stop, spinning to watch him drive toward her.

"I'm coming girl."

She wiggled her way under the fence. At least his damn dog was excited about taking care of the cows tonight.

9 Bourbon in Waterford Tumblers

Gordon and Connie were nice. Hadley was glad she'd met them. But she really needed to get a little bit done before she went to bed tonight.

Back on her boat, she pulled the short drapes on the windows closed, shutting out the world. Where to start? Those yellowed, cracked plastic covers needed to come off of the furniture.

If she was careful enough, maybe she wouldn't spill any more bug carcasses onto the carpet. Ugh! She pulled the plastic off the settee, out the door, and piled it on a trash heap on the deck.

After dusting off the tables and window ledges, she paused. Just plain tired. The bottle of wine she'd bought in town sat on the counter, calling to her. Why hadn't she thought to buy a corkscrew? *Je est tupide!*

But Dad would have had one in here somewhere, she was sure. This boat had belonged to Warren Barrington, after all. That man would have possessed all the accouterments of drinking and seducing.

She dragged open a drawer, and stared at the collection of barware and utensils. *Oui.* But of course! Everything she needed.

Including wine glasses. She found them, but they were grimy. Of course. She washed one out thoroughly at the sink, and rinsed it in very hot water, trying not to think what bugs had set up housekeeping in it during the years.

With a heavy sigh, she sank into the old settee, glass of Pinot Noir in hand. A small whisp of dust puffed out of the upholstery. She sneezed, and wiped her nose on her sleeve, and took a sip.

Here's to you, Daddy, and you, Mère, wherever you both are. She rubbed her forehead and closed her eyes.

She had to concentrate. Too much to think about. Too much to do. What a stupid, unexpected predicament. Why had Mère held on to *Black Gold* for all of those years? Had she been clinging to the memory of her time with Daddy? Was that it?

Non. She just would not have done that. It did not make sense. She'd been the one to leave, and she'd never looked back. She'd realized that she deserved better than him. And better than marriage.

With his money and his debonair good looks, Warren Barrington had pursued the wives, and even the daughters, of friend and foe alike.

Hadley stared at the vinyl ceiling, remembering her Dad's carefree laugh, the sparkle in his eye, his casual elegance, his sharp wit.

He had been a devil, but a devil surrounded by rich oil men like himself. And by beautiful, brittle women. His life and his surroundings had somehow seemed to sparkle, like expensive crystal chandeliers and bourbon in Waterford tumblers. And this boat had been exquisite at one time.

A bug crawled across the ceiling. It certainly did not shine now. She had to get busy. Do something to distract herself from the ghosts of her past. Where was that bug spray she'd bought?

After vacuuming the entire boat, Hadley faced the stateroom where she planned to spend the night, where she had slept as a pre-teen.

Sitting down on the bug-free carpet, she pulled on the handle of one of the hinged doors under the bed, and peered into a storage space where she used to stash her dirty clothes when she hadn't had time to hang them up. Yuck. A foul odor wafted out to fill the room. She wrinkled her nose.

Maybe she'd left something in there. Well, if she had, Dad probably had gotten rid of it years ago. No traces of her were left on this boat, as far as she could see.

After all, something left over from Warren's kid would just have given the wrong impression. *That man.* She shook her head, but a tolerant smile softened her eyes.

Reaching into the dark space, she pulled out a rain slicker that must have been stuffed under the bed damp. Whew! Moldy. Well, that was the smell. At least she hadn't found a dead mouse rotting in there.

Out it went. Hadley picked up the smelly yellow slicker by her finger and thumb, dangling it so that no part of it touched her as she climbed the steps leading from the cabin and dumped the offensive item on top of the trash heap.

After she and Mère had left, Daddy had turned *Black Gold* into a bachelor pad on water for his parties and women. Hadley had missed him dreadfully when she had first moved with her mother to France, but she'd gradually begun to understand, as she'd matured, how much her father had played around on Mère, how his actions had changed her.

Mère, left more and more to herself in Tulsa, had felt unloved and humiliated as her husband had moved aggressively through his world, making money and chasing other women.

Warren's philandering hadn't kept him from being upset about the divorce. Although Natalie had felt unloved, she had also known her worth in her husband's life, as a possession.

When she'd left, she'd taken herself and her daughter a long way away, to France. And she had never let another man possess her, thought Hadley proudly.

She'd made her own rules, learned to keep secrets like a French woman, maintaining a rich, internal life, what French women called their "Secret Garden," that she'd shared with few.

Well, Hadley had thought she'd been her mother's confidant. She'd thought she had known what Natalie wanted from life. She'd thought she was special. But now she wondered. Why hadn't Mère told her why she was coming back to Oklahoma? Why hadn't she told her about the boat? How had she been injured and why was she dead?

10 Hemingway

In the darkening barn, Zane parked the ATV, climbed up onto an old John Deere tractor parked under a shed, and ground the ignition to a start.

New and bigger tractors, used to plow and plant, sat in the big barn, but this one was still good enough to haul hay to the cows.

Outside, Zane backed the tractor up to a straight line of big round bales of hay.

Looking over his shoulder, he lowered the hydraulically controlled metal spike on the back of the tractor and slowly backed up. A pointed bar, mounted low, jabbed into the bottom of a hay bale.

A smile tugged the corner of his mouth. The familiar smell of hay stirred memories of how proud he'd been when he'd first learned this task as a kid. He didn't even have to think about it anymore.

Pulling a lever to raise the bale off the ground, Zane turned the tractor around. He positioned the claw-like double loader bucket to cup the side of another bale, then pushed a lever to pivot and lift the 1200 pound cylinder slowly up above his head, precariously balancing the tractor and its load. All the time, Missy barked encouragement.

"Ready girl?" Zane steered the tractor down the rutted dirt track toward the cow pasture. The track needed grading. He relaxed his body to absorb the bumps. The dog ran out in front, her tongue lolling out of her mouth.

Zane jumped down to open the gate and drove into the pasture. The sun had long past disappeared behind the trees and the moon was out, but the sky still held enough light for his purposes.

Stupid cows. Too stupid to know if they'd just get out of his way, quit crowding around the tractor, they'd get their dinner faster.

Ok girls. Get back. I know you want your supper, but you're not making it easy on me.

He positioned the claw downward and lowered the top bale to the ground, then drove a little way and dropped the back bale down. When he drove forward the spike came out, leaving the bale laying there.

He threw the gear into neutral, pulled on the brake, and jumped to the ground. Two rusty green round bale feeders sat nearby, kind of round pipe fences. The hay remnants on the ground inside of them were yesterday's leftovers.

Zane turned one feeder onto its edge and rolled it toward a bale of hay, then flipped it over the bale. *There you go, girls.*

Now they could stick their heads through for a bite, but couldn't tromp through the hay, defecate on it, or keep others from eating their share. He flipped over the second feeder. Done. Gritty sweat rolled down his arms. Nasty business.

Missy stood behind the tractor, her tail wagging. "Nope, girl. We're not going to round them up tonight. I know you want to. Save that enthusiasm for a couple weeks and you'll get your chance."

Zane jumped back onto the tractor, then hoisted himself up to stand on the seat so he could count the cows.

Damn it. Had to start over again. Couldn't they just stand still for a minute? It was almost too dark to see. Supposed to be sixty here. Yep. All accounted for. He hoped.

Time to head home. He had things to do before he met Hadley at her boat tomorrow morning. After exchanging the tractor for the four-wheeler in the dark barn, Zane and Missy headed toward the house.

Puppies ran toward them from under the deck as he parked and dismounted. He scooped one up, and lifted it to eye level. Its puppy smell brought a smile to his lips.

He rubbed it hard on the head, just the way puppies like to be rubbed, as it wiggled with pleasure. Setting the furry creature back down on the ground, he gently swatted it on its butt.

"Get back in there to your momma, rascal. She's waiting for you."

His feet heavy, he again climbed the wooden stairs to the deck. His empty stomach growled and his skin itched from the dirt of a hot dirty day.

The hummingbird feeder hanging by the back door was almost empty. He'd better add some nectar in the morning before he left.

So tired. But would he be able to sleep with everything that was going on with his dad and Hadley? In the kitchen, he found burritos in the freezer. They would work. He pulled two out and stuck them into a toaster oven.

Hadn't he stashed a bag of chips somewhere? Yep. Here it was. He tore open the bag and stuffed a handful into his mouth. Tangy and salty.

Called for another beer. He grabbed one from the fridge before munching another handful of chips, setting the bag on the table and heading for the bookcase in the living room.

Walking through the coolness, his body began to relax. He'd lived in this house since they'd built it when he was a teenager. Well, except for the years when he'd been in college.

But he'd been here a lot even then, helping Dad and hanging out with his friends at the lake. He'd never wanted to live anywhere else.

A huge native rock fireplace stretched to the vaulted wood ceiling. Three deer heads hung there in a triangular pattern.

Zane's dad loved to hunt. And it was OK if he enjoyed the sport, but Zane had never been able to get into killing animals himself.

Shelves lined one wall, full of books interspaced with crinoids stem fossils found in the local streams. And his Mom's knickknacks and amber pieces.

Zane Grey books crowded two shelves. Dog eared paperbacks leaned against collectible first editions. Dad loved them all.

But why had his parents had to name him after the western author? That used to piss Zane off so bad. He used to think he'd never forgive them for naming him Zane. Childish nonsense.

The name wasn't so bad. He'd even read a few of the man's books, mostly to please Dad. They weren't his favorites, though.

But Dad might appreciate a few of these books where he was staying. He pulled a few out, and put them aside to take with him tomorrow.

Ah, yes. A higher shelf housed Hemingway books. A diversion to take his mind off everything. He reached up and grabbed *The Complete Short Stories of Ernest Hemingway*, and thumbed over to the Nick Adams section as he headed back into the kitchen. The smell of the burritos in the toaster oven made his mouth water.

The book lay open by his plate as he devoured his supper and wished he'd cooked another burrito or two. He grabbed the chip bag and crunched a couple handfuls as he thought about his dad.

Zane figured he really should get married. Dad would like that. Grandchildren would make him really happy. He'd spoil them.

The problem was finding the right girl, though. Zane guessed he was looking. He dated, went to parties, had fun with the girls he knew. Lots of fun, in fact.

He searched his mental black book, wondering if he just hadn't noticed the right girl among his friends. Well, he'd just have to try harder. Maybe hang out with some friends in nearby towns. Or attend the college reunion coming up.

But he wasn't willing to look very far afield. He wanted a local girl, a country girl, someone who would be happy to live here, who would fit in. Be on the PTA when they had kids in school.

She'd drive a SUV and take care of this house and him and his dad. A school teacher would be nice. He needed to give that idea some more thought. Maybe next week.

Right now, it was time for a shower. He put his dishes into the dishwasher, wiped off the table, picked up his book and headed upstairs.

In the bathroom, he stuffed his shirt into the hamper and stripped off his jeans. Pulling off his boxer shorts revealed surprisingly pale skin. Most of his body was almost as dark as his dad's, but where he was always protected from the sun, he was pretty pale.

Walking into the bathroom, he reached in to turn the shower onto hot. He just tanned well, and spent a lot of time on the water and in the sun.

But, even though he was Native American on his dad's side, he was half Mom, too. His wavy hair was hers, although the color came from Dad.

As he pulled the rubber band out, and his hair fell forward into his face, he caught sight of himself in the mirror. Wonder what Hadley thought about him?

She was used to fancy French men, after all. He grabbed a towel and opened the shower door. Steam billowed out. It didn't matter what she thought!

But his body and his mind seemed to be at odds about that subject. Shit! Not again. He glanced down with disgust. That was all he needed.

He reached in and turned the shower all the way to cold and stepped in, but as he let the chilly water drench his body, leaning back his head and letting streams run down his face and his hair, he couldn't stop thinking about her, and doubted a cold shower was going to fix his problem.

11 An American Fairytale

Hadley was strong. Her mother had set an excellent example. But sometimes being a strong woman was a lonely business. Mère had been happy. Mère's life had been fulfilling. Hadley poured more wine into her glass and took a sip.

Mère had never regretted her choices. But why had she kept this annoying old boat when she'd sworn she never wanted to return to her home? When she spent her summers on yachts that would put this one to shame? Would Hadley ever know the answer to that question, with Mère gone?

Oh Mère. Her sight blurred with tears. Why? Why did you have to leave me, and why did you leave me with this problem? What would you want me to do?

Hadley set down her glass and rubbed her eyes. Darned dust making her eyes water. She stomped back out to the salon. Dragging the plastic covers off of one round swivel chair across from the settee, she threw it outside onto the pile.

Then she glared at the chair just uncovered, upholstered in a blue watered silk fabric. No telling what those stains were. Wine? Coffee?

Mère had had exquisite taste. But styles had changed drastically in the more than thirty years since this boat had last been updated.

She should really just sink this boat. Hadley stalked around the small room. And the ghosts with it. *Serve you right Dad. And you too, Mère, for saddling me with this problem.*

But could she really? Could she just take the old boat someplace deserted and chop a hole in the bottom and let it sink? Maybe row to shore or escape on a jet ski or something? Tell people she sold it?

She laughed at the mental image, all five foot two of her out chopping a hole in the bottom of the boat. Probably not too practical. Sounded like some stupid, cheap movie.

Or she could just leave it here at the dock and keep paying dock rental and maintenance, like her mom had, evidently. But why? What would that accomplish?

She really didn't want any ties back to Oklahoma, to Tulsa, or to Grand Lake. How long would it take to sell it if she just put it on the market as is?

Would someone buy it and fix it up? Or tear it apart and leave it a rotten hull in a cow pasture? She'd seen something like that on the way out here. Or they might burn it like Zane had mentioned. *Non.* That was not the answer, unfortunately.

If only she could just walk away from everything. She wished the story she'd been told about Mère's accident had been more complete. Then she'd just leave. The sentimental memories of her childhood that this boat held were just illusions, anyway.

She'd once thought she'd had a happy family. They had lived in the historic part of Tulsa, mansions built in the 1920's, kept beautiful and elegant, with sparkling Christmas trees, crystal chandeliers, and fluffy white dogs as pets.

Pretty clothes and private schools had made up her world. An American fairytale, she knew now, having lived abroad for longer than she'd lived here. Middle America wasn't really the center of the universe. Real life was elsewhere.

The old boat did have some value, according to Zane. But did that even matter? She really didn't need the money. After all, the trust funds from both of her parents provided a reliable income, and her career as a jewelry designer was starting to take off. Hadley fingered the bracelet on her wrist, her newest design.

But she needed to stay to find some answers. And who knew what might be hidden in the nooks and crannies of the boat? She might find something, cleaning it out, that would clear up some of the mysteries surrounding this whole trip and boat thing. Hadley dropped into the blue chair, head in her hands.

She knew she had to find a new owner who would take care of *Black Gold* instead of junking it, but she could hire someone to take care of the whole thing, she was sure.

Did she owe Mère the time it would take to handle the situation herself? Her stomach knotted and she rubbed it to relieve the pain.

Mère would probably think her silly for feeling guilty, for wishing she could escape this duty. Would she laugh at her daughter for taking the whole thing so seriously? Probably. She'd leave tomorrow, but except for needing to find out the facts of her mother's accident.

Hadley jumped up and grabbed the wine bottle, carrying it back over to the chair with her. She filled her glass to the brim and gulped down a drink.

She had loved Mère more than anyone in the world, and she hadn't been there for her at the end. Maybe getting to the bottom of what had happened to her and getting the boat sold would make up for not being there when she'd died?

She slipped farther down into the settee. One thing for sure. She needed sleep. Hadley closed her eyes. One glimmer of hope illuminated the gloomy picture in her mind. Maybe she didn't have to go it alone. She'd let Zane help her. Yes. Zane would help her.

She pushed herself out of the chair and headed for bed. As she stripped down for her second shower of the day, she thought of him as she stood there looking at herself in the mirror hung on the back of the door. She laughed as she watched her nipples harden and crinkle.

Maybe. He seemed to really want to help her. Was he what she needed right now, to help her get through this mess? She stepped into the head and turned the shower to cold.

12 Trails in the Darkness

Clean! Stepping out of the shower, Hadley stood staring at her old bed. She'd never been alone on the boat until today. It felt like an empty shell without the family and the life that Hadley had lost so long ago. Had even the ghosts deserted her?

What if the spirit of her mom met up with the phantom of her Dad here? A shudder passed through her as she imagined the confrontation of those two. Not pleasant. Better hollow and empty than filled with their anger and bitterness.

Too much! Connie and Gordon had mentioned stopping by for a drink before bed. Was it too late? Only one way to find out. Hadley fled the old boat in search of company and forgetfulness.

Where were Connie and Gordon? She walked by their snug little boat, but only a crack of light showed around their door. Too late. They had obviously turned in for the night, locking out the rest of the world. And her.

Hadley turned back sadly. Her boat loomed out of the shadows, where it had floated for so long, deserted. Was it still waiting for her family to come back? Or was the old boat used to its solitude and the peace that it brought?

Black Gold bobbed up and down in eerie silence. Only an occasional creak of wet wood contracting or expanding or the splash of water against its side broke the silence.

Hadley glanced back toward Gordon and Connie's boat longingly. Then a sound stopped her. She stood still, listening.

Out of the darkness, across the water, music drifted on the breeze. Where was it coming from? A light pierced the night, dimly at first. Then it brightened and lit up the dock. Another wooden boat, not as large as hers, and much different, glided into view, headed for a nearby empty slip.

The boat rode low in the water, not at all as grand and lofty as *Black Gold*, but comfy looking, somehow. Painted white with lots of gleaming wood trim, its canvas top was startlingly blue.

Hmm. Maybe *Black Gold* needed that kind of blue canvas to replace some of its old or missing covering. Might make it look as welcoming as the incoming vessel for a new owner. The boat glided into its slip, the bow crowded by boisterous men and women. No wonder the boat seemed contented.

Two men jumped off to throw dock lines to those still onboard. As the men on shore guided the craft in, keeping it from rubbing against the sides of the slip, one stumbled and almost fell into the water. He grabbed a pole and balanced himself with a laugh.

The boat glided to a stop, and the men tied her securely to the poles around the boat slip. People in damp bathing suits emerged from the interior. Some climbed down from where they'd been standing on deck. Others had been reclining on the bow.

They swarmed the dock. Someone turned on a row of parrot lights strung up high, and one man pulled the cover off a gas grill and fired it up. Others pulled up chairs around a table.

Hadley looked on wistfully, not sure if she'd be welcome if she strolled down. Unsure of dock protocol, she started to turn away again, when a friendly voice called, "Hi there!"

A tall willowy woman with a riot of long curly dark hair and the most beautiful eyes Hadley had ever seen waved her over with a friendly smile. The brunette pointed to an empty chair, her lighted cigarette leaving trails in the darkness.

"I'm Meg." Smiling, the woman plopped down into a chair opposite the one she had indicated to Hadley. "I don't think we've met. Would you like a drink?"

Hadley nodded and thankfully dropped into the empty seat, glad for any excuse to avoid being alone with her boat problem.

"Adam!" yelled Meg over her shoulder to the younger man at the grill, "We have a guest. She needs a drink!"

Adam, a slim, dark haired young man with glasses, sexy green eyes and a tired smile, glanced over from where he was adjusting the flame on the grill.

Another man, darkly tanned, with longish brown curly hair and long dark eyelashes, glanced appraisingly at Hadley. Then he quickly volunteered to bring her a drink. Adam thanked him, his hands full, as he tore the foil from a bowl of marinating hot wings and started to load them onto the rack of the grill.

"I'm Ryan." A cold frosty drink was placed in Hadley's hand. Ryan's somewhat scruffy beard and mustache, the shells around his neck, and his slightly drunken demeanor, combined to make him absolutely adorable. Hadley turned on her dimple smile.

A nice-looking guy. Hadley checked him out as he sat down in the chair beside her. Cute, with all that curly hair. And those eyelashes. This dock was a delicatessen of delicious men.

She chatted with him breezily, flirting with her eyes, but quickly realized that he really didn't turn her on. Although he was intelligent and extremely attentive, somehow, her mind kept comparing him to Zane.

Ridiculous. The handyman was fun, but nothing for her to obsess over. Barrington women did not obsess over men. Men obsessed over them, as the women reclined at ease and enjoyed it.

Hadley laughed at herself, as she leaned back in her chair and took another drink. The whole crew had obviously been drinking all day, and were having a good time. Several had sunburns. Hadley could smell the coconut of suntan lotion.

Meg clearly wanted to know all about this new girl on her dock. Hadley briefly explained her predicament with the boat to her new friends. The brunette steadily sipped her drink as she listened, laughing a bit too brightly and prompting for more details. Ryan just watched Hadley with moon-eyes.

Meg's hair was in disarray after an afternoon of sun and water. Her melon orange bathing suit showed through a sheer print cover-up. Hadley estimated her age as somewhere between her own and Connie's, maybe around forty? She seemed to be the grand dame of the gathering. Maybe the boat was hers.

Meg pumped Hadley for more information. What was her father's name again? Where did she live in France? Where had she lived in Tulsa years ago? Oh yes, she knew that neighborhood. Adam's family lived near there.

Hadley noticed that when the woman spoke to or of Adam, a possessive tone colored her voice. So that's how it was, huh? Hadley smiled. This place was not so different from home.

When Hadley told the woman about her jewelry designing, Meg's interest peaked and she just had to try on Hadley's bracelet herself. She turned her arm this way and that, admiring how the gems flashed when they caught the light and how the light metal contrasted with her tan skin.

"Oh Adam," she cooed "Come here, Lover." As he walked up behind her, Meg held up the sparkling concoction on her arm. "You know my birthday is coming soon. Hadley made this bracelet. She sells them in Paris."

"I'll just have to have a talk with Hadley, then." Adam smiled down at the woman, then bent to kiss her, just a peck in front of her ear.

Hmm, she had good taste in men. Hadley politely refused any of the food that Adam had prepared, so he brought a plate for himself and one for Meg and joined the women. Adam was a young IT whiz, Meg explained, and the boat was his.

Well, the couple and their somewhat rowdy friends were just the kind of company Hadley needed to keep the ghosts away tonight.

Someone turned up the music, and the party started to get a little noisy as people raised their voices to be heard over the beat.

13 A Slam and a Growl

"Adam, do you know of anyone who might be interested in buying my boat?" Hadley leaned over the table to be heard.

A door slammed and a dog growled. Everyone at the table looked up. The door of Connie and Gordon's boat stood open, emitting an explosion of light and barking.

"Uh Oh," muttered Adam, as an obviously unhappy Connie stomped out to lay down the law to the unruly crowd.

"How do you kids expect us to sleep?" Connie stood with her hands on her hips and glared at the young people. Toby planted his small body in front of her and barked furiously.

"All of you," and unfortunately, although Hadley was not making much noise at all, she was in Connie's direct line of vision, "All of you need to learn to be more responsible. Now turn off that music and quiet down. Now!!!"

Adam quickly rose to turn down the music, mumbling an apology, but Meg was not so easily cowed. Being a bit more tipsy, she confronted Connie.

"Listen, we didn't intend to bother you, but it's still early here. It's not our fault that you probably drank too much and Gordon had to take you to bed so early."

Ryan groaned. Glancing over, Hadley saw him stand up quietly and creep into the darkness. Could she get away with that too? Probably not.

"It's a Friday night at the lake! We come out here to have fun." Meg's voice became shriller. She was standing now, facing down Connie. "If you want peace and quiet, stay in town. But don't expect to come out here to the lake and tell us to go to bed early. We are not children, even if you are old enough to be our parents!!"

Connie's eyes flashed. Probably because she wasn't old enough to be Meg's mom. Hadley looked from one woman to the other and back again.

Who could really blame Connie if that remark pissed her off? Toby growled, and it looked for a minute as if things might get ugly. Adam stood behind Meg. Down the dock, Gordon put his hand on Connie's shoulder, whispering in her ear.

"You haven't heard the last of this, Meg. Keep that music down!" Connie hissed through gritted teeth, then turned away, and let Gordon lead her back into the boat. The little dog, growling one last warning toward the crowd, trotted in with his masters.

Gordon's and Adam's eyes met, exchanging sheepish looks. Gordon looked as if he'd almost rather be drinking with the younger crowd than calming down his angry wife and dog.

But Connie was really nice. Hadley hoped the woman wouldn't hold tonight against her. Adam comforted Meg, and someone handed her a fresh drink. Everyone breathed a sigh of relief.

"Well," Meg poked Adam's chest. "This is our dock too." Someone suggested moving the party over by his boat, which was moored at the far end of the next dock down. Everyone started grabbing chairs and drinks to take over.

"Hadley, come party with us. The night is still young, and so are we!" entreated Ryan, earnestly offering to carry her chair, and her too, if she wanted. Meg chimed in her invitations as well, but Hadley decided she'd had enough excitement.

She guessed that the party was probably going to last much of the night, and she could no longer put off facing her ghosts. Hadley said her goodbyes, and strolled toward her drifting problem.

Although she'd met some nice people today, her life and her world lay elsewhere, not here. The decisions she faced tomorrow would determine how soon she could get on a plane back to France.

She smiled. Zane would be arriving early.

14 Ghost Ship

The ship was sinking, and Hadley knew she could not escape. Water sloshed around her ankles and a thick mist hid the shore.

A voice snarled angrily. A short retort cut in, silencing the first speaker. Hadley couldn't make out the words, but she knew the voices of her mother and father arguing. Had they found each other, wherever they were now?

Their arguments from her childhood still haunted Hadley, and her stomach clenched, just as it had back then. But now, that anger was sinking the boat. The water was up to her knees. She was going to die.

Coffee, coffee. Hadley smelled coffee. Intoxicating tendrils of scent wove through her troubled dreams and subtly urged her senses toward consciousness. Away from all the anger.

She opened her eyes. For a frightening moment, the world and time didn't exactly make sense. Then the last horrible week rushed back. But at least the dream was gone. She had needed to wake up.

Hadley stumbled out of bed. Where were her silver flip flops? She wasn't quite ready to run around bare footed, just in case she'd missed any crunchy bug carcasses when she'd vacuumed.

She pulled on a clean pair of shorts. She'd never expected to be hanging around a marina in rural Oklahoma when she'd packed. She'd have to do some shopping or laundry if she stayed out here any time at all. One or the other.

Well, she'd be driving into Tulsa tomorrow or the next day. She needed to talk to the doctor who'd taken care of Mère. Maybe he could fill in the missing pieces in the story she'd heard so far. She needed to understand. And she had to pick up her mother's things. How would she be able to get through that?

But it was a new day and she had to get started. Hadley quickly brushed her hair & teeth. Then she rifled through the tops she'd hung in the tiny closet the night before. Pulling on a lime green tee shirt and fluffing her hair, she followed her nose toward the cabin door, led by the enticing smell of coffee. She stumbled out into sunlight streaking and coloring the world, mirroring off sparkling, ever-moving water. Stripes and specks of reflected brightness played and danced off all the surfaces that surrounded her.

Water lapped softly, insistently on the hull of the boat and against the dock. A gentle breeze, warm and soft, with a promise of sultry heat later tingled Hadley's skin.

Now where was that coffee? No one was stirring on the houseboat next door, so Hadley turned toward Connie and Gordon's boat.

Aha! There it was, coffee! Two steaming cups set on the couple's dock table. But Connie had been so angry last night. Hadley sighed. Not only for the loss of coffee, but for the loss of a friend she had hoped to cultivate.

And for information she'd meant to harvest. Shoulders slumping, she turned to return to her coffee-less cabin.

"Hadley!" She glanced back over her shoulder.

Connie, holding out a cup of coffee, marched toward her. Hadley watched the woman slide the cup under the rail with a sheepish smile on her face.

"Please come join us for some breakfast." Hadley hesitated a moment. "I'm really sorry about last night." Connie pushed the coffee farther toward her across the wooden deck.

"I had just gone to sleep when the music started. I had a headache and the noise just set me off. I'm so sorry you were in my line of fire. Please forgive me. Come down and have some coffee and eggs."

Hadley knew when to say yes to an invitation. She really needed someone to talk to this morning. Someone to help her dispel her disturbing dreams and listen to her as she worked out her options.

Decisions had to be made. Smiling down at her neighbor, Hadley picked up the coffee and gratefully took a long sip.

She tried to focus as she listened to Connie babble away, describing the owners of all the boats on the dock. Everyone had a story. The morning sunlight was soft. The hummingbird mamma zipped by, headed toward her nest.

Hadley's mind drifted to the neat kitchen of the apartment that she and Mère had shared. The yellow walls in the kitchen would glow in the early morning sunlight.

Natalie would be fussing at the stove as Hadley sat perched at the butcher-block topped island, watching her. Mother and daughter would chat about their day, as the noise of the Le Marais area traffic built outside the tall second story windows.

Hadley pushed away those thoughts as she greedily attacked the eggs, toast and fruit on the plate Gordon set in front of her.

"I really want to apologize again," insisted Connie. "After you left, I had a phone call from my shop. A shipment didn't arrive on time and I had to deal with an irate customer. By the time I had that all straightened out, my head was killing me."

"What kind of shop do you have?" Hadley looked up from her breakfast, buttering a piece of sourdough toast.

"An interior design shop," Connie answered proudly. "And I design a lot of boat interiors."

"Really? *Est vachement band*ante! My mother was an interior designer. She also specialized in boats. Decorated that one, of course." Hadley pointed toward *Black Gold* with her toast. "A long time ago." Hadley turned and looked at her boat thoughtfully.

"*C'est un bled* now. It's old fashioned and dirty. But when I was a little girl, it was one of the nicest boats out here."

Connie leaned forward, an eager look on her face, and even Gordon listened politely as Hadley poured out her story about childhood and happiness and divorce and sadness and death and loss, and now puzzlement and indecision.

"Hadley, I'd love to see the inside of your boat." Connie stood, purposely stacking dishes and pushing them toward Gordon.

"You girls go on and talk boat decorating. Don't mind me. I'll do the dishes," offered Gordon belatedly.

As Hadley and Connie climbed the ladder to *Black Gold*, they heard him muttering from down the dock. "No, really, I don't need any help. I love to do this shit."

The two women grinned at each other, carefully avoiding looking back at the protesting Gordon.

As Hadley and Connie entered the salon of the boat, they paused at the open door of Hadley's parents' cabin. The bed was still covered with yellowed, cracked plastic, covered with dust and bug bodies.

"Maybe you should come back when I've had time to clean more." Hadley grimaced. This boat needed a lot more cleaning before anyone was going to appreciate its potential.

"Oh, trust me. I will!" Connie was busily inspecting every inch of the salon.

"But let me just look around a little now, please. I've so wanted to look inside, ever since we moved our boat here. But, of course, I never would do so without the owner's permission."

"Well, really." She glanced sideways at Hadley with a mischievous smile. "Really Gordon wouldn't let me. You know, they call this the...."

Hadley broke in with a laugh. "I know. The Ghost Ship. I think it really is. I dreamed about my parent's ghosts in here last night." She shivered, remembering.

"I guess I'm the only live person who really remembers *Black Gold* the way she used to be, who cares, if I do...."

She opened up the door to a built-in bookcase, as much to hide the emotion on her face from Connie as to see what was inside. A photo album lay on top of a few other dusty books.

Hadley picked it up and opened it. Her family looked back at her. Her mother and father were young and sleek and tanned. And Hadley stood between them, looking tiny and pert and happy.

"You really do take after your mother, you know." Hadley jumped. She hadn't realized that Connie was looking over her shoulder.

"She was stunning, just like you." Connie took the book from her. "And your father was a very handsome fellow. I'd say he was probably a lady killer?" She glanced up at Hadley.

"Oh he was!" murmured Hadley. "He was that alright."

"I was too young to understand exactly what happened, but Mère never forgave him, and made sure he paid for whatever sins he'd committed. I don't think she ever forgave men in general for how he treated her. She learned that having a man to love is not necessary for a good life."

15 Faded Polaroids

Setting the photo album on a table, Connie pulled out the next book in the stack, a scrapbook.

"Is it OK if I look?" she asked. "I'm a terrible busybody." Hadley nodded her permission. She was going to have to deal with these memories. Maybe having a friend around would make the job easier.

When Connie opened the scrapbook, she gasped. Oh dear. What embarrassing thing had she found? Something of Daddy's? Hadley was almost afraid to look.

But no. The page was full of diagrams and carefully drawn illustrations of the space where Hadley and Connie currently stood.

Taped onto the pages were small scraps of faded fabrics, the same fabrics that covered the furniture in the room here now. It was her mother's scrapbook, her plan for this boat.

Connie eagerly thumbed through the pages, clearly in her element. She probably put together similar books when she decorated boats. The older woman made approving noises as she studied this detail or that drawing.

"What do you say we take this book back over to our place and look at it over a cold soda or something? This dust is kind of getting to me." Connie pulled a tissue out of her pocket and wiped her freckled nose.

The sunlight streaming through the window was speckled by bright motes of dust. Hadley scribbled down "fan" on a new shopping list. Maybe she could put one in the doorway and suck out some of the dust?

As she strolled with Connie back down the dock to where Gordon was finishing his cleanup, Hadley carried Mère's books carefully so they wouldn't fall apart.

Connie carelessly kissed her husband, brushing her body against his in a kind of intimate promise, not really meant to be witnessed by outsiders. With a bear-like growl, he offered to prepare soft drinks all around.

Hadley politely concentrated on the book and pretended not to notice. But as he left them to play waiter, she flashed a quick smile at his back.

He really was an awfully nice man. He and Connie were so cute together. Evidently, traditional relationships could work well, sometimes. But in Hadley's experience, most turned out badly.

While Connie looked through the scrapbook, Hadley thumbed through a photo album, lingering over a picture of her mother holding a diploma. Natalie was very young here. Maybe in her early twenties? Under the picture was written, 'Natalie Jones,' Mère's maiden name. She must have just graduated from design school.

Connie gently took the book from her and showed it to Gordon as he stepped off the boat juggling icy drinks on a bamboo tray and a dog dish of water for the little terrier at his heels.

"Doesn't Hadley look like her mother?" Gordon stood there looking back and forth between the picture in the scrapbook and Hadley.

"If I didn't know better, I'd have thought this was a picture of you, Hadley." Gordon set down the tray and the dog water, patted his wife on the shoulder, then wandered off down the dock to talk to a man who had just climbed off of another boat.

Hadley explained to Connie that her father had inherited his dad's boat, manufactured in 1955. At the time, it had been a virtual mansion on the water, and it was still bigger than any other boat on this dock, although just barely.

Her parents had met when her father had decided to have the boat redecorated. One of his older business associates had suggested that Warren consider giving the job to his daughter, freshly graduated from design school. The young boat owner and the daughter had ended up married.

"Lucky for you," commented Connie as she set the book down between them, examining a picture of *Black Gold* as it had originally looked.

All the paint was fresh, sparkly white with a bold blue stripe just under the deck and a red stripe at the water line. Flags proudly waved. Her father stood on the prow, a captain's cap jauntily topping his crisp curly dark hair.

"So handsome." Connie sighed, studying the picture intently.

As they turned the next page, two old, dog-eared Polaroid photographs fell out onto the dock. Connie leaned over and picked them up.

"This isn't your dad." She passed one faded picture to Hadley.

"Hmm?" Hadley looked up from studying the diagram on the page to take the picture from Connie. "No. That's not Daddy. Don't know who it is." She laid it aside to continue paging through the scrapbook.

"Well, your mother seemed to know him." Connie passed Hadley the second photo that had fallen out. In it, Natalie stood with the same young man, his arm around her shoulders.

Hadley examined the picture closely. Mère looked really young. It wasn't a photo of her when she'd had first begun to experiment with younger men. That had been after Hadley was born. When Warren was busy philandering.

This guy was young—and handsome—in a different way than her dad. Hadley squinted at the snapshot in the bright light. The young man looked a little familiar, but she couldn't place him. The two might have been teenagers. This picture was definitely of a very young Natalie Jones.

"Mom was out of design school when she met Daddy. She never told me about anyone before him, but—who knows?" Hadley dropped the photo beside the other one, but her eyes lingered on it for a moment.

16 A Handsome Devil

"When did your father pass away?" Connie compared the two timeworn pictures.

"He died ten years ago." Loneliness hit her, an ache in her throat that sharpened to a pain in her chest.

"I guess I'm an orphan now, with Mère gone too." The weight of the world seemed to settle on her shoulders as she realized just how much her life had changed.

"Oh, I'm so sorry I asked." But Connie's eyes sparkled with curiosity.

"No, it's all right." Hadley pulled back her shoulder blades, stretching to dislodge the heaviness pushing her down. It helped a little. She really needed to get her mind off of her own emotions.

"Really. He was so busy with business, and living the good life, that I hardly saw him after we moved to Paris. Daddy loved life, too much sometimes. He was good at making money and knew the oil business inside out. Learned it from his father." She could picture him now, always the center of attention.

"He inherited Granddaddy's company and his boat. Daddy was a social butterfly, I guess. A party wasn't a party without Warren Barrington. He knew everyone who was anyone in Tulsa, and on Grand Lake."

"And he messed around on your mother?" Connie shifted her skinny body in her chair, straining toward Hadley, her eyes wide.

Hadley looked out at the lake. "Yes. After a party, he'd lure some business acquaintance's wife, or daughter, back to a motel or the boat if we weren't there."

"A handsome devil." Connie's eye sparkled as she continued leafing through the book. Hadley suspected the woman was hoping she'd find some more "interesting" photos of Natalie.

"Where did your mother attend design school?"

"New York School of Interior Design." Hadley was proud of Mère's accomplishments. "Daddy's boat was the first one she ever decorated, but everyone who saw what she did with it wanted her to decorate theirs. Of course, it's so old-fashioned now."

"She knew what she was doing," muttered Connie as she studied a drawing. She shoved the book over so Hadley could see the design.

"That's what she did in France, too. We spent a lot of time on the Riviera, and she was *très* famous for the boats she decorated there." Hadley rattled off a few very impressive star-quality names for whom her mother had worked.

"I spent many summers exploring gorgeous boats. You know, maybe that's why she kept Daddy's old boat, because it was the first one she'd ever decorated and it started her career. I really can't think of any other reason. *Certainement* not because it started her marriage. That was a fiasco."

"So, do you have ideas for what you're going to change on the boat?"

"A little. I hate to make too many changes, but fabric for sure. And the carpet is nasty." She pulled the book over so she could study some photographs.

"I know it needs updated, *n'est-ce pas*? And if Mère were here today, she'd definitely be making changes. She'd make it look marvelous! But I'm a jewelry designer, not a boat decorator."

"But you have me to help you!" Connie leaned toward her over the table. "Your mother's designs are quite remarkable. She was clearly very talented. "She glanced down the dock to where her husband was obviously talking boats.

"I would be honored to help you come up with some ways to update your boat, staying true to your mother's vision. With her design book and my experience and contacts, we could make her proud of us." The older woman pushed herself up out of the chair. "Let me show you what I've done to our boat."

"Oh, Connie, I'd love to see." Hadley rose from her seat and followed the woman inside. As she turned, she noticed that a ray of sunshine streaked across the faded pictures, left lying on the table.

A half hour later, the friends emerged from the boat. "I love the way you've done the bedroom, Connie. The colors, and it doesn't feel claustrophobic at all."

Connie, put her hand on Hadley's arm as they paused, their eyes adjusting to the outside light. She squinted at a figure down the dock and whispered, "Who's that?"

Hadley looked up to see Gordon chatting with Zane. *Merde*, she'd forgotten that he was arriving early.

"Bonjour Zane!" Hadley smiled at the handyman.

"Connie, this is Zane Bowman, a friend of Hadley's." Gordon gave the girl from France a fatherly look. Connie glanced back and forth between her new friend and the handsome man standing on her dock.

Connie wasn't too old to admire a hunky younger guy, even though she and Gordon seemed a very committed couple. Even Connie was not immune to the fact that Zane was totally hot! Hadley was sincerely glad that she'd gotten to know the older woman.

"Uh, Zane is going to help me get my boat ready to sell." She smiled at her friend.

"Oh!" Connie nodded her head. "I remember you telling us that last night. So you work for the marina, Zane? I haven't seen you around before."

"No. I have my own shop." Zane looked out across the lake, not meeting Connie's eyes. "I restore wooden boats. You have a nice one here yourself." He ran his eyes over the well cared-for wood on Connie and Gordon's boat with an appreciative smile.

"My dad, uh, we know the manager here, and he thought that I might be able to help Hadley get *Black Gold* ready to sell."

Listening to Zane explaining how he had come to be working for her, Hadley realized that she should probably have asked more questions when she'd found him on her boat yesterday.

Connie and Gordon looked puzzled as well. All three stood there looking at Zane as if they expected him to continue with his explanation. But he just smiled at them.

17 Man of Many Secrets

Well, this was awkward. Zane's eyes dropped to the tabletop. *Oh Shit!* When he saw the old photographs lying there, he immediately recognized the couple.

"Do you know the man in these photos?" Connie squinted at Zane. She must have noticed him looking at them. He panicked. Crap. Action was required.

"Are you ready, Hadley?" He scooped up the book, along with the photos.

"Connie. Gordon. So nice to meet you guys." He shook hands with both, keeping Hadley's book firmly in his possession, then nodded to her to take the lead returning down the dock.

Zane breathed a sigh of relief, as they climbed aboard. "Where should I put this book? He leafed through it, still not relinquishing it to Hadley.

"Drawings of the boat! Is this your mom's book from when she decorated it?"

Hadley stopped, turned around and looked at him. Had he screwed up again? Don't panic. Was he supposed to know that her mother and father had met when her mother decorated this boat? He couldn't remember if they'd discussed it or not.

"Uh…." How did he get out of this mess? He made a bold move.

"Didn't you tell me that your mom and dad had met when she decorated *Black Gold* for him, or, something?"

She looked confused, then seemed to accept that they had discussed that meeting.

Whew! He'd better improve his game! Wonder what she thought about finding pictures of her mother with another man's arm around her shoulders? Natalie said she'd never known about that.

Time to change the subject.

"We need to talk about these estimates." He looked at his wrist watch. "It's almost noon. Want to grab a bite to eat while we go over these figures?" Hadley looked surprised at his invitation.

He added a little incentive. "Want a ride in the runabout?"

Hadley thought back to the wooden boat she'd seen him in the day before, how slick and almost alive it was, the way it leapt through the water like a live animal.

She was severely tempted to take that ride. But she'd just realized that he might not be exactly what he seemed. He knew more about Mère and this boat than he should. He wanted something from her. What was he up to?

She gave him her dimple smile. Well, two could play this game. He didn't know just what kind of player he was dealing with. She'd learned from the champion, her mom.

"Hey, I am hungry" Hadley lied, still full from breakfast with Connie and Gordon. "Give me just a minute to change."

Hadley threw on relaxed cotton trousers and a loose, long-sleeved shirt, tied at her waist.

As they walked past the deserted deck of the houseboat, Margo opened the door and walked out on deck.

"Hi Zane," she called. "Whatcha doing down on my end of the lake?"

"Business," he muttered, quickening his pace.

"Well, don't be a stranger." The red head picked up a couple of glasses from the night before and re-entered her nautical mansion.

Wondering how well they knew each other, Hadley watched his face, as he hurried her down the dock.

Zane, Zane. The man of many secrets. What kind of man are you?

"There's nothing that rides like a wooden boat in the water." Zane settled her into the plush red leather seat of the runabout and tucked in his lanky frame next to her.

"Rides like a Cadillac; sounds like a Harley. More fun that either." He chuckled, contentedly.

"Don't you wonder what this lake was like when woodies were the only boats out here?" He ran his hand down the smooth wood in a gesture that could only be described as possessive.

Time to find out a little more about this mystery man. Hadley leaned her head back against the softness of the leather, inhaling the masculine scent.

"Your boat?" She inquired innocently, fairly sure it was not.

"Yes. I built her." Hadley sat up straight. She stared at Zane as he started the motor and eased away from the dock.

Well, she'd sure pegged him wrong. That was her last coherent thought for a while, as the thrill of the fast ride in the long, low vessel overwhelmed her.

Wind and spray whipped her face and hair. Blue surrounded her. Blue water. Blue skies.

She and Zane were one with the elements, creatures of the water, powerful and fast. The world whipped by, as Hadley abandoned herself to the experience.

She laughed in exhilaration, and Zane laughed with her, their restraint and fears of each other swept away by the shared experience. They rounded the headland, out of the bay and into the choppier water of the main body of the lake.

They flew by sailboats and fishing boats, even a monstrous houseboat. They left a wooden skiff behind. Their sleek craft leaped from wave to wave, catching air, and then plowing through the wakes of larger vessels.

All too soon, Zane throttled back as they entered a no wake zone where speed limits were enforced. Hadley caught her breath as they slowed and the wind and spray diminished.

She relaxed once again into the red leather cushions. Her body had tensed with the excitement of the ride, but now a languor set in as they encountered other boaters, each one greeting them with a friendly wave and smile as they passed.

Hadley tried to smooth down her hair, worried about how she must look, but her short, sassy haircut easily accommodated the windblown look, and she knew it. When Zane smiled over at her, she returned his smile easily.

What the hell? She was in an extremely cool boat with an extremely good looking man. And she'd just had the ride of her life. This kind of moment occurred too rarely not to enjoy it completely.

"Wow. Now I AM hungry." She grinned at him. "Where did you say we were eating?"

18 Grand Lake O' the Cherokees

"That's where we're going." Zane nodded his head toward a marine store and dock directly in front of them.

He turned the boat to coast around and behind the store to the courtesy docks, where he parked in an empty slip. "We're here."

He killed the engines, then grabbed the rope that the teenaged worker tossed out to him, and wound it around the cleat. Hadley squinted her eyes against the sun as she gauged the distance up to the dock from the low boat. Climbing up there was going to be a challenge.

Before she had time to figure out a plan, Zane's hands encircled her waist and up she went. Before she could reach the pole and pull herself the rest of the way, a dock worker grabbed her hand and pulled her easily up to the dock and out of Zane's steadying grasp.

Hadley combed her fingers through her windblown hair. Well, she couldn't do anything about it. Where was Zane? She looked around. With his long legs and strong arms, he easily hoisted himself up onto the dock.

"In here." He opened a door and stood aside for her to enter, then led her through the crowded lakeside boat store. Cold pop and beer rivaled bikinis and sunglasses for display space.

Stopping at the counter, he removed a beer from a refrigerated case and held it up for her approval. She nodded. He paid for two meals and two beers, then led her through the front of the store, and out a door toward a deck and the lake. Several sunburned, shorts and bathing suit-clad boaters sat around wood picnic tables eating off of paper plates.

"Food's over here." A buffet set up on one end of the dock offered barbeque in foil pans. Styrofoam cups of barbeque sauce labeled hot, medium and mild with felt-tipped markers, French fries that looked not a bit French to Hadley, corn on the cob, and a tray of sliced onions and peppers. She saw iceberg lettuce salad and a few overcooked vegetables. And baked beans, of course. Yep, she was back in Oklahoma all right.

She didn't usually eat this kind of food. Back home, vegetables were always fresh and meals less meat-heavy. In contrast, the cuisine tended to focus on quality, flavor and the cooking techniques, rather than quantity. But her mouth watered at the smell, reminiscent of her childhood.

She peeked under the foil topping a pan of limp, soggy hamburger buns. That was disgusting. The smoked meat looked and smelled great and she snagged a piece. Now if they'd just had nice fresh French bread, but she couldn't handle that soggy stuff. A little barbeque sauce, though. It had been a long time.

Zane piled his plate high with every kind of meat available, and looked distressed at how little Hadley had placed on her plate.

She piled on a little more meat, just so he wouldn't think she was condescending. Silly of her. She'd probably throw a lot of it away. She added some salad and overcooked vegetables to her plate.

She usually only ate small portions. That's the way French women stayed slim. Additional pounds were not overlooked in Paris. If you started getting pudgy back home, your best friend, or even a relative stranger would not hesitate to comment on your figure.

Hadley turned in a circle to survey the area. A few seats were empty at the covered bar built into the side of the marina store. But Zane selected a small table for them down near the water, in the shade of a stripped umbrella that battled the breeze coming in off the lake.

Hadley sat facing the bar. Two girls, giggling and whispering, kept darting glances toward her. One girl had long blond hair, a very small bikini, and a dark tan that looked like it didn't stop where her bikini began.

Nice. Hadley's was the same, although not so dark. Did Grand Lake have any nude beaches? She doubted it, but maybe it had changed with the times.

"Zane, are there any nude beaches here?" She took a drink of her beer. He looked at her from underneath his eyebrows again.

He had a way of ducking his head and doing that with his eyebrow, almost a French gesture. Did he do it when he was thinking more than he said, when he was peering out at the world, or at her, from his own secret place? A slight smile quirked up one side of his mouth.

"I've heard of one, actually. A private club. Never been there. Don't really need to. Just take the boat out to Dripping

87

Springs on a Saturday and check out all the boobs on the boats. About three girls to every bikini top when the beer and rum get flowing." His eyes drifted to the girls at the bar.

The second girl had short, stylishly cut dark hair, and wore cut-off blue jeans. The zipper was only halfway zipped up, and the top of the shorts turned down so they rested on her hips and below her navel.

Her shorts and shirt covered about the same amount of skin as the other girl's bikini. The light material of her tee-shirt, cut short to show off her tan, slim midriff, hugged her full breasts tightly. Well, she isn't wearing a bra.

Hadley felt overdressed in her ankle length pants and her full cut plaid shirt of open woven fabric, cool enough for a hot Oklahoma day. And yes, she had worn a bra today.

Zane was looking at her again. "Why do you want a nude beach? Looking for an excuse to get naked?"

Hadley looked down at her food. She felt almost like he'd slapped her. What was the matter with him? She'd just asked if the damn lake had a nude beach.

He sure was touchy. Why couldn't they just relax and enjoy each other's company? The ride over in the boat had been so nice. Zane unwrapped the cheap paper napkins wrapped around a plastic spoon and fork.

"The food's pretty good here if you like barbeque." So was he trying to be nice now? "You know, this lake probably has changed quite a bit since you were a kid here. But not in the important ways. People are pretty much the same."

Hadley unrolled her napkin, avoiding his eyes. *Asshole*. She looked up as the two girls from the bar walked past their table toward the buffet. The blond brushed against Zane's blue jeans with her bare, tan leg.

So that's how it is. And he's grinning at the bitch.

The blonde looked straight ahead with a smile painted on her face. Like she didn't even notice he was there. Who cared? Hadley certainly did not care if all the girls wanted to flirt with her handyman.

She was here to eat lunch and she was hungry. Would the flimsy plastic fork cut the meat on her plate? Good. It was tender enough for the fork to deal with. Hadley tentatively tasted a bite. Zane gulped down a big swig of his beer.

"The lake has grown a lot. I mean, the boats and houses are bigger. We have a lot more stores and restaurants. A lot more people live and vacation here."

Just then, a Sea Doo plowed past their dock, spouting a plume of water. She held her breath, thinking the spray would hit them. Hadley sat there watching with a bite of meat halfway to her mouth as the machine made a sharp turn, splashing water the other way.

Suddenly, no one was driving. The Sea Doo stopped dead in the water. Two people had toppled off and were now bobbing in the water not far from the dock where she sat.

"Do you think they're OK? Should we help them?"

"Nah. Had on their life vests. Only thing wrong with them is a case of stupid. Smart enough to have the key attached to their vests so the thang stopped when they fell off. They could swim over here to the dock if they needed to." With a shrug, he took another big bite of barbeque.

The two girls who'd just brushed past them were hollering out to the couple in the water, but the wet pair just waved their hands and started swimming toward the Sea Doo.

"This side of the lake is pretty fancy. It was even when you were a kid. Even more so now. The other side is still pretty wild."

"Wild?"

"Wild as in outlaws and drugs, you know. People keep to themselves. And more Native Americans over there."

"You're a Native American?"

"Cherokee. At least my dad is. This is 'The Grand Lake O' the Cherokees,' you know."

"Grand Lake of the Cherokees?"

"No. Grand Lake O' the Cherokees. Over the Cherokees." He took another drink of his beer and sat back, looking at her. "Lake was built over the Cherokees. Over their land, their culture, and over the bodies of all the Cherokees buried here. Ever since they were run out of the East Coast."

"The Trail of Tears. I remember that from Oklahoma History, before I left. Haven't thought of it for a long, long time. It was so unfair that even Native Americans who were educated and held professional jobs were just herded out here to live. It was unfair for all of them, of course."

Hadley picked at her food, not meeting his eyes. "So your mother isn't Cherokee?"

Zane didn't say anything for a few minutes. He sat there, staring out at the lake, his chin propped on his hand.

"Nope. She wasn't."

"Wasn't? Oh, I'm sorry, Zane." She looked up at him. When he met her eyes she saw pain there, pain she recognized. The same pain she was feeling over the loss of her mother.

She opened her mouth to say she was sorry, but before she could get a word out, he started fumbling in his pocket and dragged out some folded papers.

"Here's what I figured out last night." Obviously changing the subject, he smoothed out the crumpled and slightly moist lined paper. The page was covered with figures and a few drawings.

"We need to refinish the toe rail for sure." He jabbed a finger at the first item, then continued down the list of repairs that he felt necessary to get her boat ready to sell.

"We have to replace that Bimini top. I've always thought that "*Black Gold*" needed a blue Bimini instead of that old rotted tan one."

Always thought? Was that what he'd said?

And just how long was "always"? How long had he been thinking about what her boat needed? From what Margo had said to him, he didn't even get down to her part of the lake very often.

About time she found out a little more about Monsieur Zane.

19 An Unexpected Gift

"Natalie?"

Hadley jumped at the sound of her mother's name, and looked up into the perplexed, wrinkled face of a man leaning on a cane, staring at her.

Did he think she was Mère or something? Hadley stared back as Zane quickly rose to his feet and offered his hand to the oldster.

"Mr. Halloway! So glad to see you, Sir. Let me introduce you to Hadley. She's Natalie and Warren Barrington's daughter." Hadley stood to shake the elderly man's hand in confusion. Had she ever told Zane her father's name?

"You know, my dear, you look just like your mother." The old man returned his gaze from Zane to Hadley. "How is she doing these days? I haven't seen her around these parts since you were this little."

He balanced on his cane and held his hand flat to show how tall she'd been back then. Hadley, dragged back into her recent tragedy, explained her mother's sudden death to the old gentleman. A tear leaked out of his eye.

"Dear? What's wrong? Is something the matter?"

An elderly woman, all of her clothing brilliant white, including her oversized straw hat, walked up behind Mr. Halloway.

"Oh, Norma, did you know that Natalie Barrington passed away this week? I can't believe it. And this," he took Hadley's hand and pulled her closer to him. "is her daughter. Can't you tell? Doesn't she look just like Natalie?" He stepped back and Hadley found herself face to face with Norma Halloway.

"Oh, my poor dear." The woman put her hand on Hadley's shoulder and peered at the younger girl. Although wrinkled and faded, Norma's eyes were sharp. Hadley could tell that every detail about her was being analyzed.

"Natalie, gone…" She looked over at Zane, then back at Hadley. She reached out for her husband's arm. Probably for comfort.

"Oh my darling girl. Your mother was very dear to me, as was your father. I could tell you some tales." Hadley's eyes widened. What kinds of tales of her mother and father might be out there?

Norma, chuckled softly, "No, not those. Some are better left untold, but your mother and father shared some very special times, Hadley. You should hear about them. We have to find time to talk. Are you here for long?"

Norma's warmth touched Hadley. A friend of her mother's, and her father's, who wanted to share some of their good times together. What an unexpected gift.

Maybe this woman could also shed some light on the mystery of why Mère had hung on to *Black Gold* for all of those years.

"I think I'll be here for a few days, at least. "Zane," she gestured to indicate her companion, "was just showing me a list of things that need to be done on Mom's boat." Both Mr. and Mrs. Halloway's eyes widened. That had gotten their attention.

"I found out yesterday that Mère still owned *Black Gold*. And now, I guess I own her." She shrugged her shoulders. "I don't know what to do except fix her up and sell her. I live in France, you know."

Mrs. Halloway turned to Zane. "How do you do?" She reached out to shake his hand. "I don't believe we've met?"

Her husband introduced Zane to his wife. "Honey, this is Zane. You know, Sonny Bowman's son. You remember Sonny?"

"Oh yes, Sonny's son, huh?" Norma looked thoughtful. "How interesting that you would be helping Hadley fix up her boat, Zane."

Was she protecting Hadley or was she just nosy? The older woman's curiosity reminded Hadley of Connie. They might even know each other.

Norma turned back to Hadley. "Sweetheart, we really must have a talk. You know, we're having a little get-together at our house tomorrow night. Many of your parents' friends will be there. I realize that this must be a very sad time for you."

Hadley noticed the older woman glance to Zane and back to her again. "But you really must take this opportunity to meet a few people who knew you and your parents way back when. I'm sure that even a few of your childhood playmates might be there. Let me think. Anyway, please do come, won't you?"

Merde. The last thing Hadley wanted to do right now was explain to more people how her mother had died alone in Oklahoma while her only daughter pursued her career in France.

But this wasn't about her. She owed it to Mère, she guessed. And anyway, this was her opportunity to ask questions about her boat. Someone surely had some idea. In fact, Norma Halloway seemed to have something she wanted to tell her, and not in front of Zane. Hadley couldn't pass up this opportunity.

"I would be delighted." Norma looked relieved at her response, and Earl carefully drew directions to their house on one of the cheap napkins that had come with dinner.

Then the old couple excused themselves and headed for the bar. Hadley wondered if they would also have barbeque.

Barbeque. Hadley and Zane looked down in dismay at their cold lunch. Grease had congealed around the edges. They looked up at each other.

"I think the fish are hungry." Zane glanced around to see if anyone was paying attention to them. The blond girl at the bar caught his eye, winked, then turned back to her companion. Ignoring her, Zane slid the contents of his paper plate over the side of the dock into the water.

"Go ahead. It's not pollution. The fish love this stuff."

Sure enough, a catfish surfaced to suck down a floating French fry. The water churned with hungry fish, and since they were obviously enjoying Zane's meal, Hadley followed his lead. After a quick glance to make sure no one was watching, she dumped in her cold, greasy food.

"We paid for an all-you-can eat buffet." Zane stood up. "Let's go for seconds." Over new plates of food, Zane and Hadley ran through his list again.

"If you tell me which things on this list you want done, I'll get the materials today, and I'll try my best to have everything finished in one week. That means you'll see quite a lot of me, you know. I'll be there early and work late. No sleeping in for either of us."

Hadley reviewed the list. The cost was not insignificant, but cost wasn't the issue here. Hadley had never really wanted for money. Both sides of her family had profited from the oil boom in Oklahoma through the years. They were definitely from the "Oily" side of Grand Lake.

This whole fix up the boat, sell the boat exercise was about tying up loose ends, not making money. She gave him her go-ahead to make the repairs on his list.

"Do you need me to pay for the supplies up front?" This handyman probably did not have that kind of money to invest in this job without a preliminary payment. In fact, she should probably have insisted on paying for lunch.

Zane looked taken aback. "No, no... that's not necessary. The total cost of the job is written there on the paper I gave you. You can pay me when I've finished to your satisfaction."

The trip home was fast and the water and the sky were just as blue as before, but Hadley felt somewhat subdued. Her plans were made. The wheels were turning. She would be gone from here in a week or ten days max.

She'd never have to come back to Oklahoma or Grand Lake again. She could get on with her life and her career. Just as she wanted.

Her body felt heavy, probably from all that food. She could really use a nap. Right now, she was just glad to get back to the dock.

Zane shook her hand and assured her he would purchase the supplies and be over early the next morning.

As Hadley walked down the dock toward *Black Gold*, she overtook Connie carrying a bag of groceries from her car down to her boat.

"Oh, Hadley. Zane is so yummy. How did you find him?" Connie giggled. "You did hire him, didn't you? Of course you did. If you're going to have a man working on your boat, why pick someone old and smelly? Zane will definitely improve the scenery around here. We'll ALL enjoy him working on your boat."

She glanced over at Hadley, her eyes sparkling with mischief. "Well, not the guys. They'll be jealous and suck in their guts and maybe even put on clean shirts, but we girls certainly will. Be sure and stop by tonight."

"Thanks, Connie. I'm pretty tired and I have a lot to do this afternoon. We'll see." She turned to walk down to the back of her boat, then turned back.

"Hey, Connie, do you know the Halloways? Norma Halloway, and I'm not sure what her husband's name was. Mr. Halloway?"

"Norma and Earl Halloway?" Connie stopped and looked back at Hadley.

Oh she'd seen that look before. Curiosity sparkled in Connie's eyes. "I know OF them. Mr. Halloway is a benefactor to several charities and arts groups in Tulsa. Everyone knows Earl Halloway."

"Oh. Well, I met them today. Zane knows him, and they knew my parents. I'm going to a party at their house tomorrow night. I have the directions here." She pulled the rumpled napkin out of her pocket. "Should be kind of interesting. I thought maybe someone there might have an idea of why Mère held on to this boat. Who knows?"

"Wow. A party at the Halloway's." Connie looked impressed. "Well, I want to hear about every minute of it. Everyone you meet and all the details. OK? Promise me!"

"*Oui.*" Hadley turned and climbed up the back of her boat, where her parents' ghosts awaited her.

20 *Knights in Shining Armor*

She'd never be able to get these sacks to the dumpster. Hadley slowly dragged two over-filled garbage bags off her boat, the results of a three-hour battle with bugs and dust.

Walking backwards, she strained to tug them along the dock. They had to go all the way to the trash bins at the top of the hill. Although they slid across the old wooden planks just fine, she was afraid the shale in the parking lot would tear holes in the super-tuff plastic.

Half way up the ramp, she stopped to catch her breath, pushing back sweaty bangs as she stared at the black plastic sacks. She heard flip flops coming up behind her and turned.

"We're your knights in shining armor!" The cute guy from last night's party, Ryan, brandished a stick as a make-believe sword in the air. He assumed the stance of some kind of storybook hero, grinning at her impishly. Behind him, Adam shrugged and rolled his blue eyes, as he reached for a garbage bag with a brotherly smile. But Ryan was not through with his act.

"Let us help you. Then let us take you far away from this dilapidated dock and this scorching sun and ply you with food and wine."

Ryan's leer was not at all brotherly. "Or rum. Or vodka. Just let us ply you." Hadley couldn't help laughing. Back down by Adam's boat, Meg waved at her as she strolled toward the trio.

"Seriously, Hadley, and I realize that no one can take Ryan seriously, we really would love to take you with us tonight." Meg caught up with them and raised up on her tiptoes to give Adam a kiss on the ear. "We're going to Jimmz for drinks and dancing. Why don't you come along? We know you've been down here cleaning your fingers to the bone. You need a boat ride."

Images of how much fun it had been out on the water with Zane earlier in the day flashed through Hadley's mind. She wiped her hands on the seat of her shorts.

She was filthy. Tired. Hungry. Thirsty. She did deserve a little fun. For a second, she wondered what Zane's plans for the evening were. Well, they definitely didn't include her. She was alone. Just ghosts waited for her back in the boat.

"You go clean up, Hadley, and we'll take care of these bags." Ryan swung one of the huge bags over his shoulder and pretended to stumble to one knee under its weight, then grinned up at her.

"You've just got to go out on Adam's boat with us, and Jimmz is a rockin' joint!" His smile was infectious.

Hadley looked around for any trace of Gordon and Connie. When she'd spoken to them earlier, they'd mentioned getting together with her, but the couple was nowhere to be seen.

"OK. Sounds like fun. Let me clean up." Hadley felt a tickling sensation on her leg. "*Merde!*" She swiped wildly at a tiny spider, sending it spinning off into the lake.

Ryan sat down his bag and knelt to examine her leg. "Let Dr. Ryan have a look at that leg, young lady." Hadley jumped back.

"She's already had to deal with one creepy crawling insect, Ryan." Adam swatted his friend on top of the head with the palm of his hand.

"Leave her alone or you'll scare her so badly she won't come with us." He tipped his ball cap at Hadley. "Let me apologize for m'friend here. We'll just be on our way, Ma'am."

Ryan recovered his trash bag, and before Hadley could rethink her acceptance to their invitation, the guys were halfway to the trash bins. She glanced back at Meg, who was strolling back toward her boat.

"Thanks!' Hadley smiled at Meg's back. The woman turned to flash Hadley a quick smile and saluted her with the glass in her hand, before heading back down the dock. Hadley tuned back to *Black Gold*.

The steaming hot water felt so good on her back. She'd never appreciated being clean so much until she'd been exposed to Oklahoma dirt.

Now what to wear? Hadley poked around in her closet and suitcase. Not much there, since she hadn't planned a trip to the lake when she'd packed. Ah yes. She'd brought that short black skirt. Simple and casual. Didn't she have a black camisole somewhere? Yup. It would be cool and sexy. Perfect.

What could she do to dress the outfit up just a little? That wide stretchy red belt would be perfect. And she had a pair of red sandals somewhere, and, of course she'd brought more jewelry than clothes suitable for wearing at the lake.

She fastened a large lime green and red necklace carved with black hieroglyphs around her neck. The overlapping pattern of ivory discs was held together by green and red woven leather. And the matching earrings. Yes. Quite nice.

Hadley had started using leather in combination with expensive gems this year, and the pieces were a hit in Paris. The large green Amazonite centerpiece of the necklace contrasted starkly with her black skimpy outfit. *Très chic.* She swept her lips with coral lipstick and fluffed her still damp hair. She'd do.

As she approached Adam's and Meg's slip, Ryan, catching sight of her, froze where he stood, and his mouth drooped open.

He groped in the general direction of his heart with both hands, seeming not to be able to find it.

"I lost my heart when I saw you." He walked toward her, holding out his arms as if beseeching her. "Kiss me, my lady and save my life!"

He collapsed limply on the dock at her feet. Hadley glanced over at Meg, who stood, hands on hips, looking down at the collapsed figure in disgust. Ryan sat back up, his hands clutched beneath his chin as if pleading. "Let me gaze upon you. You are a goddess!"

Meg took Hadley's hand, pulling her around behind the kneeling Ryan and toward the boat. Then she turned to give him a light kick in the leg, as he remained there gazing toward where Hadley had been standing a moment before.

Hadley walked off with her friend, ignoring the clown. He was funny, but irritating.

"You haven't seen the inside of *Rum-Runner*, our boat. Come on in." The older woman ushered Hadley into the salon, all rich woods and bright fabrics.

The floors were parquet and the wooden furniture was built-in, leaving plenty of room to move around. The cabinets in the tiny kitchen on the same level were crowded with the ingredients and accoutrements for boat drinks.

"Help yourself." Meg followed her own advice, clinking a few ice cubes from an icemaker into her half empty glass and opening a cabinet door to show her friend an array of glasses from which to choose.

Drinks in hand, Meg led Hadley on the grand tour of their boat. It was not a Saint Tropez yacht, but it was cute and cozy. Hadley liked it.

Meg explained that Marine Traders were built in Taiwan and were designed for comfort, not show. Everything was charming and neat as a pin. The couple had a snug and pleasant home away from home.

Hopefully the right buyer would appreciate *Black Gold* just as much as this couple seemed to love *Rum Runner*. Her family had enjoyed some really good times on their boat, and some really bad ones.

"Ready to cast off?" Adam called down from the fly bridge.

"Ready, my Captain." Meg winked at Hadley.

The motor thrummed steadily as Adam checked all the systems.

"Ryan?" He rang the ship's bell to get his friend's attention. "Anchors away!" The boat glided smoothly out of its slip and into the twilight.

21 The Wild and Wooly Side

"Come on, Hadley. Let's go up on top with the boys." Meg led the way up a short stairway to emerge on the fly bridge under the bright blue canvas Bimini as they motored out of the bay.

The two women settled into a comfortable white wicker settee on the aft deck behind where Adam steered. They watched the wake churn and the gulls dip to take advantage of any injured fish.

"Do you know where the Halloways—Norma and Earl Halloway—live?" Meg's eyes narrowed at the question.

"Up near the Yacht Club. Not far from here. One of those big houses right on the lake. I'm not sure exactly how to get there. I mean, you can see their house from the water, but those little roads that go to those houses are a maze back in there. Why?"

"Oh, they invited me to a party, and I'm thinking about it." Meg's eyebrows arched up over her eyes. "They knew my parents."

Hadley was having second thoughts about attending the event. Her heart still protested that a party was the last place she wanted to be right now.

But then, again, she was kind of going to one tonight, she guessed. Sitting by herself in her old boat was just not helping her cope with her loss. But would anything help right now?

Going home would help. Or would it? Back home to that empty apartment that she'd always shared with Mère? She took another drink and pushed the dark thoughts to the back of her mind.

Adam took it slow. No hot rodding from that boy, Hadley noticed. Ryan put on some mellow country music, and Meg pointed out the sites along the lake as they passed, the marinas and the mansions.

Hadley, used to the grandeur of the Riveria, was still impressed by some of the homes perched on the bluffs here. Had there been such impressive mansions when Hadley had spent her summers here as a child? Who knew?

Actually Zane had indicated that this side was much more developed now. The "rich oily" side. He came from the other side. The wild and wooly side. But it was a big lake, stretching miles north, with many estuaries, coves and bays. A lot of room for different kinds of communities.

She probably hadn't really noticed the palatial homes much back when she was a kid. When you grew up in a place, you just took everything for granted. But when you went away for many years, and then saw the same thing with fresh eyes, you noticed.

"That's the Halloway house right up there.

"Where?" Hadley scanned the houses with property that led down to the waterfront. Not easy to do at night, but all these houses had lots of lights.

"The one on top of that hill, with the lawn that comes all the way down to the water and the cool boat dock with the room built up on top of it. See the tile roof? By that light pole. And the balconies? The one with the trees down by the water over there. See it? I'm pointing right at it."

"Oh, that one. The one we're passing right now? With the arches?"

"Yeah, that one."

"*C'est super!* Very nice. Wonder if I'll be able to figure out how to get there. If I decide to go."

22 *The Turquoise Guitar*

They motored on down the lake, waving to the people on all the boats they met. Finally they came to a marina back in a bay, perched up on a hill.

Behind the boat store, hovering high up in the trees, was a deck sporting a couple of lit up fake palm trees and a big sign that read, "Jimmz."

As the two men and two women climbed the steep steps up to the deck, everyone but Hadley waved to people they knew. She just looked around.

The bar area looked like a tiki hut. Actually, it looked like a very fake tiki hut. The music was Jimmy Buffet and Kenny Chesney. That kind of thing.

The group snared a table outside by the wooden rail, where they could look out over the water and watch the boats arriving and leaving. The reflection of the lights of the dock and boats swirled and shimmered on the dark water below.

A waitress materialized to take their order. No wonder the boys liked to come here. She looked about sixteen, with long, almost white hair. She wore white cowboy boots. The glittery rear pockets on cut-off blue-jean shorts emphasized her perky butt.

A wide, ornate belt circled her hips below her bare midriff, and her pierced belly button sported a sparkly dangly ornament. She was extremely tan, heavily made up, and very beautiful. She smiled and made eye contact with the men, but not the girls, as she took their orders.

"Hey Meg!" A short, buxom woman with dark hair streaked with blond and red highlights appeared from the shadows of the tiki hut bar, carrying a turquoise guitar.

"Randi!" Meg hopped up, arms spread wide. Randi, dropping her guitar on the table, hurled herself into Meg's arms, squealing. After several enthusiastic hugs, Meg held her friend out from her and examined her closely. "Are you playing here tonight?"

"Oh, I am, but I can take a break." Randi laughed and collapsed into a chair next to Ryan. Her black vest topped a red tee-shirt and her tight blue jeans accentuated her ample curves. Huge earrings peeped from underneath her layered, shoulder-length hair.

"You know Adam and Ryan." Ryan stood and made a courtly bow to the pretty woman. "And this is Hadley."

"Howdy, Hadley." Randi reached around Ryan to shake her hand. "Oh! Look at that necklace you have on, girl! Where'd you get it? I love jewelry! She flipped her long silver necklace, made of silver loops with occasional tiny padlocks attached here and there to the chain. "I made this 'un myself."

"Hadley makes jewelry in Paris!" Meg leaned over to get into the conversation between her two friends. "That's what she does."

"Oh wow! Did you make that stuff you have on?" Randi's eyes grew large as she stared at Hadley.

"Yes." Hadley smiled at Randi. "And I really like your necklace. That's such an interesting design. I would never have thought of it, myself."

Hadley really did find Randi's chain interesting and unique, and kind of wished Meg had just kept quiet about her jewelry business. Most people didn't have the opportunities she'd had to attend the French National Institute of Gemology in Nice and intern with a famous gemologist—one of her mother's friends.

But the comparison of their necklaces didn't seem to bother the woman with the turquoise guitar and the big smile.

"How did you all get this table? It's usually always taken." Randi leaned forward, resting her chin in her hands, elbows on the table.

"Really lucky, I guess." Ryan scooted closer to Hadley. "But it's a good one. Now we can spot any cougars coming this way."

He stage whispered. "Jimmz is cougar central on weekends, but some of 'em slink around during the week too. You know, man is the cougar's number one prey."

Hadley flipped the hand he rested on her shoulder with her fingers.

"Ouch!" He frowned at her as he removed his hand.

"Yeah." Randi leaned toward him. "Don't be so down on older women, Ryan. You really shouldn't run so hard. You might like you a little cougar if you tried it. Why should a beautiful woman be stuck with a hairless, big gutted, man who can only talk about his insurance premiums and has the TV remote control permanently attached to his hand? Why would she choose that guy, when she has her choice of all the dumb hunks like you to be had on every dock?"

Silence fell around the table as Adam and Ryan seemed to contemplate Randi's comment.

"In fact, I can kind of understand why they might prefer to hunt for themselves rather than be hunted." Randi stared back defiantly at a drunk who looked like he might be thinking about approaching their table.

"You'd better be careful, Ryan." Meg seemed to be trying her best to look like a stern schoolmarm, her lips pursed. "You might not have a boat ride home. Lots of people think I'm a cougar!" She laughed as she pinched his cheek.

"Oh no, Meg. That's ludicrous. You're one of us. And you look so young. And you're not THAT much older than Adam." He wrinkled his forehead as he started counting off years on his fingers.

Adam slapped Ryan on the back of his head. "Shut up dude. Before you get hurt." He put his arm around Meg's shoulders and she looked into his eyes lovingly.

"Oh no!" Ryan rose half-way out of his chair, peeking over the wooden railing as some commotion on the dock below drew his attention. "It's the friggin' cougar brigade, come to call."

Hadley glanced down at the dock.

"Where?" I only see Margo from the marina."

"Cougar woman makes up a brigade all by herself." Ryan slumped into his seat and fortified his masculine courage with another drink of his beer. "Well, at least they don't ask you to call 'em later."

"Oh?" Randi sat up straight and stared into Ryan's eyes with a slow smile. "Would you like to tell us how you know that?"

Adam and Meg snickered. Ryan sat silent, for once, as everyone stared at him.

23 *Carpe Diem*

As Hadley struggled to keep her face straight, she once again felt a hand settle on her shoulder. Preparing to tell Ryan to keep his hands to himself, she turned with a snarl. But what she saw was only a golden arm that was not attached to Ryan at all, but to someone she hadn't seen approaching.

She knew before her eyes reached the muscled shoulder that it belonged to Zane. He had obviously been standing there a few minutes, because he was laughing with them at Ryan's discomfort.

Hadley's snarl quickly melted into an easy smile as she met Zane's eyes. At least their expressions started relaxed and friendly. But as they looked at each other, fire seemed to build, and she fell into his gaze, catching her breath. Heat radiated from her shoulder where his hand softly but confidently rested.

Ryan and Adam seemed to take an interest in the fact that she didn't push him away. Meg and Randi looked from Zane to Hadley and back again, then at each other with knowing smiles.

Hadley stood, managing to dislodge the big, tan hand in the process, and moved over to the balcony rail. She didn't want anyone to think she was easy prey, and certainly not for Zane. He was just the guy working on her boat!

She'd learned to keep men guessing. She knew hot and cold drove them crazy. But did she want to drive Zane crazy?

She didn't entirely trust him. Keeping him off-balance was surely the smartest move.

She leaned over into the night, hiding the flush she knew must show on her face, or maybe not, since her cheeks and nose were a little sunburned from that morning's boat ride.

Zane turned to the men at the table with a confident smile, offering his hand. "Hi. I'm Zane Bowman. I'm helping Hadley get her boat ready to sell."

"Hi up there!" Margo waved up at Hadley and started climbing the steps to the deck. Hadley smiled and waved back.

"Now you've gone and done it." Ryan slumped in his chair. "Here she comes. She'll want to sit with us, and she'll be feeling us up with her toes and stuff. Crap."

"Sorry." Hadley turned back to the table, laughing.

"I know!" Adam jumped up and pulled Meg after him. "Let's dance. Everyone! Get up and dance. Don't leave anyone at the table. Come on!"

"Sounds like a good idea to me. Hadley?" Zane grabbed her hand and pulled her toward the dance floor out by the florescent pink flamingo lights.

Ryan grabbed Randi, then pulled some sweaty bills from his pocket and thrust them toward the band with a request, and the music picked up.

It felt good to let loose and dance. The music was country. Hadley improvised.

She'd danced to every kind of music in the clubs and on the yachts of the Côte d'Azur. She and her friends had partied though many sultry nights, drinking Cristal, and often ending up spraying each other with bottles of the expensive champagne.

She was a long way from France now, but Zane sure knew what he was doing on the dance floor. He twirled her, swinging her around, and she suddenly found herself wrapped in his arms, their eyes and lips inches apart for just a moment. The world around them faded away for just that second, then they swung apart again.

The music ended and Ryan yelled, "Again!" All three couples whirled and spun energetically. When that dance was over, they stumbled over and collapsed into their seats at the table, gulping their drinks and looking for the cute little waitress to order another round.

"You kids are certainly full of vim and vigor tonight." Margo's high heels clicked on the wooden deck, as she approached their table carrying a drink decorated with a tiny umbrella.

"Randi, Jim's looking for you. They're ready for you to sing." She smiled smugly as Randi grabbed her guitar and headed for the stage. Then she casually seated herself in the empty seat next to Ryan, who squirmed uncomfortably. Hadley scooted her chair closer to Adam's to make room as Zane dragged an empty chair from the next table over and placed it between Hadley's and Ryan's.

The little waitress sashayed over to the rearranged table. Margo ordered tequila shots all around, and scooted her chair a little closer to Ryan's.

A little later, when Margo ordered another round of shots. Hadley and Zane both pushed theirs away and nursed their beers, rolling their eyes at each other as the other members of the party rapidly grew louder and sloppier.

"I don't think you should ride home with this crew, do you?" Zane whispered into her ear. "I don't think it would be prudent. And as your loyal employee, I think it's my duty make sure you get home safely."

Hadley considered the situation. The man had a good point. When he arched that quizzical eyebrow at her, she nodded.

"Hey, gonna dance?" Meg slurred the question as Hadley and Zane stood up. "We might too. Uh, Adam?"

"Yeah! Let's dance!" Adam stood up, a bit wobbly, and draped his arm around his girlfriend's shoulder. "Come on e'vbody!"

Interesting, Ryan didn't seem to be fighting off Margo quite so valiantly anymore. The older woman pulled him up out of his seat and led him toward the dance floor.

"Hey, Meg, Adam" Hadley called to her friends as they headed toward the music.

"Huh? Ya'all comin'?" Meg squinted at them.

"No. No. Uh, Zane's going to give me a ride home." Meg stopped and turned back toward them, directing a cockeyed leer at the two.

"Oh. I see."

"I'm, Uh, tired. That's all. And it's awfully hot." Hadley shrugged her shoulders and wiped her sweaty palms on the seat of her skirt.

"Yeah. I see it is. Well," Meg came over and looked Hadley directly in the face. "You come over, tomrra, hear? Don' be a stranger. Promise?"

She directed an appraising glance at Zane that started with his face and wandered slowly down the rest of his body, stopping strategically at his zipper.

"Yeah, it is pretty hot." She giggled and turned to follow Adam.

"Geez." Zane guided Hadley toward the exit, his hand on the small of her back. "Let's get out of here."

A table stationed at the top of the stairs leading down to the dock held an ice bucket with free bottled water.

Zane grabbed two as they passed, handing one to Hadley. Music and laughter from Jimmz trailed them as they walked down the dock to a white wooden boat, tied up beside Adam's *Rum Runner*.

"This is my dad's boat. He's had it for a long time. It's almost as old as *Black Gold*, but it's a day boat. I mean, it does have a vee-berth up front, but it's not very comfortable. See? All of it is deck. It makes a great fishing boat, and a pretty good party boat too. And it's pretty fast. Light. Really scoots across the water."

Hadley ran her hand down the side of the carefully maintained varnished toe rail. "What's its name?"

"Carpe Diem."

"Seize the day." muttered Hadley, "*Profitez de l'instant présent*. My mother's favorite phrase."

She sighed. Was it a little cooler down by the water, or was it just her imagination? The sound of water sloshing against the dock at least fooled her senses into imagining that she felt a breeze.

"Can you cast us off?" Zane climbed into the boat. Hadley was used to being a passenger on yachts more recently than she'd been on many private boats where the passengers were also the crew, but she remembered the drill. She'd done it enough as a kid. She stayed on the dock while Zane boarded and fired up the engines.

"OK!"

When he yelled, she slipped the ropes off of the post and tossed them into the boat, swinging herself lightly up and over the side.

As Zane eased the boat away from the courtesy dock, he grinned at her over his shoulder. She opened one of the bottles of water from Jimmz and handed it to him, then opened one for herself.

Perched up on the table in the small, open cabin, she could see where they were headed. The lake was dark. Red and green navigational lights of a few boats in the distance moved slowly, but Hadley and Zane were practically alone.

"I'm really glad we got out of there when we did." Zane smoothly guided the boat around a turn, and out onto the main body of the lake.

"When Jimmz closes, a herd of boats full of by people way too drunk to drive will be out here trying to kill each other."

Hadley glanced over at him. A brisk breeze from the side window blew in on him, molding his shirt to his chest. His hair swept backward off his face. The muscles in his arms knotted as he controlled the craft.

Meg was right. He was definitely hot.

24 *Good Clean Oklahoma Fun*

Zane steered the boat through the darkness, glad that he'd been there to rescue Hadley from that crew. Not that he was all that sober. Probably not as bad off as most of the partiers leaving the bars, though.

And he'd been driving a boat on this lake since he was about six, with his dad's supervision at first. And he knew the lake, where the channels ran, where it was shallow, where an anchor would hold, and where the good swimming holes were.

In fact, swimming really sounded good right now. He wiped the sweat from his forehead before it could drip into his eyes. Even though the night was sweltering, he knew the water would be cool.

"Oklahoma is HOT!" Hadley pushed her hair up off of the nape of her neck. "Can't wait to jump into the shower when I get home."

Zane wondered if she'd go for the idea that had just popped into his mind. A nice cool swim with this beautiful Parisian expat was just what he needed tonight, even if his dad would kill him if he found out about it.

Crap. Since when was he interested in anyone but Grand Lake girls? What was wrong with him? He'd always shied away from anyone the least bit foreign or exotic. For good reason.

But, something about this girl made him reckless. He was having a hard time schooling his desires tonight. Hot summer nights were dangerous that way.

He watched her out of the corner of his eye to gauge her reaction to what he was about to propose. She was staring out into the night. Her mouth was slightly open, and her chest and breasts heaved as she took a deep breath.

"I don't know about you, Hadley, but I can't stand this stickiness anymore."

He knew he should cool down. His body was clearly in charge of his head. He watched her pour a little water from the plastic bottle into her hand and rub her face with it.

"You may not remember, since you've lived in Paris so long, but sometimes, in Oklahoma, it stays hot right through the night." She turned to him. Her eyes liquid in the dark.

"We might jump into the water real quick and rinse off before we go on home. I know a place right over there," He pointed toward a little cove to their right. "A great place to anchor and swim."

Hadley looked out the window at the dark water, then shut her eyes and rested her forehead on the edge of the window.

She could imagine how the water would feel. The coolness was so close, right outside the boat window. It splashed temptingly against the outside of the boat.

She opened her eyes and looked over at him.

"I didn't bring a bathing suit."

Zane laughed. "Your clothes are pretty sweaty too, Hadley. They could use a wash, or we could always skinny dip."

Hey, it was a shot. Heaven knows he'd love to see her naked. The memory of her firm breasts under the wet cloth of her blouse the day before overwhelmed any thoughts of what his dad would say if he knew what his son was doing right now.

They'd had a few drinks. They were alone, late at night out on the lake. It wasn't as if he hadn't been in this situation before, and no one had gotten hurt. Not when everyone wanted the same thing. Good clean Oklahoma fun.

Hadley, groggy from the drinks at Jimmz and limp from the heat, wondered how it would feel, jumping into the water bare. The fresh cool liquid would slide over her. Zane's naked body would brush by, then their bodies would come together.

Whoo. She shook her head to dispel the image and gather her wits, which seemed to have a mind of their own tonight.

"Oh, ok. I think I'd like to jump in and cool off, just for a minute." The boat's name was *Carpe Diem*. How many women had been influenced by that name and let Zane seize the day and have his way on this boat?

"And my clothes do need a wash too!" Better keep at least that barrier between them, tonight at least. After all, she didn't know him. He was just the guy fixing her boat.

No reason to be hasty, except, when he looked at her like that, from under his brows, like he knew what she was thinking, or at least hoped he knew, her body didn't want to wait. It knew what it wanted.

It was ready to race, even if her mind was trying to keep on the brakes. She needed the coolness of the water right this minute!

25 Lake Monsters and Water Sprites

"Here. Sit up here in the captain's seat. You don't have to do anything. The motor is idling. I'm going to throw out the anchor."

Zane slipped out of the high captain's chair, then took her hand as she climbed up, enjoying the view. Her short knit skirt didn't hide much.

With pride in his own restraint, Zane exited the cabin, and made his way around the outside of the boat to the bow. He knelt to unfasten the heavy anchor and hoist it over the side, playing out the rope until it pulled taunt.

Back in the cabin, he reached around in front of Hadley to pull back on the levers, reversing the engines and setting the anchor.

"There. All set." He backed up a step and held out his hand to help her down. She jumped, but underestimated the height and landed almost in his arms.

He reached out to prevent her falling. And there she was, close. He wanted to wrap his arms around her and kiss her, but she laughed up at him and sprinted toward the back of the boat.

Dropping her jewelry into a chair, she quickly disappeared over the transom and into the water.

He'd never seen a girl swim in a skirt before, but it was so short, it wouldn't bother her. Zane stripped to his underwear and jumped in after her. He sucked in his breath at the initial shock of the cool water. Now, where had Hadley gone? He scanned the darkness.

There she was, floating on her back out behind the boat. He dove beneath the surface and then exploded out the water right beside her. She uttered a small scream.

"Don't do that Zane. I don't know what kind of monsters live in this lake. Well, really I do. I swam in it enough as a kid, but not usually at night."

"Sorry, Hadley. I won't scare you again." He floated beside her. "Here, hold my hand so we don't get separated. I'll protect you from any monsters." They floated companionably for a few minutes.

"So, what do you think of Oklahoma, after living in Paris so long?"

"Exotic!" she exclaimed, to his surprise. She let loose of his hand and disappeared beneath the water, only to surface again on the other side of him.

"Exotic?" When she was once more floating on her back, he lazily turned over in the water, floating on his stomach, his face turned to her. "How can you say that when you came here from France?"

"It just depends on your point of view." She looked over at him. Her lips were so close. "France is home to me. America is no longer my home. It's foreign. Even though I lived here long ago, looking at it through adult eyes, it's not home anymore. It's different and exotic."

Her comment kind of made sense when you reflected on it. He'd just never thought of it that way. He turned back over on his back and stared up at the stars.

Actually, it disturbed him that anyone else would think of his home that way. He had never wanted exotic or foreign or different. He'd only wanted to be a part of his community.

Hadley struck out toward the boat, leaving him floating there. She was the exotic one, so different from the other Grand Lake girls. So why was he was attracted to her? It had to just be physical. Nothing else.

His mother had been different too. He missed her terribly and her going had left a giant black hole in his heart, but he'd grown up wishing she had been more like everyone else's mom.

A girl from far away could never be someone he'd take seriously. But maybe they could be friends. Friends with privileges, maybe? He could handle that, as long as his dad didn't get wind of it.

He rolled over in the water and swam after Hadley. It would be nice to get to know her better, even though she confused him. He grabbed at her playfully, but her slim, wet body slipped through his arms like a fish and she was up on the teak swim platform, then up the side of the boat before he could recover.

Her wet clothing clung to every slim curve, her hair was spiked with water, her nipples jutted out from the breeze against her wet body and clothing. Looking like a mermaid or a water sprite, she sat on the side of the boat, laughing down at him.

"And I think you are exotic, Zane." She grinned wickedly, her voice mischievous. "You are nothing like the men I know in Paris." She climbed into the boat. Moonlight reflected on her dark wet hair, adding golden highlights. "You were so right about swimming. I feel so much better now."

Zane started to climb aboard after her, but became aware that he'd better not right away, for his clothing would cling too. He was sure that the tell-tale sign of his need for her would be apparent.

So he turned and swam, hard, with thrusting, strong stokes, to the opposite side of the cove and back. By the time he returned to the boat, he had worn himself out enough to gain some control.

He climbed into the boat and grabbed two towels from the vee berth. He tied one around his waist, and carried the other one back to wrap around Hadley's shoulders.

As he started to back away—he didn't want to frighten her—she sighed and leaned back against him, her wet hair resting on his chest.

He stood there with his hands on her shoulders as they looked out over the dark lake. The partiers were headed home. Zane could just make out lights passing the opening of the cove. One was traveling way too fast for nighttime conditions, and he hoped those people made it home safely.

The moon was out, playing its light across the main body of the lake, and stars reflected off of the water. Beautiful. But he felt Hadley shiver. The night was finally cooling off.

"Would you like a jacket?" She gratefully nodded, so he grabbed the one he always kept tucked away in the boat, even in the summer.

She took it from him with a smile, but just stood there for a minute facing him. Then she rose up on her tiptoes and touched her lips to his, softly and fleetingly.

His lips parted, ready for more. But instead of allowing him to kiss her the way she should be kissed, she backed away and put on the jacket, leaving him breathless and throbbing. Good thing he'd put on that towel.

26 The Sounds of Home

"What can I do to help you bring in the anchor? We'd better get home." Hadley backed up a few more steps to put distance between her and Zane.

She didn't want to. She wanted to open up the door behind him and drag him down the steps to the vee berth and experience the hardness she could see beneath his towel.

She took a deep breath. He worked for her. He was keeping secrets. It was all too confusing. She was really attracted to him, but wasn't sure if she wanted to complicate her stay on Grand Lake and the job of getting the boat ready to sell. She needed to stay in control.

So for now, she'd keep her distance. But before she left, hmm. Her body ached for him, physically ached for that beautiful golden physique.

His wet hair hung down in his eyes, his full lips were parted as if ready to continue the kiss she'd unwisely started.

His eyes smoldered from under those dark brows and she knew he was feeling the same desire that she felt for him. They'd better get out of here quickly, or they'd still be here in the morning.

To her relief (or was it disappointment?), Zane turned away. After flashing her a lazy smile, he eased himself into the captain's chair and started the engines. The lights played out over the water and highlighted the trees on the shore. A slight smell of gasoline permeated the night air.

She'd thought she might have to fight him off, and a part of her may even have hoped for that, and for losing the fight. It wouldn't have taken much, she admitted to herself.

But Zane went about getting them underway in a polite and even rather distant manner. He brought pulled up the anchor, then guided the boat out of the cove and played the tour guide on the way home, pointing out landmarks, shadowy in the night, that she'd never remember.

Her mind was elsewhere. When they arrived at the dock, *Rum Runner* was parked securely in its slip. No one was around. Everyone must have succumbed to their evening of partying and drinking. Zane tied up his boat and offered to escort her to her ghost ship.

"Thanks, but it's not far. Thanks a lot for the safe ride home." From the smile in his eyes, she knew he was thinking that the safe part had been in doubt for a while there.

"I'll be over early."

"That sounds good. See you tomorrow."

She walked down the dock between bobbing, silent boats.

As she passed Margo's houseboat, Hadley noticed a tell-tale rocking that was more than the normal rhythm of a boat on the water. She giggled and rolled her eyes. Soft voices drifted from inside as she hurried on to *Black Gold.*

She hugged Zane's jacket that he'd forgotten to reclaim around herself, glancing back at the gently rolling houseboat.

Was she was a little jealous? That was silly. She had more important matters to see to. Hadley climbed the swim ladder and entered her cabin alone.

Hadley woke up early and checked her phone.

"Rentrer à la maison," read the text message. *"*Come home."

Violette, Hadley's assistant, did not understand what was keeping her employer and friend away from Paris and her studio. Customers were calling, complaining, she wrote. Gems were arriving. Come home.

The woman's *petit ami,* Jules, kept complaining of the long hours Violette had to work. He resented the stress she was under. And it was all Hadley's fault because she wouldn't come back to Paris where she belonged.

Hadley glanced at her watch and made a quick mental calculation to French time. She'd call Violette later. Right now, the Frenchwoman wouldn't be awake, much less at the studio.

She laid down her phone, rubbing her eyes. Why wasn't there a coffee maker on this boat? Her dad used to drink buckets of coffee, especially after a night of partying and seducing. Maybe she hadn't checked every place one could be hidden. But why bother? If she found one, it would be too old and dirty anyway. Hadley added a coffee pot to her list. A cheap one.

She hadn't slept very soundly, tossing and turning, and, yes, thinking of Zane. Although she wasn't sure what she was thinking about him.

All of Hadley's problems kept swirling around in her head, along with memories of last night's swim. Really, though, she couldn't believe that this local guy kept invading her thoughts. Probably just her subconscious awareness of the activities next door.

Opening the drapes just a little, Hadley peeked out toward Margo's houseboat. Sure enough, Ryan was creeping off the boat, trying not to attract any attention. When he glanced her way, she quickly ducked into the shadows.

His eyes lingered on the window a second. Had he seen her, or was she just on his mind? Well, either way, he was the least of her worries. Zane, on the other hand....

After a quick shower, Hadley searched through her clothing for something clean and appropriate. The wardrobe situation was getting serious.

Good thing she was driving into Tulsa tomorrow. She'd pick up some lake clothes, shorts and tops that she wouldn't feel bad about getting dirty. And a coffee maker.

Maybe Connie was up and had some coffee made? Hadley walked out onto the deck of the old boat but she seemed to be the only person stirring.

A bug carcass crunched under her bare foot. Ridiculous. Her broom was leaning against the wall just inside the sliding door, so she grabbed it and started sweeping.

She'd spent yesterday working inside. Zane was going to start working out here today and he'd probably make a big mess. But at least she could get rid of the dead bugs.

She focused all her energy on trying to clean every inch of the deck. Then she attacked a few spider webs she could reach with the broom.

Would the hose reach up here? The broom was only removing loose material. Dirt was caked on the boards, the result of years of neglect.

She hummed along as she swept, then began to sing softly, sweeping to the rhythm.

"...Heaven sighs...." She grimaced at the pile of dead bugs and other filth she'd piled up and continued to sweep. "...la vie en rose...."

How many times she'd heard that song belted out in the streets of Paris. She closed her eyes, remembering the smells, the sounds of home.

As she stopped humming, standing there with her broom still in her hands, she realized that she could actually hear the song. It wasn't merely her imagination. And the smell of coffee drifted in the breeze. Was she going crazy?

Walking around the cabin of the boat to see where the song originated, she realized that it was coming from Margo's boat.

Hadley had only heard trop-rock belting from the houseboat's music system before, but now the lyrics of Edith Piaf floated softly from the giant speakers.

Margo sat at a small table on the spacious deck of her boat. A simple short white satiny wrap, tied around her waist, exposed her generous cleavage.

She took a sip of coffee from a porcelain cup as she gazed out over the lake. Then her look drifted up to Hadley, standing above her, holding her broom, and staring down in amazement.

Margo smiled warmly, and held up her coffee cup as if for a toast. Hadley smiled back, unsure what to say.

"Would you like to join me for some coffee?" The older woman stood and walked over to the tiki bar, refilling her cup from an electric coffee maker. "Have you had breakfast? I was just going to have some fruit and croissants."

"Croissants?" Where would Margo have gotten croissants out here in the middle of nowhere? "Be right down. Just a second."

Propping her broom against the wooden cabin, Hadley slipped inside and washed her hands, then made her way down to the dock and over to Margo's boat. She wanted to know what this was all about, French music, croissants, as well as coffee!

By the time she arrived on the houseboat, Margo had set down two small plates with forks and napkins. Two dishes had also appeared, one with sliced fruit and the other with hot crusty croissants.

Hadley's eyes widened as she realized they were chocolate croissants. *A pain au chocolat.* But how? She looked at Margo in wonder, and the older woman laughed gently, mischievousness sparkling in her eyes.

"My secret? No. I don't have a French chef hidden in my boat, although I do know one who does make the most divine Cherry Clafoutis."

"But, you didn't make these yourself, did you?" Hadley reached for a crusty pastry as the mother hummingbird zipped by right over the women's head, fulfilling her motherly duties.

"No. Well, in a way, yes. But I cheat. I'm no one's 'wifey-poo.' These are from William Sonoma. No. Really they are."

She laughed again at the look of disbelief on her guest's face. "They're frozen, you see."

Hadley took a delicious bite and shook her head.

"I don't believe you. You MUST have a handsome French chef hidden in that boat. Where is he?"

"No. They are frozen. But you have to let them rise overnight, and then just put them in your toaster oven."

"*Non!* It cannot be so easy! But these are wonderful, and make me think of home. And the music. So you have been to Paris."

It was a statement, not a question. For some reason she just knew, although she would never have expected it from her previous encounters with this woman.

"A few times." Margo seemed so different, sitting here relaxing, enjoying the early morning breeze and friendly girl talk.

"You know, you're really lucky that I decided to make more than one this morning." She licked her chocolaty fork.

"I thought I was going to have a breakfast guest." She frowned. "But the scoundrel took off before I could tempt him with a civilized breakfast. One aspect of young men I enjoy is teaching them the subtler arts of pleasure."

Hadley could tell Margo was watching for her reaction to her statement. Did the woman think she'd be shocked? Ha. Margo should have known Natalie.

Hadley sunk her teeth into her croissant, first encountering the crisp/crunchy flakes that tasted of butter, then the bread so light it was hardly discernible, except for its warmth.

Finally there was the chocolate, rich, sweet, an almost sexual sensation. Hadley shut her eyes, the better to experience the explosion of taste.

"*C'est magnifique!*" She opened her eyes and smiled at her hostess. "I must thank Ryan for enabling me to have such a wonderful breakfast."

"He's still young. Still has time to learn. I have hope for him." Margo rose to refill their coffee cups. "And speaking of men, that one of yours is pretty tempting. I'm just warning you."

"Zane?" Hadley's head jerked toward Margo's back. Taking a deep breath, she looked down at her plate as she bit her lip.

What did she care if her handyman signed up for a few lessons in the 'subtler arts of pleasure'? Her lips stretched into what she certainly hoped was a breezy smile as the woman returned and set a full cup of coffee in front of her.

"And speaking of delicious young Zane..." Margo looked up toward the marina. Sure enough, he was striding toward them, carrying a tool box.

"Mornin' Hadley. Mornin' Margo." Zane stopped on the dock, right behind where Hadley was sitting.

"Good Morning, Zane. Looks like you're ready to get busy. I really should as well." Hadley took a last sip of coffee as she prepared to leave.

"Oh, Hadley. Sit still, girl. Zane, would you like a chocolate croissant, still a tiny bit warm? How about some coffee? You just come here now, and let us feed you some breakfast."

As Margo opened the gate in the railing for Zane to enter, she stood so close that he almost had to brush her cleavage as he walked through the opening.

The neckline of the woman's satin wrap mysteriously, but strategically seemed to gap more than it had a few minutes earlier, when Hadley had been her only guest.

Zane met Hadley's eyes as he carefully avoided touching the woman without seeming rude or awkward. Margo seemed to amuse Zane rather than tempt him.

The man was not shy about eating, clearly appreciating Margo's food and coffee. Margo kept up a flirtatious chatter, seeming to forget Hadley's presence. When only crumbs remained on his plate, Zane politely excused himself to get busy working on the boat.

"I'll be there in a few minutes, and we'll talk about today's agenda." Hadley finished her coffee as he made his way around and up onto her boat.

"Thank you for a delightful breakfast, Margo. It reminded me so much of home. You should have met my mother. In many ways you remind me of her."

"Thank you Hadley. Actually, I did meet your mother, and I'm flattered. Maybe I'll even get to the point where she was someday. Not sure if I should add, 'if I'm lucky' or not. I thought maybe she was lucky then, but her luck ran out. I am so sorry. I liked her."

Hadley sat perfectly still, and studied Margo though narrowed eyes. The woman's eyebrows arched as she waited for Hadley's response.

What in hell was this woman talking about, and when had she met Natalie? Hadley struggled to form the questions she needed to ask.

"Hadley, I need to ask you some questions before I can get started. Are you finished with breakfast?" Zane leaned over the rail of the boat.

She set down her coffee cup, and pushed back her chair.

"Yes. I'll be up in just a minute." She forced a smile for her hostess.

"Thank you Margo, for breakfast. We really must continue this conversation later, but I have to go."

"Yes, Zane seems anxious to get you all to himself." Margo's feline smile softened.

"We'll talk, Honey. We will. I'm glad my croissants didn't go to waste this morning. If you see Ryan, you might mention how much you enjoyed them."

Hadley shook her head as she walked around the boat and started to climb up. What had Margo meant when she had said that she might get to the point where Natalie had been someday?

27 Reflections under a Velvet Sky

Hadley had a party to attend. Both she and Zane had worked hard all day, on their separate projects. She'd watched him inject some substance into soft places in the wood, using a giant syringe.

It would toughen up the wood, he'd assured her. And when he painted over it, no one would ever know that the wood had rotted.

Connie had come down, and insisted on meeting her in Tulsa the next day. She and Hadley had planned what they needed to pick out, fabric for curtains and upholstery. Carpet for sure.

Connie had connections to get the curtains made quickly and Zane knew a man who installed carpet in boats for a living.

They were going to look at furniture tomorrow, too. They'd probably replace the settee and just re-cover the chairs. And somewhere in that city, Hadley was going to find a good, cheap coffee maker.

The list of errands to run in the city was long, but Hadley was looking forward to that part of the day, the easy part. But she also had to visit the doctor who had cared for Mère.

Attending the Halloway's party tonight would keep her mind off of tomorrow and thinking about visiting the place that Mère had died. And off of picking up her mother's belongings, which would be boxed and waiting for her.

She'd briefly considered asking Zane if he wanted to accompany her to the party. But tonight's event was a fact-finding mission as much as anything else. She needed to travel light and cover ground.

She showered, fluffing her hair to dry tousled and curly. What did you wear to a party on Grand Lake? She poked through her sparse clothing options.

She didn't have that much choice, and she had never followed fashion trends anyway. Good thing, because when Hadley had packed, a party with old friends of her parents had never entered her mind.

Oh well. In her tiny closet, she'd hung a short off-white ruffled skirt in slightly sheer fabric.

And she'd brought the blouse that matched it, with a button-down front, plain collar and three-quarter-length sleeves. She'd planned to wear this outfit on the trip home with Mère.

Of course, when the call had come, she'd already been at the airport. *Dieu merci.* She wrapped a black belt around her waist and slipped her feet into red pumps with heels.

She paused to consider where she was going to be walking and slipped them back off, placing them in her red handbag.

She was absolutely not going to take the chance of ruining those heels on the dock or in the gravel of a Grand Lake driveway. Not with how much they'd cost.

She surveyed her reflection in the mirror. Her nose was a little burned, she noticed. The sun was intense in Oklahoma. She added a few touches of makeup. It would have to do.

The directions on the napkin were simple to follow, although the roads to the Halloway's lake house were curved and treacherous. On the banks of Grand Lake sat mansions that would fit right in on the Riviera.

But to get to them by road, you had to bypass trailer parks. In these humble homes resided Tulsans who could not afford a mansion or even a vacation house at the lake, retirees, and some people who had lived there all their lives.

Did Zane live in a trailer house? Oh what did it matter? She really needed to focus on what she needed to accomplish tonight.

But her mind wandered back to floating in the cool water last night with her hand in his, and that brief but potent kiss. She almost missed a turn. Well, the party would help her get her mind off Zane. She would be talking to people and trying to gather information.

She squinted though the twilight to find the correct road sign. No one bothered to light these country lanes. Not that different from the French countryside, but difficult to navigate if you didn't know the way.

Past a steep downhill curve, she saw the lake. It'd be fun to meet some more interesting men tonight. Maybe there'd be someone cosmopolitan, modern, suave well-travelled. Someone very different than Zane.

The Halloway's lake house was built out on a point, with a verdant lawn stretching down to the lake. The surrounding shoreline was sprinkled with more beautiful homes.

This area seemed to be a bay or something, and the opposite shore was twinkling with the lights of even more picturesque houses.

Music and laughter mingled with the noise of boats motoring by. Were those people heading toward other parties or toward no destination except to be out on the water?

The lights reflected on the lake and sounds floated on the evening breeze. Almost like a fairyland. All it needed was a Prince Charming. Hadley didn't remember Grand Lake quite like this. It really was quite grand.

She pulled into the wide drive, crowded with every kind of car and truck and SUV. Vehicles were so big here. Americans seemed to like those giant Hummers that looked like assault vehicles to Hadley.

They wouldn't even fit on many European roads and streets. And even worse, they took up so much of the parking space here.

The drive curved around a landscaped green, encircling a lively fountain. The house was Tuscan design, but new, not like the authentic old beauties that Hadley was used to. But this was the United States, after all.

Hadley pushed the button to raise the top of her convertible. She slipped on her red pumps, glanced at her reflection in the rearview mirror, and took a deep breath. She was as ready as she'd ever be.

The open door led to an elegant entryway, where Norma Halloway greeted Hadley and ushered her into a living room designed for comfort. Deep leather chairs flanked the rustic rock fireplace under rough timber rafters.

"I wondered if you were coming. I'm so glad you could make it." The older woman's charm and warmth enveloped

Hadley. So comfortable and familiar. They could have known each other for years.

Hadley felt at home with her. Together they strolled over to a group chattering and laughing by the stairs. These guests cordially welcomed Hadley as she was introduced.

Warren Barrington would have been right at home here, and Norma seemed to have known him quite well. Would she have been of an age to have been one of his conquests?

Not a road Hadley wanted to go down right now. She accepted a glass of wine and let the older woman drag her around, meeting more friends and acquaintances.

Yes, it was definitely her father's kind of party. Hadley strolled out onto the marble patio where perfectly made-up and expensively dressed women and their men gossiped.

A few danced under the arches and beneath the stars that were just starting to appear, their reflections twinkling in the sparkling blue water of the swimming pool.

A heady mixture of scents from expensive perfume and flowers swirled, floating in the fresh breeze from the lake. Out over the banister, she could see a stunning view of the bay, although Norma assured her it was really a "creek."

Duck Creek held most of the businesses on the southern end of Grand Lake. Tonight it was alive with lights and reflections under a velvet sky. A few guests rambled down toward where a boat pulled into the private dock, discharging more guests.

A young, handsome musician in a tuxedo sat at a grand piano, inside open French doors. His hands flew over the ivory keys, playing a Cole Porter tune as he conversed with a middle-aged admirer who lounged on his piano, holding an iced drink in her hand. She was very thin, and her low-cut sequin studded dress exposed her ample cleavage to advantage.

Out on the deck, Norma paused. "Hadley, I'd like you to meet my grandson, Kip." A tall, blond-haired cutie, a few years younger than Hadley, turned around with a lopsided smile.

A heavy stubble enhanced his handsome, chiseled face. His chestnut hair was long enough to curl over his collar. His black jeans fit his slim hips snuggly and a dark tweed sports jacket causally topped a black tee-shirt.

The glasses perched on his nose gave Kip a bookish look that heightened his attractiveness. His startling blue eyes smiled appreciatively at Hadley.

"Kip is attending Georgetown University in D.C. "Norma was obviously bursting with pride. "I don't know if you knew him growing up here or not. Kip, Hadley is Warren Barrington's daughter." She beamed at her grandson. "I told you about her visiting from France."

"Hadley." Kip took the hand she offered to shake, but held it instead, in his own well-manicured hand. For a minute she thought he was going to kiss it.

"I do remember you, you know. I was just a little pipsqueak when you lived here, but I always thought you should notice me because you were no taller than I was. But, no, you were always busy with all the older kids. I would have died to have had you pay attention me back then."

What was I thinking? Age must matter much more when you're twelve, Hadley mused. Childhood memories had been all too prominent in her thoughts lately. Well, young Kip probably didn't have that problem now. Hadley smiled warmly at the charming man who oozed sex appeal.

28 The Cobblestone Path

Hadley smiled around the group surrounding Kip, but several of the girls eyed her suspiciously, including that same dark-haired girl she had seen at the barbeque buffet at the marina the day before.

No cutoffs tonight. She was wearing a long slinky dress split up to the thigh. Her blond friend, the one who had so obviously brushed against Zane when she was passing their table, didn't seem to be around.

But one girl in the group looked familiar. Hadley couldn't place the pretty girl with a big grin on her face. She had long legs and a slim build. Her curly hair, strawberry blond, hung down to the middle of her back. Wisps surrounded a freckled face with green eyes. She wore a short frilly, baby doll style dress in an old fashioned print. It suited her. The girl's eyes sparkled with recognition as she stepped forward.

"Hadley. It's Paula. Paula Saunders. How have you been, girl? I couldn't believe you left and never came back!" Hadley laughed as the girl hugged her, and hugged back enthusiastically. With an apologetic and rather wistful look at cute Kip, she and her childhood friend slipped through an archway to a seating area.

The smell of fragrant pinion wood burning in a clay chiminea filled the air. Hadley snagged another glass of wine from the tray of a passing waiter as they found a quiet corner where they could talk.

Artful indirect lighting softly illuminated a few couples who had also found their way to this shadowed corner. A slight breeze ruffled Hadley's short dark hair and blew Paula's red hair across her face.

The girl reached up to brush the strand out of her eyes, then twirled it into a tiny hair rope with her fingers, a habit that Hadley remembered from their childhood. She'd always done that when she was nervous, thought Hadley. She wondered what was bothering her friend now.

"I heard that you and your mom moved to France after the divorce." The statement was really more of a question.

"Yes. Mom wanted to get as far away from Oklahoma and Daddy as she could." Hadley settled onto a padded wrought iron settee.

"Is Natalie here with you?"

Of course. Paula didn't know! Holding back tears, Hadley told her friend how her mother had died and how she, Hadley, had ended up on Grand Lake.

"So there you have it, Paula. I'm just here to sell that old boat. It's the only thing binding me to Oklahoma now. France is my home, and I can't wait to get back."

"Don't you miss the lake, and us, at all? Aren't you even tempted to stay?" Paula sounded sincere, but for some reason, when Hadley assured her friend that she really didn't feel any temptation to stick around any longer than she had to, the girl looked relieved. She quit twirling her hair and sipped her drink serenely.

"I love your bling, by the way." Paula touched the raw quartz stone on Hadley's wide silver cuff bracelet, then admired the matching earrings and the necklace of four faceted amethyst beads on a chain, accented with a metal dye-cut flower on one side. "Where did you get them? Paris?"

Hadley told her friend about her jewelry design studio, about the pieces she was wearing, and how, each season, she played with a different stone in her designs. "These are from my quartz year."

"But you said the necklace is amethyst."

"Well, amethyst is a kind of quartz. So I wasn't cheating." Not many thirty-year-olds knew as much about gems as Hadley. Paula would never guess that she had a degree in gemology.

As the two girls giggled over a childhood adventure that had occurred one time Paula had spent the night with Hadley's family on *Black Gold*, Kip appeared in the archway. Paula stopped talking suddenly and started twirling her hair again.

"Hey there!" Norma's handsome grandson, managed to plant himself firmly between the two girls. After complementing Paula and making her giggle, he turned to Hadley.

"You know, my granddad has a story he always tells about your dad. They were on a business trip once, in Houston, and a hurricane was about to hit.

No one knew how bad it'd be, but at that time, computers were big and clunky, and they didn't have the backup options we do today.

"Anyway, the guys started thinking about all the important information that was stored on the computers in the Houston office and they got worried.

Most of the employees down there had their families to worry about and the storm was getting closer, so Granddad and Warren loaded all those computers up in a greasy old oilfield truck and struck out for Tulsa.

"It was raining hard by then, and about midnight. I guess it was quite an adventure. Sounds like grandmother and your mom were pretty much nervous wrecks by the time Granddad and Warren got here."

"Thank you for telling me that story, Kip. I'd love to know more about my parents, back then."

"Hey. Can I show you around the place?" Kip grabbed Hadley's hand as he stood up, pulling her to her feet.

"Sure. That sounds like fun." She turned to make her excuses to Paula, but the girl was disappearing through the doorway. Well, she'd catch up with her later.

Hadley let Kip lead her down the cobblestone path that led to the water and dock. They passed couples and groups, who called out to Kip, but although he returned their greetings, he didn't pause to introduce Hadley.

"My grandparents bought this land back in the 70s. The oil boom days. Back when your grandparents made their money. You know, my family didn't live far from you when you lived in Tulsa. We lived closer to the museum."

Memories flooded through her. "That's the mansion side. My side was just the gracious home side."

"Not really. Your side of the street has some mansions, as well. They're older than the ones on my side. Yours are from the real first oil boom, from the 1920s and 1030s. Prohibition days."

"Does Oklahoma still have Prohibition?" His question reminded Hadley, how hard she'd found it to buy a bottle of wine the day before.

Kip laughed down at her. "You know, you're adorable, Hadley. No. Oklahoma doesn't still have prohibition. Although it is a little behind France in some ways, including where alcohol is concerned.

"Of course, no one who lives here lets it bother them. Just like during prohibition, they figure out how to get and to do what they want." The couple made their way down some rock steps to the dock.

Waving at another boat approaching, Kip opened a door into the back of the dock structure. Hadley supposed it would lead to where the boat had slipped out of sight to unload its passengers, but instead it led to a rustic landing with a wooden stairway. He turned on a light, and motioned her up.

"I want to show you one of the best views on the lake." Hadley looked back over her shoulder and smiled demurely, controlling the laughter that threatened to escape.

She'd heard better excuses before from men who wanted to get her to themselves, but she could handle this cutie. As soon as she decided just how she wanted to handle him.

They emerged into a lodge room, the second story of the private dock. The walls were paneled with unfinished wood. Rustic rafters supported a slanted timber ceiling with skylights. Cow skins and thick oriental rugs overlapped haphazardly on the tile floor.

Oversized furniture filled the space with warm color. Indian blankets draped casually over the backs of chairs and loveseats.

In one corner, a compact kitchen glowed with charming red appliances. Above the stove hung a kitschy Roy Rogers and Dale Evans clock. The wall that faced the lake was composed entirely of glass doors.

Kip escorted Hadley out onto a balcony where a couple of rustic willow chairs were piled high with cushy pillows. Hadley leaned forward, her hands on the rail of the deck, enjoying the lively view of lake, listening to music drifting from a dozen sources. She stood there a few minutes taking it all in.

Hadley and Mère's life had been glamorous in France and on the Riviera, but she had to admit that this lake community had a unique elegance and charm all its own.

"Nice, isn't it?" While she was admiring the view, Kip had slipped back inside to procure a cold bottle of wine and two glasses.

He sat in one of the rustic chairs as he uncorked the wine, and Hadley settled down in the other one. Kip was telling her about his studies at Georgetown. He was studying International Business.

"What do your parents and grandparents think about that major? Do they expect you to take over their oil company?"

"Sure." He filled her glass. "But more and more, an oil company is an international business. We're investing in South America and around the Caspian Sea.

"I can hire engineers, but the business end needs a leader who understands how to guide a company into the future. And out of Oklahoma. But don't tell Grandma and Grandpa I said that."

Hadley noticed Paula wandering along the bank of the river. She seemed a little unsteady. Calling Kip's attention to her friend, she asked if he thought they should make sure the red-haired girl was OK. He sighed, as if in resignation, and pushed his hair back off his forehead.

"Hadley, let me handle this. Paula has a habit of needing to be rescued, I'm afraid. I'm sorry. I'd really like to spend some more time with you before you leave." He smiled down at her, reaching for her hand to help her up.

"You know, I get to Paris every once in a while. Let's have dinner before you go back home, please?" He escorted her back down to the dock, and disappeared into the dark toward the direction in which Paula had been headed.

Instead of immediately strolling back up the cobblestone path toward the music and lights, Hadley took off her shoes and climbed up to the top of a slide on the dock. She was tempted to let go and slide down in, splashing into the cool water below.

Last night had been a lot more fun than tonight had been. She'd half way wanted to meet a handsome, urban man to take her mind off Zane, and she had. But it hadn't worked. Well, she still had questions to ask. The night wasn't over yet.

As she sat there, enjoying the breeze on her face, she saw Kip and Paula slip out of the shadows and pause at the door that led up to the loft apartment. They didn't see her.

Paula seemed to be crying. Hadley tried not to overhear what they were saying, but the girl's sob was clearly audible over the waves splashing against the dock and the music drifting down the hill from the house. "But I love you Kip."

Poor Paula. She hadn't picked wisely. Kip was not for her. She was an Oklahoma girl to the core, and this boy had moved on from Oklahoma.

The couple slipped in the door to the stairs, and closed it behind them. Hadley shook her head and climbed down the ladder. Kip was cute and interesting. She liked him. She hoped he would be kind to Paula.

She hadn't seen her friend since they were twelve, but she knew the girl had no chance of winning Kip's love. She wondered again what Zane was doing tonight as she retraced her steps up to the house.

29 Breakfast Burritos

"Just how well do you know Zane Bowman?" Norma Halloway had asked Hadley last night as they'd said their goodbyes. Norma had dragged her around to meet a few more of Natalie and Warren's friends, but no one knew anything about the boat or Mère's visit here.

Everyone had been polite and curious, but Hadley had not learned anything that might help her solve the mystery of why she now owned *Black Gold*. Or how her mother had been injured.

During the few moments she and Norma had been able to chat alone, Hadley had explained Zane showing up on her boat and offering his assistance. Norma had hesitated, as if wanting to be careful how she phrased her next sentences.

"Hadley, according to my husband, Earl, Zane is an outstanding young man, a real artist with wood. He loves wooden boats, as you may have noticed.

"His father is a good man too, a pillar of the Grand Lake community. But I find it strange that when you first showed up here, Zane was at your boat waiting for you.

"We didn't have much time to chat tonight, but call me. Let's have lunch. Or come to dinner. Anytime. I do need to tell you a few things about your mother that you may not know." Norma had patted her arm affectionately and repeated, "Call me, Dear."

After the party, Hadley had barely found her way out of the maze of roads that led from the Halloway's house. But, with the car top down, she's actually enjoyed the ride back to the marina. The stars had been startlingly bright. She loved the lights of Paris, but they did tend to overpower the brilliance of the stars. And she had slept soundly.

Now Hadley stretched in the bed where she had slept as a child. But what was that noise outside? She tried burrowing back under her covers, but the pounding would not go away. Groggily, she admitted to herself that someone was knocking on the door to the boat.

She ignored it. Her eyes drifted closed again. The boat's horn reverberated, obliterating any chance of drifting back into sleep. Whoever was up there had obviously never seen her in a bad mood, or they would have left her alone.

She reached up with one hand and tweaked open the curtains covering the tiny window. Weak, rose-tinted light reflecting from the water outside danced over the walls and her face.

Well, Merde. She pushed herself to a sitting position, then reached down and searched for her flip flops before getting up, still wary of crunchy bug remnants.

Smoothing the oversized tee-shirt she wore as a nightdress, Hadley climbed the stairs to the salon and peeped out of the door. Zane stood there with a fresh cup of coffee in his hand. When their eyes made contact, he cocked a quizzical eyebrow at her.

Hadley laughed. Connie had supplied coffee one day and Margo another. Today Zane was doing so. Pretty good room service, if you thought about it. She opened the door to admit the coffee and the man who was carrying it.

"I'm a little early." Zane handed her a steaming thermal cup. Hadley nodded her head emphatically, but then took a sip of coffee and managed a smile.

The place was looking better, and cleaner. As Zane watched Hadley sip her coffee, he asked himself how the hell he had thought that this plan was a good idea. His father would be furious.

What had he gotten himself into? He should just get to work on the damned boat. So what if he'd turned up earlier than any lake handyman in the history of time? He'd warned her that she wouldn't be able to sleep in.

Oh hell. His willpower failed him. What could it hurt to have a little fun? She'd be gone in a few days anyway. No one would ever know.

"Want some breakfast?" He entered the cabin as she strolled over to the sofa and eased herself down into the cushions, taking care not to spill her coffee. Zane was unable to resist the temptation of this tiny mop-haired girl, even if she was French.

"We both have a lot of work to do here today. I know I work better with a full stomach, and it's a little early to get started. Sun's just coming up. As my dad used to say, it's the butt crack of dawn."

"No kidding." She looked up at him through slightly squinted eyes, as if she didn't entirely trust his motives. Well, if she knew what he knew. But she didn't.

He watched her sip her coffee. She might have found something out at the Halloway's party last night. But she wasn't saying anything, so he and his dad were probably safe. For now.

"Look, Zane, I just got out of bed." Hadley yawned like a kitten, all fluffy and disheveled. "You woke me up. I need a shower." Her legs curled under her. Her hair was a mess. He wanted to touch her.

"Just put on some shorts. You don't need to dress up where I'm taking you."

"You're such a guy." She laughed. "Give me a few minutes. I can't go back to sleep now anyway." Hadley headed to the guest stateroom, still sipping her coffee, and shut the door behind her.

Through the door he heard her muttering. "But don't do this tomorrow, OK? This hour is obscene. Or the day after either, OK?"

She stuck her head out of the door. "If I'm encouraging you in this folly, tell me right now and I won't go today." She shut the door again, and didn't appear again for a half hour.

When Hadley emerged from the cabin, Zane was outside pacing the deck. She smiled at him, her face illuminated by morning sunshine. "Now, where's that food? I'm hungry."

The dock was quiet this morning. They were obviously the only people awake yet. Birds called from across the water, which still reflected remnants of pink from the sunrise.

Zane led Hadley over to the courtesy dock, where the Sea Skiff was tied up. She squinted up at him with a quizzical look, but he just offered her a hand up to board. Shrugging her shoulders, she climbed in, her empty coffee cup still in her hand.

Zane idled out of the dock, trying not to make much noise. Neither one of them said a word, but he pointed at a thermos of coffee and Hadley opened it and refilled her cup. He lifted the empty cup from the holder near the captain's seat and handed it to her. She refilled it as well.

As they left the bay for the main body of the lake, no words spoken, she quietly gazed out on the still surface of the water, so tranquil and motionless that it was hard to imagine how it looked when disrupted by personal water craft and fast boats, or wind.

They had the lake all to themselves, except for the gulls that wheeled overhead, occasionally diving for a fish. A slight fog clung to the banks, softening the trees there like a vintage romantic photograph.

Très beau, was all Hadley could think as they sipped coffee in companionable silence. Last night the lake had been vibrant, alive with music and action. Today it was deserted except for their boat.

She felt like the two of them were alone in the world. She could almost see how someone could learn to love this lake. Nothing like Paris, or even the Côte d'Azur. She hadn't expected to find anything here that appealed to her. But, as she looked out over Grand Lake, in some ways, it felt like home. Both the sparkling social life and the sense of being one with nature that she felt right now. She laughed gently to herself.

She could understand it, if she had never been to France. She knew where her home and heart were, and it was not Grand Lake, Oklahoma. But she would enjoy it while she was here. She glanced over at Zane, silently piloting the boat into a quiet, fog-shrouded bay.

"Where are we going?" She broke the silence gently. "Is there a restaurant in here, Zane?"

He smiled at her, and put his finger to his lips. Why was he shushing her? Did he think she was a child to be told to be quiet? But the smile in his eyes, crinkling the corners, intrigued her.

What did Zane have up his sleeve this morning? She checked that she'd remembered to put her cell phone in her pocket. It wasn't that she didn't trust him. Well, actually, she didn't entirely trust him. And she liked to live life on her own terms. She didn't very much like anyone else making decisions for her.

As the boat drifted through the fog, close to the shore, Zane silently pointed to an opening that had softly appeared in the fog, and Hadley caught her breath as she glimpsed a small herd of deer muted and softened by tendrils of fog floating hauntingly around them.

Now she was glad she had heeded his warning and stayed silent. As they drifted, the fog closed in on the magical scene. As they proceeded deeper into the bay, Zane smiled over at her.

He was proud he could show her the deer. How cute. He was like a little boy showing his mother the first flower he found in spring.

But, little boy… She admired the way his tee shirt clung to the muscles of his back and shoulders as he turned the wheel of the boat. …*I'm not your mother.*

Zane slowed the boat, then stopped it. He hopped down from the captain's seat and ran around the cabin to the bow so he could drop the anchor.

"If you think you're going to talk me into another swim."

He laughed at her.

"Actually, I'd rather have some breakfast than swim, but maybe you'd rather undress?" He leered at her cheerfully.

"Breakfast? Where? Zane, I am starved and I don't see any restaurant."

Her voice trailed off as he set up a folding card table and draped a white tablecloth over it. From an insulated bag, he brought out a covered bowl of fruit, peaches, strawberries, apples and bananas.

"Oh!" Hadley bit into a juicy strawberry she'd snagged from the bowl as soon as he set it down. "So sweet!" She licked a drop of juice off her lip.

Zane set out two slim stemmed glasses and filled them half full of orange juice, then topped them off from a bottle of champagne that he'd had stashed in his insulated bag of goodies.

Next he pulled out a couple of long, foil-covered cylinders and set them on two plates. From another covered bowl, he spooned out some cubed fried potatoes, and then set out plastic containers of salsa and chopped avocado.

"There you go." He poured fresh coffee and settled into the chair across the table from Hadley. His smile was infuriatingly self-satisfied, but the food looked and smelled so delicious that Hadley decided not to punish him for it, not just now anyway.

The cool morning air and the beauty of their surroundings heightened Hadley's appetite. What fun! *Well I won't be here long, so I'll just enjoy myself before I leave.* She watched Zane as he unwrapped a foil-covered cylinder.

"My specialty." Zane held up a burrito looking object. "Breakfast burritos. Try them. They aren't French but they sure are good. I made them this morning." He beamed with an appealing pride at his accomplishment, and she couldn't help but chuckle.

Plop. What was that? Plop. A big raindrop plopped onto Hadley's plate. She looked up at the sky. So did Zane, just as the raindrops begin to fall more steadily.

"Oh crap!" Zane began to gather food and drinks from the table on the deck. Hadley scurried to help him. She didn't want her wonderful breakfast to be drowned!

Although they both grabbed and ran, the rain was on them before they and their breakfast were safely under cover.

"I think the food is still edible." Hadley grabbed a wet strawberry. "But my drink is all watered down. Did we get in with the champagne?"

"You are a greedy woman." Zane ducked his head as he ran back through the rain to grab the champagne.

You have no idea how greedy. Hadley studied the way his wet tee shirt clung to his chest, and sighed. Her trip here wouldn't last much longer, but she had to admit to herself that she'd was very tempted.

Young Kip was pretty, but this guy was much more than pretty. She could dawdle with little boys like Kip anytime she wanted. Zane was something different, and French women appreciated different, even a little dangerous maybe.

The tiny open cabin area of the day boat contained a captain's seat, a cabinet with a sink, and a dinette booth. Hadley and Zane reclined on upholstered benches on opposite sides of the booth, finishing their breakfast and the champagne.

Coffee was forgotten. The burritos were spicy, tortillas filled with scrambled eggs and bacon, onions and peppers, sharp cheese and a fiery salsa. Hadley licked her fingers delicately.

"And you expected us to work after drinking champagne for breakfast?" She leaned back in her seat, feeling very relaxed as the rain drummed down on the roof of the old boat.

She peered out of the window. Although they'd anchored near the shore, she could hardly see the trees. The raindrops plopped into the water with a steady staccato beat. Zane looked sheepishly at her.

"I didn't really expect us to drink the whole bottle of champagne. I thought just a little with the coffee would be fun, but I didn't count on the rain."

"Well, now look what you've gotten us into." Hadley laughed. "What do we do now?" She was starting to get some interesting ideas about what she'd like to do now. She snagged the last strawberry, and nibbled a bite from the side, licking the juices that ran down her fingers.

Zane unfolded himself from the seat across from her, standing up and stretching, his muscles flexing under his still damp tee-shirt. Hadley watched him with a smile as she nibbled her strawberry.

Zane stood there taking her in, with a long lazy smile, then sighed deeply.

Turning, he strode toward the back of the boat, then dashed out to the open back deck of the Sea Skiff, jumped up onto the side and ran nimbly forward along the cabin to the bow through driving rain.

He pulled up the anchor, then, quick as a flash, he was back inside, soaked to the skin. He jumped up into the captain's chair and started the engine before the boat could be swept onto the shore.

Hadley watched the whole show as she finished her strawberry, her eyes wide with surprise and curiosity. Zane turned the boat around in the cove and carefully guided it around the bend and back into the main body of the lake, as Hadley prudently crammed the remaining food and utensils into the bag he'd brought them in.

She wasn't very familiar with the lake, and wasn't at all sure of her directions in the rain. Zane seemed to have turned in the wrong direction, but she wasn't going to second-guess him.

She was, however, concerned by his decision to leave the cove. She held onto the table and seat of the booth as the wind picked up and tossed the boat in the high waves of the stormy lake.

"Are you trying to kill us?" Hadley yelled at Zane as they plowed through the downpour. Earlier she'd seen a pile of life vests under the table, near her feet.

Now she pulled one out and fastened it around her, although it was way too big. A child's vest would have fit her better. She cinched the straps tightly, as the boat bucked, unbalancing her.

Hadley fell back into the seat as a gust, swirling in through the open back of the cabin, blew Zane's hair around his face wildly. He just laughed!

She could see he was enjoying the wind and the danger. And he was laughing at her too, as she cowered in the corner of the booth, trying to stay dry and warm. She held on tightly to keep from being thrown around as the boat careened from wave to wave.

"Hold on!" She heard Zane shout at her above the sound of the wind and the water battering the little wooden boat. "We're crossing the lake."

Hadley stared at him in disbelief. Her marina was on this side of the lake. Where was this wild man taking her? She gritted her teeth in anger.

Well, different might have been fun, but crazy was not. She considered calling the Lake Patrol from her cell phone to rescue her. Her plans did not involve drowning in the middle of Oklahoma.

A huge wave broke over the bow of the boat, completely covering the front windshield with water that ran along the roof and splashed down onto the back deck, rushing down the stairs and swirling around her feet. She huddled on the bench and held on tighter.

This was insane. If she ever got out of here alive, she'd fire this mad man, burn her damn boat and get on a plane out of here. Today.

The effects of the champagne had long since worn off. Hadley was wet and cold and scared and angry. Most of all, she was angry. If that crazy man driving this boat would get them someplace where she was not afraid for her life, he'd find out just how angry she was.

Hadley screamed as another wave broke over the boat and the spray of water hitting the back deck splashed in on her, drenching her once again.

Her teeth were clenched, but Zane only laughed at her. She screeched at him, but didn't dare loosen her grip on the booth.

Then Hadley sensed the boat gaining some control of its direction, both horizontal and vertical. The wind had lessened and the waves were only about half the size they had been a few minutes before.

Peering out the window, through the rain, she saw that a headland was shielding them from the brunt of the storm. Would they soon pass it and face that fury again?

She shuddered in anticipation, but soon realized that Zane had navigated them into some kind of a cove or bay. The rain still fell and the wind still blew, but the little wooden boat chugged along and then turned down a kind of a creek that was almost calm.

Hadley worked up her courage and struggled to a standing position, so she could snarl at Zane. "What was that supposed to prove? Why on earth would you take us out into the lake in that storm? Does that make you a big man?"

Zane looked her up and down, standing there. She realized how she must look, all five foot of her, drenched to the skin—probably like a starving, half drowned cat.

She almost laughed, partly from that image of herself in her mind's eye and partly from relief that she had survived the ordeal. But she didn't laugh. No way was Zane going to hear a laugh or see a smile from her.

The boat motored smoothly into an old slip in a small dock next to some worn buildings. A beat-up work truck was parked there, with a pile of soaked lumber stacked in the back.

Zane smoothly killed the motor, threw out the bumpers, and climbed onto the dock in the still driving rain to tie up the boat. He offered a hand to Hadley to help her out, but she pointedly ignored him and managed to struggle over the side on her own.

The rain hadn't let up, but she couldn't get much wetter. Arms crossed, she stared at him as he finished tying up his boat. He was deliberately taking his time. Hadley fumed.

She was sure he just wanted to make her miserable. What had she ever done to him? She'd given the jerk a job. She was his boss. *But not for much longer, Buster.*

Hadley seethed, waiting for him. The rain plastered his shirt to his strong shoulders. The muscles of his arms flexed, stretching the wet fabric as he manhandled the boat.

As Zane turned toward Hadley, she quickly tore her eyes from his torso, realizing that she had been staring, almost in a trance. He gestured her to lead the way up the path toward a nearby metal building.

Head back, she marched ahead of him, but when they reached the door, she turned to him, hands on hips and glared up into his face.

"So why are we here? What is this place and why should I go in there with you?" Zane reached around her, almost touching her shoulder. She drew back with a jerk, trying to avoid contact, but he only opened the door.

She peeked sideways to see what was inside, but couldn't see anything in the darkness. Although the welcome warmth emanating from inside tempted her, she waited for an answer to her question.

"It's dry?" Zane shrugged his shoulders.

Just at that moment a streak of lightning illuminated the dark day and crashed way too near them. Hadley was inside the warm, dry building before the thunder rolled in, straining to see in the dark.

As Zane followed her in, he flipped on the light in the cavernous metal building. Now she could see more wood stacked neatly to one side. She saw a variety of machines that might be saws.

She also observed neat bins and shelves full of something. She didn't know what. It kind of reminded her of her jewelry workshop, only on a much larger scale. Whatever was built here was much bigger than earrings!

"Where are we? And how dare you risk my life dragging me over here without even asking? Who do you think I am? Who do you think you are?"

As Zane leaned against the wall, not looking very proud of himself. He'd better not be! She steeled her face to show no mercy, and kept her eyes off the shirt plastered to his chest.

"Uh, Hadley." Zane pushed back his hair. "I should have checked the weather, but Oklahoma's climate is so unpredictable that it might not have mattered.

"I'd planned us to just have a pleasant breakfast, then to run over here to pick up what I needed to work on your boat today. If it hadn't been for the rain, we'd probably be back at the marina working by now." He peered at her closely.

He seemed to be looking for a hint of forgiveness, but she was still very angry.

"You could have killed us."

"No. I'm sorry but I've been out there in much worse weather than this. We really weren't in danger. The Sea Skiff is a very safe boat. You could drive that thing in the ocean. Much smaller craft than that are working off shore. But I'm really sorry that I scared you."

"You could have at least told me where we were going."

"You're right. I should have, but once we were out in the storm, I needed to concentrate on getting us here."

"You were LOVING it out there." Hadley growled at him, pacing now. "You loved the danger. I don't care if you kill yourself tomorrow, but you won't have another opportunity to risk my life.

In fact, I think we should end this business relationship right now. You are irresponsible, and I frankly do not trust you." Well, she guessed she'd told him. Ball in his court.

30 The Warning

He'd done it now. Damn, but he'd messed things up. His dad would kill him if he ever found out what Zane had done. All of it.

Being attracted to Hadley despite what he knew, almost letting himself get out of hand at breakfast, and risking her life, a little, not much, but a little, to keep himself out of even more trouble back there in that cove.

He tried his best to banish thoughts of where he might be and what he might be doing right now if he hadn't made the rash decision to brave the storm.

How could he explain what happened without hurting his dad? How could he protect him now? Dad had warned him.

Zane gritted his teeth. He was going to have to grovel when all he wanted to do was to kiss this girl. Back there at breakfast, she'd made it clear that she had wanted to kiss him too, but he'd blown any chance of that.

He knew she deserved to be mad. That's what he had wanted. At a responsible, rational level. But he had to grovel now and do the best he could to clean up his mess.

"I am really sorry I scared you, Hadley." He really tried to look humble, which wasn't easy because Zane was not a humble man. "Look, let's just get that boat of yours ready to sell. No more breakfasts. No more boat rides. You won't even know I'm around.

"I've, I've…" This was killing him. "I've already bought the supplies." That was a lie. He'd already had everything he needed to work on her boat before she ever met him.

He wasn't out any money on the job, but he couldn't tell her that. He peeked at her while trying to look like he was staring at the floor. Was his ploy working?

She was still dripping. Her tee-shirt and shorts clung to her tiny body. Her dark hair curled slightly and stood out in every direction. Her green eyes flashed angrily.

Not many women could look that sexy under these conditions. Why oh why did she have to be Natalie Barrington's daughter? But she was.

His dad had no idea what he was asking. Then Zane realized. His dad knew exactly what he was asking of his son.

"Is there a place I can freshen up in this barn?" Hadley stood with her hands on her hips. The glint in her eye warned him that he should still tread carefully. She needed some time to cool off—or warm up. Zane showed her to a slightly grungy bathroom.

"Sorry, I know it's not very nice." She didn't respond because her cell phone was ringing and she was digging it out of her wet pocket as she closed the door in his face.

He stood there, listening to her conversation, eavesdropping shamelessly.

"Hi, Connie? Uh, I'm afraid that I'll be a little late. Do we have reservations? Oh, Good. I should be in Tulsa by…" She must be checking her wristwatch. Zane hoped it was waterproof. "I should be there by one o'clock. I'll see you then."

She must be working on getting some of the interior work on the boat done. That meant she'd be gone soon. His mind knew that was a good thing, but his heart was not convinced.

When Hadley returned, she seemed to have settled down a little.

"Look Zane. I need to get back to my boat. I must go into Tulsa today to take care of some business. I really don't feel like another boat ride. And I think you're right. We should eliminate any future boating adventures."

He nodded his head. Did that mean she was going to let him continue to work on her boat? He repressed a sigh of relief, both for the success of his mission and for the fact that he would see her again.

"I had planned to take my truck, anyway. All the supplies I need are already in the back. I loaded them last night." The rain had let up, and he opened the door of the shop.

Hadley peeked out. "I'm ready."

He opened the passenger side door for her. "Jump in and I'll drive you back to the marina."

"OK. That'll work."

Zane climbed into the truck, watching Hadley. She seemed preoccupied. Just as Zane started the truck up, Hadley's phone rang again.

"Hello, Hadley Barrington here. Yes, I am Natalie's daughter. I'm stopping by today to pick up my mother's belongings.

"No, What? No, I have no idea who was visiting her when she died. I didn't even know. We'll talk this afternoon. I'll be there as soon as I can."

Oh Dad. Zane shifted gears in the manual transmission. This plan may not work. I'm afraid we're in trouble now.

31 A Carved Cane

Just wait until she told Connie about her wild morning! Hadley pushed the elevator button for the thirty-first floor. She was late, but the trip to Tulsa had taken a little longer than she'd planned.

Hadley stepped out into the elegant foyer, glancing through the wall of windows overlooking the winding Arkansas River, which stretched out to the horizon.

Following Connie's instructions and a vague memory of dining here as child, she turned into the hall leading to the lunch buffet.

Well-dressed business people doing lunch crowded the dining room. Wait staff, dressed all in black, saw to their every need. Hadley scanned the crowd. There was Connie, over by another bank of windows that overlooked the charming art deco downtown of Tulsa, Oklahoma.

The friends ordered glasses of wine and filled their plates at the buffet, selecting salads of delicate designer greens, topped with berries and grilled shrimp.

"Well, tell me everything." Connie's eyes sparkled as she examined her friend. She settled back into her chair and took a sip of wine.

"How was the party? We came back to Tulsa late yesterday, and I've been dying of curiosity!"

So Hadley described the party, the house, and the people she had met, but decided not to mention delicious young Kip, or the flowers that had been waiting at her boat when she'd gotten back from her disastrous morning with Zane.

She was going to have to let Kip know, kindly, since she did like him and his grandparents, that their friendship was just that, and nothing more.

That situation needed to stay private. She did not, however, skimp on the details of her morning with Zane.

Connie's eyes widened when Hadley described the romantic picnic breakfast. She laughed when Hadley told her how the rain had surprised them.

Hadley carefully did not mention what she speculated might have been the cause of Zane's mad decision to expose them to the storm. She didn't understand that herself. She wasn't used to men running away when they realized that she was attracted to them.

After filling up their plates from the entrée section of the buffet, the women continued their conversation.

"I thought he was going to drown us both." She did not feel at all guilty leaving out the juicy parts and portraying Zane as a mad man. "And you should have seen the bathroom in that barn of his. Yuck! That's where I was when you called me."

"So did you fire him?" Connie asked, somewhat wistfully. She was obviously hoping for spicy updates to the story at a later date.

"Almost. But I need to get that boat fixed up, and that's why I'm here, so you can help me pick out fabric today. But,

Connie, I also need to run by the hospital where my mom was staying. They still have some of her stuff, and…."

"What is it, Honey?" Connie was nosy, as always, but also seemed genuinely concerned for her friend.

"When the nurse at the hospital called me this morning, she said that some man had left his cane in Mère's room. I don't know who would have been visiting her."

"Oh, maybe a clergyman. When someone is sick, those places often have someone who kind of makes rounds and comforts people."

Connie finished the last bite of her roast beef, and glanced back at the display behind her.

"Look at that dessert bar. Come on. Let's live a little." She motioned to a waitress. "Could I have a cup of coffee, please? Hadley?"

"Sure. Coffee would be great."

Connie reached out and patted Hadley's arm. "Then, if you'd like, I'll go with you to the hospital. That's going to be kind of hard on you. Let's get it out of the way, then we'll shop for fabric, OK?"

"You're on." Hadley followed Connie to the desert bar to see what kind of chocolate was available. Having a friend by her side when she faced the hospital would be a big relief. She'd been dreading that visit.

Later, when the two women entered the medical center office, the nurse rang to have someone bring Natalie's belongs and asked if they'd like some water or coffee.

"Is it possible, I mean, it probably isn't, but I think I'd like to see where, where…" The nurse clicked a few keys on her computer. Her eyes scanned the screen, then she smiled over at Hadley.

"Actually, that room just happens to be unoccupied right now." She rang again and changed her instructions, directing the orderly to take the boxes and luggage to Room 614.

Then she efficiently rose from her desk and indicated that they follow her. "Just this way, ladies."

Down a corridor and around a corner was the room that Natalie had occupied. Hadley was relieved that the décor was tasteful. Her mother had spent her last few days here, alone.

A deeply recessed window overlooked a lush garden with a fountain. That was nice. As she looked down at the lovely garden, Hadley tried to imagine her elegant mother here.

Natalie had thought she'd be going home in a few days, never guessing that a blood clot was forming in her lungs, a blood clot that would end her vivacious life.

Connie walked up behind Hadley, and put a warm arm around her shoulders, understanding that she needed comfort. Hadley put her hand on Connie's arm to acknowledge the gesture.

"Thank you Taylor." The nurse turned to Hadley. "Here are Natalie's things." The orderly had set two pieces of designer luggage and a box on the bed.

"The man who was here with her that last day left this." The nurse laid a beautifully carved wooden cane beside the other objects.

"I can't imagine who he might have been. Do you have any ideas?" Hadley picked up the cane, turning it slowly and examining the carvings. "You should probably keep it here, in case he comes back looking for it."

"Why don't you take it? I'm afraid we don't have room to store personal belongings for very long. Oh, and he may have left this book, or it might have been your mother's." The nurse took a small photo album out of the box and handed it to Hadley. "It was laying on the table over where they were sitting when your mother..."

Hadley didn't want to imagine Mère sitting in the love seat near the window, so alive one minute and the next—Tears seeped from her eyes.

"Here, Miss Barrington. Let's sit down." The nurse tried to comfort her, the way nurses are taught to do.

Connie took the book and sat down in a rocking chair. She opened the album and thumbed through it. Her quick intake of breath startled Hadley.

"What's wrong?" Hadley glanced at Connie, just sitting there, staring at the page of the album. She turned several more pages, over to the back. She looked stunned.

"Hadley," The older woman rose from the rocking chair. "You need to look at this album."

"Should I let you two have a few minutes?" The nurse looked from woman to woman. "I can go get someone to help you carry these things to your car."

"No." Connie surprised Hadley by insisting that the nurse stay. "I think we may have some questions for you."

She handed Hadley the album, opened to the first page. There was a picture of the young man, the same one they'd seen in her mother's photo album.

Connie then turned to another page she had marked with her finger. Hadley took the book from her, staring at the picture of a young man beside a beautiful boat. He was younger there. He looked more innocent, but she knew that face.

She'd seen it that morning with hair blowing wildly around it. She'd seen it glorying in the danger and excitement of battling the elements.

"I don't understand." She looked through the rest of the pages of the scrapbook, which held photos of different vintages.

There were faded photos of the first man. And a picture that had to be of the Sea Skiff. That was Zane's father's boat, he'd told her.

Some pictures showed the older man in uniform, on a battleship, she thought. Then there were pictures of him with an exotic-looking woman. Very pretty. And a wedding picture, then pictures of the couple with a baby.

This must be Zane's family, but what was the book doing in Mère's room? Had Zane's father known her parents? If so, why hadn't Zane mentioned it?

"Was the person visiting Natalie one of these men?" Connie gently took the album from Hadley and showed the nurse the latest picture of Zane, where he was standing with the older man in the album.

"Yes, that older man." The nurse pointed to the picture. "The other one was here too." Both Connie and Hadley stared at the nurse. "The young one brought the older one, then left." She looked worried at their reaction. "They'd been here every day, you know."

"No, I didn't know." Hadley walked over to the window and looked down into the garden.

"When your mother had her—stroke—the older man called us. You know that there was nothing we could do for her. He stayed here with us until the doctors confirmed that she'd passed.

He held her hand for as long as we'd let him. That younger fellow showed up and took him away. The old man was so distressed that the younger one, he might have been his son, had to help him out.

I guess that's why he forgot his cane. And the album. I'm sorry. I wish I could tell you more, but that's all I know. I'll go get help for your mother's belongings." The nurse left the room.

"Why would Zane and his dad be visiting Mère in the hospital?" Hadley turned as she asked the question.

"I don't know what's going on here. None of this makes sense." She put down the album and picked up the cane.

It was carved from a wood with a swirled grain and was sanded and varnished until it shinned. It was as beautiful as a museum piece. Hadley laid it on the loveseat, wondering where Zane's father had gotten it.

Just then, a middle-aged doctor walked in.

"Hello, Hadley. I'm Dr. Symonds. I know you're Hadley because you look so much like Natalie." He shook her hand, then turned to shake Connie's hand.

"So glad to meet you, Dr. Symonds. This is my friend, Connie Kent. I have quite a few questions I'd like to ask you." The doctor and the two women sat down.

"I'm sure you do." Dr. Symonds removed his glasses. "Your mother's case was a real tragedy. She was such a beautiful and warm person."

Yes, he had felt her charm. Hadley recognized the symptoms. Mère had had this man wrapped around her little finger. Like every other man she'd ever met. Hadley knew her mother.

"I see you have her cane."

"Her Cane?" Hadley glanced down to where it was lying beside her. "I thought it belonged to some older man who visited her. The man in this photo album. This man."

Hadley reached for the album to show the doctor Zane's father's photograph. As she picked it up, a paper fell out and drifted to the floor. Dr. Symonds picked it up and handed it to her.

She glanced at the check for $20,000 she held in her hand. Shoving the album, opened to the man's picture, into the doctor's hands, she held the check under Connie's nose. It was made out to Zane Bowman.

Stuffing the check into her tiny purse, Hadley turned to the Doctor. "Do you know why that man," She pointed to the album. "Those two men, the men in that picture, were visiting my mother?"

"Mr. Bowman was an old friend of your mother's, from what I understood." The doctor shrugged and handed back the album.

"She was with him when she fell. He and his son brought her to the hospital. From what they told me, I think she had fallen on a boat or something."

As Hadley stared at the doctor, her thoughts whirling around in her head. That morning, on the boat in the storm, Zane had recklessly risked her life.

What if the same thing had happened to Mère? She pictured her on the same boat, falling, breaking her leg and hitting her head.

Whatever had happened, it had ended her life. And Zane. Zane had been there and he'd never told her. And that check was made out to him. Why had Mère written a $20,000 check to Zane?

Something was so wrong here. Hadley had been flirting with, and having a good time with, the man who might be responsible for her mother's death. The tears started, then wouldn't stop.

Hadley collapsed on the loveseat, overcome with grief. And anger. Anger at herself for being gullible to whatever Zane was up to, at Zane for his part in Mère's death and for lying to her.

And, she realized as she wept in Connie's arms, she was angry with Mère too. Why had her mother felt she had to come back to Tulsa?

How had she gotten mixed up with these Grand Lake characters? What was Zane's dad to her? Why had she kept all this from her daughter? Why had she died?

32 Wifey-Poo

"What do you think they wanted from Mère?" Hadley asked Connie. The two women had searched the fabric and carpet stores and made their choices for the boat. Now they were headed back downtown.

"Well, any man would be flattered by your mother's attention, from what you've told me. The real question is, what was your mother doing over here in the first place? Why did she come? Did she tell you anything?"

"No." What had Mère said? Almost nothing. That hadn't been typical of her, but Hadley had been too busy with her show to think about it then.

'Do you have any idea at all? You said she hadn't visited the states since she divorced your dad? That was..." Connie concentrated on the math problem for a minute. "Eighteen years ago? Why now?"

"I don't know! Mère was vague about her reasons, said she'd tell me more later. Ha!" Hadley's laugh was bitter. "Let that be a lesson to you. 'Later' may never come."

The two women drove in silence for a few minutes, staring out the window at Tulsa. They could see the 1920s high rises of the downtown skyline in the distance as they drove through the newer, more modern part of the city.

Hadley's car was parked in one of the tallest, the building where the restaurant where they'd had lunch occupied the top three floors.

"I don't even know where to start looking to find out why she was here and why she was with Zane and his dad. I'm confused and tired." Hadley sighed and leaned back against the seat, her face grim.

"Why not start with Zane?" Connie glanced sideways at her as she drove. "Ask him."

Like he'd tell her the truth. Then Hadley remembered Norma Halloway's invitation. Actually, it had been more than an invitation. The friend of her parents had insisted that Hadley call her because the woman had things to tell her about her mother.

She explained last night's conversation to Connie, who agreed that she really should call Norma and see what the woman knew. So Hadley placed a call to the Holloways. Norma answered promptly. Yes, she would love to see Natalie.

Yes today was fine. No, the hour was no problem. In fact, would Natalie consider staying for dinner? Did she need directions to their house?

Mrs. Halloway insisted that she couldn't wait to see Hadley and finally have that talk. As Connie drove into the downtown area of Tulsa, Hadley leaned back and finally relaxed a bit.

"I had an interesting breakfast with Margo yesterday." Hadley watched for Connie's reaction, but her friend only grinned.

"Surprise you?"

"Yes. Actually, the whole thing was pretty strange. I'm not sure what she's really all about. Sometimes she reminds me of my mother. Then....." Hadley recounted the events of that morning and Connie chuckled.

"Don't let her put you off balance. There's more to that woman than you realize."

"Really?"

"She plays pretty loose when she's at the lake, but if you were to meet her in Tulsa, you'd never guess. She does a lot of volunteer work. Lives in the neighborhood near your friend Norma."

"I guess I just never thought of her aside from what I've seen at the lake. The houseboat, the boys. I, of all people, should know better, shouldn't I?"

Hadley suddenly wondered how other people had seen Mère when she'd dated younger men. It had all seemed so natural to her, but it might not have to everyone. She turned to Connie as they waited at a stoplight.

"It was the same way with my mom. Sometimes I wished she'd find someone her own age and settle down, but eventually, I realized that would never happen, that she was perfectly happy with her life as it was. She could afford the younger men. She was beautiful enough that they—or at least most of them—really enjoyed her company and her attention."

"Margo's a widow. Her husband died just a few years ago. I don't know much more about her, but I've seen her at some events in town, and she came across as a very different person that what she is up at the lake. I'm sure there's an interesting story back there somewhere."

Connie pulled into a parking place next to where Hadley's car was parked, and got out to help her friend load the luggage and boxes into her rental car.

"Your mother was never serious about any men her own age?" Connie scooted the box of Natalie's belongings into the back seat.

"No. Not after Daddy. I don't think she ever believed in love again after the way he made her feel."

"That's sad" Beads of sweat had formed on Connie's upper lip. Unsurprisingly, the day had turned hot.

"Not to ever have experienced real love. Sex cannot take the place of love." She looked at the younger woman pointedly.

"Is it actually so wonderful, Connie? To live with the same man for years and years? You can't really live your own life, or be a truly free woman, or follow your own desires. Is it worth just being a 'wifey-poo' as Margo put it?"

Connie laughed. "Do you think I'm just a 'wifey-poo,' Hadley?" The question was good natured and light. "Gordon and I have two children and three grandchildren.

We have a life of memories, good and bad. And we have each other. For better or worse. I have someone to take care of me and someone I can take care of. Think about it, Hadley."

She slid into her SUV and started the engine, then rolled down her window to say goodbye. "I'll talk to you later. Call me. We need to get the seamstress lined out. I know just the person and the fabric will be here day after tomorrow."

Hadley stood there, watching her as her friend rounded a corner and disappeared behind a building, going back to her home and husband. She turned to her own car, trying to ignore the hollow feeling in her stomach.

Susan Vineyard

33 Shenanigans

At the property entrance, Hadley entered the code that Norma had given her. Then, as the ornamental wrought iron gates creaked open, she eased her car down the circle drive of the Halloways' Tulsa home.

In a neighborhood of imposing houses, theirs dominated. It resembled a gingerbread castle, with its blue tile roof, many steep gables, and entryway turret. Two stories of tall French doors overlooked green manicured lawns and a splashing fountain.

Since it was only a few blocks from here, Hadley had driven by her parents' old house, on what had once been called *Black Gold* Boulevard.

While elegant and impressive in its own right, that residence didn't hold a candle to this property. Both neighborhoods contained houses built by oil millionaires years ago, when Tulsa was the 'Oil Capitol of the World.'

Other structures, being built now, shared the streets with the grand old dwellings from the past. Some of the newer houses were blatant icons of modern architecture that sent shivers of disgust down the spines of their traditionalist neighbors.

On the other hand, some new mansions were built to match the gracious and opulent style of the older homes. Like this one. Earl opened the door when Hadley rang the bell, a delighted smile etched into his weathered face.

182

"I love opening the door and finding a beautiful woman standing there!" He ushered her through the octagonal turreted foyer and down a hall.

As they passed an open door, Hadley noticed a well-designed formal living room with a cathedral ceiling. An opulent oriental rug covered the floor.

Through the French doors and arching windows at the far end of the room, she could see the blue of a swimming pool.

On the other side of the hall, through another arched doorway, Earl and Hadley entered a more causal room. The message of this space was clearly that, although their home might be stately and elegant, Earl and Norma were world travelers.

A kudu head hung high on a wall that angled up to another cathedral ceiling. No wonder this house had so many steep gables. They accommodated the dramatic ceilings.

The walls looked like stucco, and heavy dark beams highlighted several of the angles. Comfortable, dark leather furniture invited plopping down and curling up.

The floor was tile and partially covered by a colorful tribal rug. Impressed, Hadley recognized the primitive figures of a Gabbeh rug, created by the Qashqai weavers of Iran.

She knew anything from Iran was hard to come by in the United States these days, but France had no such restrictions. These rugs were common in the elegant homes of Paris and the French Riviera.

Norma, rising from a comfortable sofa, greeted Hadley warmly, and shooed Earl off to bring them coffee. She settled her guest down beside her.

"You were at the hospital today?" She grasped the younger woman's hands with her own, her gaze softening in understanding.

Looking back into Norma's eyes, surrounded by the wrinkles of a lifetime, Hadley realized that every woman must, at some time in her life, go through what she was experiencing, losing her mother.

"When my mother passed away, I felt like an orphan, although I was in my fifties. I know today must have been hard for you.

"But then, it's been a hard week, hasn't it, Hadley? I'm so glad you came by tonight. I've been wanting to talk to you.

"I loved your mother and your father. They were wonderful people, in their own ways. Yes, they were flawed, just as we all are, and I have a feeling that the best thing either one of them ever did was to bring you into this world.

"You have a proud legacy, my dear, being the daughter of Natalie Jones and Warren Barrington."

Although she struggled, Hadley couldn't hold back the tears overflowing her eyes, forming drops on her thick lashes, and blurring Norma's face.

Her anger at Zane and his father had temporarily subdued her grief. But the memory of that lonesome box and Mère's luggage, out in her car, pushed other emotions into the background.

Two suitcases and a box. And that damned boat. All that was left of her mother, who had always been her best friend and confidant, the only family she had had in a world of acquaintances.

Sure, she had friends whom she'd known since she was a schoolgirl, and she'd had lovers who had made her laugh and sigh, but Mère had been her family.

Even though Natalie had had many men in her glamorous life, she had never belonged to any of them. She had belonged to Hadley, her daughter. Natalie griped the older woman's wrinkled hands tightly as she sobbed, and Norma tightened her own grip in return.

As Earl entered the room, balancing a tray with three cups, Hadley sat up straight, reclaiming her hands to rub away the tears, and smiling bravely as she accepted her cup of steaming coffee.

"Oh, now Hadley, dear." Earl stared at her with a dismayed look on his face.

"I must look a mess," Hadley stood up. "Do you have a powder room I can use? I'm so sorry. It's just that…. I picked up Mère's things and…"

She looked down at Norma, sitting there with that understanding expression. Hadley lowered her voice. "I feel like an orphan today."

As Hadley splashed water on her face, she reflected that Norma's smile had been as understanding as any mother's smile could be, except for Natalie's smile.

If she didn't get herself under control, she was not going to find out anything useful tonight. Hadley steeled herself as she applied her lipstick.

As she turned to leave the elegant powder room, she caught a glimpse out the window of someone diving into the pool and moved closer to have a look. A head surfaced, water cascading from Kip's blond hair and blue eyes.

Oh, of course Kip was here. She really didn't need that. Hadley let the curtain fall back into place, but before gravity could save her, Kip's blue eyes caught hers for just a second. She sat down heavily on the marble bench below the window.

She was going to have to deal with Kip sooner or later, and she needed his grandparents' information. She could do this. She closed her eyes for a minute.

Mère, I'm going to get to the bottom of this whole affair. I don't know why you came back to Tulsa, and I don't know the whole story of how you were injured. I don't know why Zane and his father were visiting you when you died, but I'm going to figure it all out.

As she stood, she tossed back her hair, and took a deep breath. Then she opened the door, clearing her mind for the task she had set herself.

"They were very good friends." Norma and Earl looked through the small picture album.

"Before she met your father. Sonny was just a lake boy, and your grandparents certainly didn't encourage any relationship between them," Norma explained.

"I don't think there was any relationship. Not like that." Earl scowled and rumbled his thoughts. "Your grandparents wouldn't have allowed that."

Oh, it was like that, was it? Hadley glanced up at the kindly old oil man, her father's friend. True, the very thought of Mère being in any kind relationship with Zane's father had almost disgusted her, even though she'd never met the man.

On the other hand, she could certainly understand the attraction, if he was anything like as sexy as his son. The thought that her grandparents would have disapproved of an innocent friendship, just because they perceived that some boy who lived at Grand Lake and was part Native American was not suitable for their daughter disturbed her in a different way.

But she wouldn't hold those attitudes against Norma and Earl. She hoped that kind of thinking had died out with their generation, but being angry with them wouldn't accomplish anything. It sure wouldn't get her the information she needed.

Still, the story they were telling her didn't explain why Mère had been with those two when she was injured. Or why Zane had never mentioned that he or his father knew her mother, or that he knew anything about the way she'd been injured. Something was fishy. What was that check made out to Zane all about?

Hadley smiled and gently nodded at Earl to continue, but Norma cut in.

"Your grandparents sent your mother back east to design school, hoping she'd meet someone special out there. They really wanted the best for their little girl, Hadley. You understand."

"But she came back here to work." Earl interrupted his wife. "Wanted to decorate boats. That girl loved the lake. So her daddy got her a job redoing Warren's boat—*Black Gold*."

"I knew that's how she met Daddy, decorating his boat." Hadley had always known that, but now she had the feeling that the simple romance story she'd grown up with might not have been so simple after all.

Norma stared at Hadley, her chin cupped in one hand.

"Earl, I think it's cocktail time. What would you like, Hadley? I'll take a dirty martini, Earl. Will you be a dear?" Hadley requested a vermouth.

Norma watched her husband walk to the bar at the other end of the room before she again focused her attention on Hadley.

"I don't know for sure, Dear, but I think your mother, and Zane's father, Sonny…. Well, I don't know how close they were, but I think they cared about each other. Life was simpler then, in a way. You know, you got married. Not like today when everyone's living together, or not even that, just, you know.

"And you married someone who could give you and your children a good life." She laughed self-consciously.

"I know what that sounds like, but, my mother always told me that you can fall in love with a rich man as easily as you can a poor man. Understand, I certainly would not trade Earl for any other man in the world, even if he couldn't give me all of this."

Her eyes swept the room with its tall ceilings, French doors out to the garden and expensive furnishings. "And when we were young, younger than you, we, your mother and I, we all dreamed of a Prince Charming. If we were lucky, we found ours. I did.

"Life was not so kind to your Natalie. I think, I think she was pressured to marry your father. I don't know how much she fought it. Like I said, a good marriage was what a girl did. But…" The older woman rubbed her face as if trying to find just the right words.

"I don't think your father would have been her first choice… if she had followed her heart."

"And Zane's father would have?" What Hadley was hearing began to sink in.

"I don't know. I'm not sure. I wasn't a confidant of your mother's back then. We knew each other, but we didn't share that kind of thing. I was older and already married to Earl when she came back from school."

"I haven't been around Sonny that much. But I do know one thing. Your daddy and Sonny Bowman, they never really liked each other, or it seemed that way.

"I've wondered. I would not be surprised if your daddy knew or suspected that he was not Natalie's first choice. In fact, makes you wonder if knowing that played any part in all his shenanigans, doesn't it?"

Hadley leaned back into the sofa, dumbfounded, as Earl re-joined the women with drinks. She had so many questions.

If Mère had loved that man (and she was having a hard time accepting that possibility), why had she married Daddy? And had that really had anything to do with the decisions that Daddy had made, with his running around with other women?

Whew! She knew that Natalie was no angel after the divorce. Life had taught her that love was an illusion, that men were fun, but not to be trusted, that a woman must take care of herself and not depend on some man for her happiness or success. Wow. So many questions.

"Hey Hadley!" Kip breezed into the room, full of fresh, young enthusiasm. He flashed a bright smile as he strode over to give his grandmother a quick hug. His chestnut hair was still damp from the pool. "What's for dinner, Gran? I'm hungry!" Norma fondly patted the hand he rested on her shoulder.

"You promised you'd join us, Hadley. Our girl has the day off, so I hope you don't mind eating my cooking."

"No one minds eating your cooking, Sweetie Pie." Earl offered his wife his hand to help her stand. Norma's eyes crinkled as she smiled up at her husband.

"I'll set the table," he proclaimed, eyes twinkling as she let him help her up, then turned to Hadley and his grandson.

"Kip, why don't you show Hadley around the place? We'll have dinner ready soon. Come on Norma, I could smell that roast cooking when I was over at the bar. My mouth's a waterin'. Hadley, you're in for a real treat." He led his wife toward the kitchen.

Sipping the last of her vermouth, Hadley watched the couple walking away, holding hands and chatting about dinner, and she wondered if her parents had ever experienced that simple companionship.

34 *False Pretenses*

"Come on, Hadley!"

Kip held out his hand to help her up. She wondered if he realized that he was mirroring his grandfather's actions.

Well, Hadley didn't need any help up from a low, cushiony seat, but she couldn't exactly ignore his offer, so she allowed him to pretend to help her up, then reclaimed her hand.

The last thing Hadley wanted to do right now was to deal with Kip Halloway, but she realized that this was an opportunity to accomplish something she'd been thinking about, so she smiled brightly at the young man and allowed him to guide her though his grandparents' stately manor.

Being an International Business student, Kip enthusiastically pointed out where many of the house's treasures had originated. Hadley listened politely, remembering how many of her parents' friends had also been collectors.

Many couples, and even families, who worked in the oil business had spent time overseas in places like Indonesia, Libya, Egypt, Nigeria, and Saudi Arabia, since those locations were where oil had been abundant.

She thanked Kip for the flowers he'd sent.

"Did you like them?" He searched her eyes, but she hid the truth, that they were more disturbing to her than welcome, and assured him that they were beautiful.

Kip led Hadley out by the pool where she had seen him swimming earlier. Even though she was used to palatial homes back home, Hadley was impressed by this pool, long and rectangular, reflecting the white and blue mansion. The water looked cool and inviting.

If she could just jump in and swim a few laps right now, maybe she could clear her mind a bit and figure out—what?

She pretended to listen to Kip's chatter, smiling and nodding. How had what she had just learned changed her view of her parents? But what had she learned? Just guesses, speculations.

And what about the accident? She'd never had a chance to even mention that, but there was still dinner. She could bring it up then. Now she had to have a serious talk with sweet young Kip.

Past the pool was a veranda where two wicker chairs faced a carefully groomed rose garden. With a challenging backward look at Kip, Hadley settled down into one of the chairs, indicating that he take the other one.

They both sat, rocking for a moment, enjoying the profusion of roses of every style and color. A hummingbird darted past, a colorful, dashing male, free and carefree.

"I'm so glad you stopped by, Hadley. I've been wanting to talk to you again. I'm sorry about the other night. About Paula…."

"Don't Kip." Hadley interrupted him before he could continue. "I mean, you don't have to explain, really."

"But I want to, Hadley. Paula, well, well…."

"Kip, I know. It's OK."

"But that's not something I chose, not something I want. I, I, I'd like to spend some time with you Hadley, get to know you. We have so much more in common, and Paula is just not…."

She wished he would just stop whining. Hadley forced herself to keep smiling. Ok, she'd better get to the point and tell this boy what to do.

"Kip." He started to interrupt again. "No. Listen to me, please. Just. Listen. I see what's happening with you and Paula. I'm sorry. No. Just listen.

"Paula used to be my friend, but I know that you and she are not cut out for each other, and I can see the ways she's trying to hang on to you." The younger man looked relieved.

"Do you want my advice, as a friend?"

"Oh yes." Kip leaned toward her. "Yes, Hadley, I do. How do I get out of this relationship with Paula? I'm so glad you understand."

The expectant, hopeful look on his young face dismayed Hadley. This was by far not the easiest conversation she'd ever had, but nothing had been easy today.

"Kip, if you keep hanging out at the lake this summer, this situation will only get harder to deal with, you know. Paula has to accept the reality that you aren't in love with her and get on with her life. Stringing her along isn't good for either one of you."

Kip looked down at his hands. "Yeah, I know." He sighed. "I just wanted one last summer on Grand Lake. I graduate next year, you know, and I'm not coming back to Tulsa right away. I have some other offers in companies that have more opportunities overseas.

"Granddad knows my plans. And he agrees, for a few years, to let me go my own way. After all, dad's here to help him out. Anyway, this is my last free summer to just be a kid, kind of. So, that's why you and I have so much in common. I'll be in Europe a lot. I'd love to see you there."

"Stop, Kip. Stop right there. I want to be your friend. I like you. I really do. But that's as far as we go. No." She looked at him sternly.

"Don't say anything. We can be great friends, just not anything else, OK? You are very young, and you're going to have a very good time finding the girl of your dreams.

"Hey, don't look so down, silly. You've just made a lifelong friend, if you want one. We'll be laughing over this day when we're old and wrinkled, Kip.

"And about this summer. The choice is yours. I really do understand you wanting to enjoy being here. It's a decision you'll have to make."

Kip was obviously trying to look pathetic, but Hadley didn't buy it at all. He'd find his older woman to have a fling with. Boys like Kip always did. But it wouldn't be her.

She wasn't exactly sure why either. She'd enjoyed a few flings with younger men, and Kip was very attractive. But for some reason, she just wasn't interested this time, and it was more than Paula.

Nope, it had nothing to do with Zane. How stupid of her to even think about him right now, after what she'd found out. That man had some explaining to do and that conversation was going to be rougher than this one.

Earl rounded the corner of the house.

"Oh, there you two are. Well, come on in. You don't want to upset Norma by letting dinner get cold, now."

The three strolled around the house.

"Grans." Kip put his hand on his Grandfather's shoulder as they walked.

"I'm thinking about going ahead and taking that emersion course in Arabic that I was telling you about."

"I thought you didn't want to go abroad this summer." Earl turned his head toward his grandson. "I thought you wanted to play at the lake."

"I've been thinking." Kip caught Hadley's eye. "If I go, I'll be able to skip a language class required for my degree next semester and take that engineering class you recommended."

Earl gave his grandson a speculative glance and smiled.

"Norma." He led the two younger people through a door into a large kitchen. "I think our boy's growing up." He patted Kip on the back, and the young man seemed to stand a little straighter. Hadley smiled.

The kitchen where his wife served her succulent pot-roast, on a stoneware platter, surrounded by tender carrots and onions, looked a little like some French country kitchens Hadley had eaten in, but on a larger, grander scale. Like almost everywhere else in their house, French doors opened up one wall. The floor was tile. The table was massive and rustic. The big stove was designed for serious cooking.

When Hadley had thought of Tulsa and Oklahoma all those years while she'd lived in France, she had never thought of it like this: eating delicious, simple meals with people who made her feel so welcome. It was almost like coming home in an odd kind of way, a home she'd never had any desire to come back to.

Hadley hated to disturb such a peaceful family dinner by bringing up a painful subject, but she could not let this opportunity pass.

She had to get Norma and Earl's input on what she had discovered today, so she told them what she'd heard from the doctor, about how her mother had fallen on a boat.

She also told them about her experience that morning with Zane, the storm part, anyway. The three of them listened intently to her story, asking a few questions to make sure they understood it all. Kip muttered under his breath when Hadley described the boat ride, something that was probably not very complementary to Zane.

After she'd told them all she had to tell, she waited to hear what they thought. All three of the Halloways sat there for a few minutes without saying anything. Earl peered at her sharply under shaggy eyebrows.

"So, are you saying that you think Zane was driving a boat recklessly when your mother was injured?" Norma quizzed her pointedly.

"I don't know." And that was the truth, Hadley admitted to herself. She didn't really know anything. "But he scared me this morning. He made some stupid decisions. He endangered my life.

"I don't think he's very responsible, so, I just don't know about that, but there's more. I told you Zane's dad was there when she, she had her attack. Well, when I found that photo album, something fell out of it." All of them had stopped eating, waiting.

"A check fell out of the book. My mom had made out a check to Zane for $20,000. I just don't know what any of this means, but the thing that makes me most suspicious is that Zane has been lying to me."

"Lying?" Kip's eyes narrowed.

Hadley looked down at her hands. "Yes. He was there waiting for me on the boat when I drove down after the funeral. He told me he knew the dock manager and that's why he came to help me. He never said anything about knowing my mom or his dad knowing my mom, or being there when she was injured, or being in the hospital or anything.

"He came to work for me under false pretenses. I guess he didn't get that check that my mom was going to give him for some reason, so he had to come to me to make the money?"

Earl cleared his throat.

"Hadley, I don't know why Zane did any of that, and I think if I were you, I'd want to find out. Hell. I want to find out, myself. In fact, why don't you let me have a little talk with that boy?"

"Me too!" Kip echoed Earl. "Granddad, I'll go with you. He can't treat Hadley like that. I want to know what that sucker is up to!"

"Kip, you've got to get packed up and get overseas. I can handle this, but…" Earl once again focused on Hadley. "There's something you need to know. Zane doesn't need your money. And he didn't need your mother's money."

"What do you mean?" Hadley focused on Earl. "I mean, I saw his shop, and it was OK, I guess." She wrinkled her nose. "Except for the bathroom. But he works on boats and lives at the lake. He can't make that much money being a handyman."

"Well, he makes more than you probably know in that shop, because he only works on the best boats, and he builds boats. And he races them. Hasn't he ever told you that about himself?"

Hadley shook her head.

"That's strange." Earl tapped his fingers on the table. "Just strange. Besides that, his family, his father, they do alright too.

"That family owned a lot of land before Grand Lake was built. Not much else, but a lot of land. And some of their land was taken to build the lake, but a lot of it became that town up north on the lake.

"Now restaurants and hotels and other business are built on it. And Sonny and that foreign wife of his invested the money wisely. They still own some of that land and lease it out, and they own part of several businesses in town, along with the ranch that Zane pretty much runs now."

Hadley squinted her eyes at Earl. Her head hurt. She knew her brain was in information overload. When Kip poured her another glass of wine, she smiled a completely sincere thank you at him and gulped down half the glass. OK. That numbed the pain a little bit. She took another sip. Norma laughed.

"I see that you didn't know much about that young man you hired." Her smile turned into a frown. "But that still doesn't explain why he kept so many secrets from you.

"In fact, it's really looking like he deliberately deceived you for some reason. I don't like it. I don't like it at all." She turned to her husband, who was looking rather fierce.

"Earl, I want you to go up there tomorrow and have a talk with Sonny and see if you can get to the bottom of this. I want to know where and how Natalie was injured and I want to know the reason for this deliberate deception."

Earl nodded solemnly. Hadley couldn't help smiling to herself to watch Kip once again unconsciously mirroring his grandfather by nodding just as solemnly.

Cute. He had a good role model. But as endearing as these men were, Hadley's style was not to let men run around solving her problems for her.

Unless those problems had to do with fixing a boat, she admitted. Letting a man step in and solve a problem for her was exactly what had gotten her into this mess.

"Thank you so much." Hadley smiled at each person around the table. "But please let me see if I can figure this mess out on my own first."

Earl's mouth tightened into a stubborn line and Norma looked worried. "I promise you that I'll call on your help if I can't handle this situation, but I want to meet this man, this Sonny. I want to see if he'll answer my questions."

Their expressions didn't change much. "And I promise that if I can't get to the bottom of this mystery, I'll let you step in and help me, Earl." But she was determined that asking his help would not be necessary.

Why had she let her guard down with Zane? She was attracted to him, yes. She pictured his golden skin and piercing eyes, his gentle mouth, how he had looked with his shirt open the first time she'd seen him. And then she thought of how wild and uncontrolled he'd been just this morning.

Now that she wasn't so frightened, the thought of him in the boat, riding the waves, his hair blowing, his face clenched in concentration and a wild joy at battling the elements, made her weak, even though she was extremely angry with him.

How could she have let a physical attraction get the best of her common sense? Well, that wouldn't happen again.

Just wait. Just wait until she saw Zane Bowman again. She would see who had the upper hand then. He'd have an opportunity to see the real Hadley. No more secrets. No more lies.

35 So Much Baggage

She had to walk out the door. Or at least open it. She couldn't cower in her boat all day.

Hadley peeked out the window. He was still on the deck, prying off pieces of her boat with a crowbar. The day was heating up early, and his worn tee-shirt strained across his muscular back as he pulled and pushed with the tool, carefully popping every piece off intact and adding each to a growing pile.

She'd used some pretty strong language when she'd almost fallen over some of his supplies in the dark coming home last night.

The deck of her boat was a mess right now. He'd done that on purpose so she wouldn't dare fire him. She was sure of it.

But why would he care if she fired him or not, since he didn't need the money? She dropped the curtain and stood back. And shouldn't he be building race boats or managing his family ranch? What was this man doing working on her boat?

Although her cleaning in here could keep her busy all day, sooner or later, Hadley was going to have to go out there and ask the man questions. She peaked out the window again, then hastily dropped the curtain when Zane stood up to stretch his back, probably tired from hunching over that way. Through the tiniest opening, she watched the muscles in his arms and chest flex as he stretched.

Guiltily she glanced over to the galley, at Kip's flowers on the table. A fresh pot of coffee sat next to it. Zane would probably like a cup. Or was it already too hot outside for that?

She'd picked up an electric coffee maker yesterday. She'd probably gone through the free coffee that seemed to magically appear for her at the dock.

It was time she fended for herself. She'd just leave the pot for whoever bought the boat. They'd need it.

Was it just yesterday that Zane had prepared her breakfast? And almost killed her? Hadley sighed. What she had to do next would be so much easier if the sight of him didn't take her breath away.

As she watched, Zane closed his eyes, and leaned back his head, rolling his neck and shoulder muscles.

He looked like he was really enjoying that stretch. She realized her heart was pounding and she was breathing deeply.

She had to get herself in hand, when all she wanted was to get her hands on Zane. Hadley never fooled herself that she was immune to a good looking man.

They were the desserts in life, dark chocolate, meant to be savored. But this situation was different, and she had a conversation to carefully maneuver. She couldn't put it off for much longer. She had to go out there.

He knew what had happened to Mère. He had been there. Hadley let the anger wash over her. That was safer than the feelings that had previously been washing over her.

She let the anger build. She was ready for battle. Her eyes narrowed, she took a deep breath, and opened the door.

Zane, who had just picked up his crow bar to start working again, turned toward her with a smile, a smile that quickly died when he saw her expression.

He put the crow bar back down slowly and sighed. He had been afraid of this. What had those doctors told her? He thought he'd probably really messed up this mission.

Sorry Dad. Sorry Natalie. Zane tensed, waiting for Hadley to speak, dreading what she might say.

She marched toward him, back stiff, head high, her look thunderous, kicking aside a piece of wood in her way.

He sucked in a breath. She stopped right in front of him, almost touching him, and glared up at him, her eyes flashing.

Then she hit him. She just clenched her tiny fist and hit him in the middle of his chest. Then she turned away and stomped toward her door, her head down.

"Hadley?" Zane took one long legged step and put his hand on her shoulder to stop her. What was he supposed to do?

She shrugged off his hand, wrenched open the door, walked inside and slammed it behind her. He could hear her crying in there.

He knocked on the door, thinking he should probably just gather up his tools and leave. But that wouldn't solve any of his problems at this point. He had to see this scene out. What did she know? When she didn't answer the door, Zane called out to her.

"Hadley, let me in. What's wrong?" As if he didn't have a pretty good idea.

He knocked again. After a minute, she opened the door just a crack. He could see that she was trying to stop crying.

I am such a jerk, he thought. But…but…, but what? I have had a very good reason to keep my secrets. It's better for everybody.

Standing there, however, looking at her, his reasons didn't seem quite so noble. He sighed and pushed the door the rest of the way open. Hadley stared at him, then took a step backwards so he could enter.

As he stood in the middle of the salon, he couldn't miss the vase of flowers sitting on the table. A sudden burst of jealousy hit him head on. She'd probably bought them in Tulsa, to cheer herself up. Except what if she hadn't?

She probably had a lover in France who was missing her, and she'd attended that party the other night. If she had such a strong effect on him, the man who had every reason to stay away from her, surely other men would be attracted to her too.

But so what? She was leaving. He'd live. He wasn't that far gone on this chick. No. He. Was. Not.

He looked around. Hadley had obviously been busy. An oriental patterned rug now covered the cuts in the carpet that led to the bilge and the engines. The colors were still old-fashioned and dark, but everything looked clean and bug-free.

Hadley turned from him and picked up a book from a bentwood end table, a familiar-looking book. Zane groaned.

Hadley eyed him suspiciously as she pulled a piece of paper out of the book and handed it to him.

He knew what it was. He didn't even have to look. He started to tear the check in two, but Hadley put out a hand to stop him.

"Don't, Zane. My mother wanted you to have that check. She made it out to you. And then she had to die on you before you had a chance to get your hands on it."

Her face was one angry question, and he couldn't answer. But he knew what he had to do. He'd talked to Dad the night before, thinking he'd be furious with his son for botching up the job so badly, but his father had just chuckled softly.

"I should have known better," Zane could hear his father muttering softly, as he'd looked out the window toward the clouds.

"Well, I tried to keep your secrets, Natalie, old girl. But I couldn't. And now it's up to me to set things right with that daughter of yours. I'll do the best that I can."

It had broken Zane's heart last night to see the tear that slid down Sonny's wrinkled, sun-worn face. It had broken his heart, because in the past year, he had seen his father crying way too much, over his mother's death, and then Natalie's.

Recently, what had broken Zane's heart had been that his father's latest tears had not been for his wife, but for another woman. He turned his back on Hadley and walked out the door and back onto the deck of the old Chris Craft.

Hadley wasn't going to let him just walk out on her. She followed him until he reached the back of the boat, then walked around him to see what his face was telling her, since he wasn't talking.

Zane didn't look defensive or angry. She'd seen both of those expressions on his handsome face before. He looked sad.

She hoped, hoped badly, that Zane would be able to explain her suspicions away. She hoped that neither Zane nor his father had been in any way responsible for Mère's death.

But Zane had kept secrets from her, had even lied to her. She was deeply afraid that no explanation would ever make anything right with this man.

And why did she care? What was he to her? She would be leaving this lake, this state, this country very soon. Maybe tomorrow. She'd never see him again.

He'd continue to live his stupid life out on this lake and she would live her life in France, and never, ever come back here again. Never see any of them again, not Connie and Gordon, nor Meg and Adam, nor Earl and Norma.

A wisp, a tendril of sadness wormed its way through her thoughts and clouded her eyes for a moment, but, swallowing hard, she forced it out of her consciousness.

Wasn't Zane going to say anything in his own defense? Was he just going to walk away? She stood there, biting her lip, waiting. He seemed to be looking far away, like a sailor gazing out to sea, standing so quietly.

As he leaned over the back railing, he lifted the check she'd given him, looked at it for a minute, then slowly and deliberately tore it into four pieces.

Hadley reached out, but he held them out over the rail and let each piece drift lazily down until it kissed the water and floated away, bobbing in the slight ripples of the lake.

He turned, running his fingers through his hair, pulling it back from his tanned forehead. He looked down, not meeting her eyes.

"Hadley." His voice was hardly more than a whisper. She moved forward a step to hear what he had to say. Was he finally going to answer her questions? Was she finally going to learn the truth? Zane raised his still sad eyes to hers.

"I, we, owe you some answers. My father wants to talk to you, but I'll need to take you to him."

Hadley tried to read his eyes. Was he pleading with her to accept, to wait, to listen? She couldn't interpret what she was seeing there.

All she knew was that the answers to all of her questions were once again being denied her, and that was unacceptable.

"Goodbye Zane." She turned and walked to the salon door. She entered and shut the door behind her. She'd call Earl later. Now she was crying too hard.

In the small cabin where she'd slept during her idyllic childhood summers, she threw herself on the single berth and cried huge gulping sobs.

Her world had crashed down around her, again. Mère had deserted her. Oh how that hurt. This stupid boat had kept her from leaving, but no more.

She had always been so content to never visit Oklahoma again. Her life had been so, what? Easy? Civilized? Sane?

She and Mère had been so happy. With their comfortable Paris apartment, their many friends to visit in other parts of France.

Her life had been blissful as she had nurtured her blossoming talents, and immersed herself in a creative career. Like Mère, she had surrounded herself with casual friends and lovers.

Her future had held no fears or anxieties, only Paris in the spring and the Mediterranean coastline, the Côte d'Azur in the summer.

And now? Now her memories of childhood, memories she had sealed away in the dark caverns of her mind, were surrounding and crushing her. Friends of her parents, her own childhood friends, this boat.

She wasn't the little girl who had moved away from Oklahoma any more. She was a free spirit, without the baggage all of these people had: kids and grandkids and people who loved them and trapped them. So much baggage.

She couldn't breathe here. When Hadley sniffed, no air would enter her nasal passages, swollen with crying. She gulped in air through her mouth. Her eyelids felt like sandpaper as she blinked away tears.

How dare these people play on her emotions? She grabbed her bags out of the hanging locker.

How dare Zane refuse to tell her what had happened to her mother? She yanked open a drawer and dumped the contents into one bag, stuffing the mess down and tugging the zipper closed.

How dare that man make her feel bad when he was the one hiding things and probably lying to her? She grabbed the few clothes hanging in the locker and stuffed them into another bag, followed by a traveler's jewelry bag, a hairbrush, and a few toiletries from the adjoining head.

She stormed out of the cabin, but stopped in the salon, looking down at the picture album lying open on the table there. Dropping her bags on the sofa, she picked up the small album, and sighed.

36 Broken Glass

A squeak startled her. The door opened, and Zane stood there, head bent, biting his bottom lip.

"Please, Please let me take you to meet my dad tomorrow. He's not home today. I can't take you today. He's seeing his doctor. But tomorrow, we will answer any questions you ask us. Both of us."

He walked toward her, and took the album out of her hand. A single tear rolled down his cheek, and Hadley sighed, realizing that she had to hear the story.

She could not leave this lake forever without knowing Mère's story, the story of her youth and the story of her death.

"OK, Zane. Tomorrow. But I need to be alone now. And after I talk to your father, I'm leaving for home. I'm going to book my flight tonight." She indicated the open door with her eyes.

Zane nodded, turning to leave, then turned back unexpectedly. He bent down, cupped her chin in his hand, and before she knew what was happening, tilted her face up and touched his lips to hers, just a brushing touch, a touch that sent ripples of sensation from the soft skin of her lips, throughout her whole body, waking a need she had never felt.

Not the pure carnal need with which she was familiar. Not the need to control any relationship, to hold herself apart emotionally while immersed in physical pleasure and uncomplicated desire.

She felt something more, as she opened her lips to Zane, but his mouth was not where she expected it to be. Her eyes fluttered open to see him disappearing out the door, his hair flowing down his back.

As he disappeared from her sight, she heard him murmur, "Tomorrow."

Hadley sat on the aft deck of her boat. A few tatters of its old canvas cover remained attached to the rusty framework of what used to be the party room, spacious, with teak flooring and a wet bar.

The teak was worn and faded now. It needed to be varnished. Some of the wood should probably be replaced, but that had been too big an undertaking to end up on Zane's to do list.

She had dragged one of the deck chairs back here where she could look out over the bay and be away from all the people and parties going on up and down the dock.

Margo's houseboat was just leaving its slip for parts unknown, the throbbing music competing with Meg and Adam's music, down the dock. Who was Margo's plaything tonight?

Who would she, herself, have chosen if she were in Margo's position? Hadley knew the answer to that question too.

She stretched out her legs, bare feet propped on the top of the rail. She really needed to do something about her toenails. The polish was chipped. Soon.

On the Dock: A Tale of Grand Lake

Everyone was at the lake today. It was the Friday before the Fourth of July on Sunday, and everyone was in a party mood.

Yes, as she'd explained to Meg earlier, they did celebrate the Fourth of July in Paris, kind of seeing the United States as having followed France to freedom. Hadley knew that the way it was celebrated on Grand Lake was very different.

But who cared? She wouldn't be here to see it this year. But back during her childhood summers, she remembered the hot dogs and hamburgers and cold pop served in frosty bottles. By the fourth, she'd be back in Paris, alone.

A streak of lightening cracked the sky open, followed by the echo of that rupture. A single bloated drop of rain hit her foot where it was unprotected on the rail. She watched it flatten and roll down her leg. Then another drop fell, and then another, until the steady rhythm of a soft, steady rain softened the throb of music down the dock.

Hadley pulled her feet back in out of the rain and leaned the folding chair back under the overhang of her slip, where she could easily watch the drops falling out of the dark sky, illuminated by the dock's safety lights.

Each drop reflected the world in its tiny circumference. Mère had loved the rain. She had loved the colors of autumn and Paris in the rain.

Did Mère know her daughter was sitting here on *Black Gold* tonight? If she did, what did she think about that? Why had she come to this stupid place anyway?

Well, Mère, I hope I find the answer to those questions tomorrow. Then I'm going home. The next time I sit in the rain will be in Paris.

Hadley couldn't imagine what home was going to be like when she got there. Would she do anything different with the apartment, now that it was hers alone? Guess someday she'd have to pack up some of Mère's things.

Hadley had never really lived alone. Sure, her mother sometimes traveled, but the flat had always been so full of life, with its floor to ceiling windows looking out on Rue Commines. It would feel different when she returned there by herself.

She could almost feel Zane's feathery kiss on her lips again, and how she'd felt, needing more of him than flesh on flesh, needing to cling to him, something she'd never felt before.

She'd had never lacked for lovers in France, friends with privileges, but never anything more. What had she felt when Zane had kissed her? Whatever it was, that feeling had to be a result of her loneliness and frustration…. That was all.

Her mind wandered. Sitting there in the rainy night, she imagined Zane in her bedroom in Paris, with the sun shining in through the long white curtains, the sounds and business of the city ignored as he stood outlined in the light, standing over the bed where she waited for him to come to her.

Angrily, Hadley stood up, shaking her head to rid herself of the thoughts that were consuming her senses uncomfortably on a night that she would spend alone. It was just stupid to think like that. She's going back to Paris. She couldn't wait to get home!

The raindrops had slowed a bit, but a mist still fell on her where she stood, looking out at the lake. Reflections of lights from the dock swirled in the dark water, picking out the circular ripples made by the rain.

Hadley carefully made her way down onto the swim platform and quietly slipped into the cool wet darkness. It felt so good. She swam out a bit, where she could float and watch the partiers on the dock.

Gordon and Connie were strolling over toward Meg and Adam's boat to join the crowd there. Chairs were pulled up. Drinks were poured. Laughter drifted through the air.

Hadley strolled back over to her own boat to prepare for tomorrow and for leaving the lake, for getting back to her own world, where she knew her place and had a plan for her life.

These last few days had been a waste of her time. Her boat wasn't ready to sell, and she hadn't solved the mystery of Mère's death. She crawled back up onto the swim platform and slipped, unseen onto the cabin.

After a shower, she packed all of her belongings. When she picked up the photo album, it fell open to the picture of Mère and Sonny. They looked happy. Had they been lovers?

She brushed her finger over the picture, from her mother's face to the face of Zane's father. But her own father had been very handsome as well. And Mère had chosen to marry him for reasons Hadley might never know.

She opened the cabinet door to retrieve her mother's scrapbooks, then looked around to see if she'd missed any other mementos of her parents.

She didn't intend to ever see this boat again, so now was the time to take anything she wanted. She opened a drawer under the bookshelves. A framed picture lay upside down. She picked up the dusty object and turned it over.

Her childhood self looked back at her through broken glass. It was a family portrait of her parents and their young daughter, Hadley.

Her mother's hand rested on the young girl's shoulder. Natalie had always been so protective and supportive. Warren Barrington's arm was around Natalie's shoulders. A loving gesture or a possessive one?

Well, Mère had done well enough without him. They'd both been happy in Paris. Her mother had had so many good times, the companionship of many wonderful men. She'd never looked back.

And Hadley would do the same. She'd visit Sonny tomorrow, then she'd leave Grand Lake and she would never look back. She carefully wrapped the picture in several layers of paper towel and placed it carefully into her bag.

37 Neon Signs

Soon she would be home. With the time difference, she would be in Paris late on the Fourth of July, Paris time. She might even see fireworks as she landed, because the French do celebrate America's Independence Day.

It would hurt to walk into the empty flat, but she had to get past it. She would learn to live alone. She would go on with her life. It was time.

Today, she'd get to the bottom of the mystery surrounding her mother, then be on her way back home. Hadley stretched languorously under the worn sheets.

Her body felt good this morning, lithe and limber and ready for any task she asked of it. As she pushed off the sheets, she noticed that her nipples were hard, and realized just what her body was ready for.

She did have one more day here. And it would be spent be with Zane. The way he'd acted yesterday, offering to tell her everything, she really didn't think, really hoped that he had done anything wrong.

She hoped there was an explanation she could live with. Maybe, just maybe, since he knew she was leaving, they might say goodbye with more than words.

She wiggled, thinking of how his lips had felt on hers the day before. And he had kissed her. He wasn't immune to her charms.

She cupped her breasts in her hands and closed her eyes, drifting into a fantasy of how his bronze skin would feel against hers, how those lips would feel on her breasts.

Were those steps on the deck of her boat? *Merde!* Hadley was out of bed in a flash, grabbing a short skirt and sweater that she'd hung on the back of her cabin door, pushing her feet into a pair of sandals and dragging a brush quickly through her hair before rushing to the door.

Zane stood there with a paper cup of steaming coffee and a bag that smelled deliciously of eggs and bacon. Hadley badly wanted to reach out and push that strand of hair out of his eyes, but instead she accepted the coffee and took a long sip to steady herself.

"Just a minute." Zane retrieved another cup of coffee that he'd left sitting near the edge of the boat. Hadley held the door open in an unspoken invitation for him to enter.

An invitation from the spider to the fly, she thought to herself. *Enter at your own risk.* She watched him spread out the contents of his sack on the dinette in the galley and slid in across from him.

"Here we are again." Hadley watched the way he moved. "You do this kind of thing so well. You're very domestic."

But she was really thinking. *You'd make a good cabana boy, you know.* She smiled to herself, thinking back to her recent fantasies, very aware that she wasn't wearing any underwear.

Her plane left tomorrow. She'd promised her assistant that she was coming home. She'd committed to meet Zane's father today. And until she was clear about what had happened with Mère, she was keeping her distance, but she really deserved one bout with this summer boy.

That's all it was. A passing fancy. She looked up at him through long lashes and smiled her dimple smile.

Hadley was trying to put her anger on hold until she'd heard the Bowmans' story. Her attraction to this man was making forgiveness or forgetfulness easier. She'd know the truth soon, and then she'd know what these men's relationship with Mère had been.

She calculated that an easy, sexy manner would open more doors, and secrets, than would anger. And the thought that this was her last chance to seduce Zane made sexy easy to do.

On the other side of the booth, Zane kept his eyes on Hadley's face and tried not let them wander down. Sure, lots of girls around the lake wore very little in the summer, bikinis and tee shirts with no bra. Hell, he'd been to more than a few wet tee-shirt contests when he was younger. That wasn't his style now.

But for some reason, Hadley's casualness in displaying her body was both hard to ignore and enticing enough to keep him off-balance.

Like today. Her lime green sweater was casual and draped her body loosely, but it was also thin and somewhat see-through. It fell off her shoulders. The ruffled sleeves were wide and might offer tantalizing peeks if he really wanted to look.

Zane wanted to look, but he focused deliberately, first on his food, then on her face. He couldn't help noticing that the outlines of her breasts were plainly visible underneath the lose weave. And that her nipples were hard.

Oh, he wanted to look. And he wanted to touch. And he wanted to taste. And they'd better get out of here before he lost control completely.

He took the last sip of his coffee and stood, frantically trying to think of some non-offensive way to suggest that she change before he took her to meet his father.

Hadley sipped her coffee so he wouldn't notice her satisfied smile. Yeah, Zane was distracted. Hadley hadn't really had time to think how she'd look in this sweater without a bra when she'd been surprised by Zane this morning. And, truthfully, in the mood she'd been in right then, it probably wouldn't have mattered.

And her breasts would not be quite so noticeable if they weren't swollen by her desire for this man. She was very aware of her body this morning, and so was Zane, obviously.

Sliding out of the dinette, she stood, casually stretching so her sweater strained over her breasts and the loose weave became even more transparent. Zane stared.

She'd finally gotten him to take a good long look and she could see evidence that her arousal was contagious. She stifled a laugh.

"Just a sec, Zane. Give me a minute to freshen up?" The relief on his face was hilarious. She knew she needed to change clothes before she met his father, but breakfast had been fun, watching him squirm.

And wasn't that a thought. Hadley felt sure that Zane would carry the image of her as she looked now in his head all day, no matter how conservatively she dressed.

She loved the thought of him thinking of her body all day. Because she knew she'd be thinking of his as well. Tough. He shouldn't have kissed her last night.

Back in her cabin, Hadley considered her options, and chose to leave on the sweater, but add a tank top with a built-in bra, which made all the difference. Now she looked significantly covered up, but Zane would be continually reminded of exactly what was being covered up.

She brushed her hair, added just a touch of lipstick, slid a bracelet up her arm and inserted matching earrings into her ear lobes.

Grabbing an oversized pair of sunglasses and her bag, she glanced once more at herself in the mirror mounted on the back of the cabin door, then walked out into the galley.

Zane had his back turned to her as he leafed through the small album. The thought of the pictures it contained and the day ahead sobered Hadley. She never took her eyes off him as she walked up the steps to the salon and took the album from him.

"This belongs to your father, doesn't it?" He nodded. "We'll take it back to him today, then." She put the album into her purse.

"Ready?" Zane's eyes raked her, seeming to approve of what he saw. Hadley gave him just a hint of her dimple smile, and led the way outside as he held the door for her.

"You have a choice today." Zane stopped where the dock divided. "I brought my run-about, but we can go in your car if you like."

Hadley was torn. She'd told Zane that she'd never go out in a boat with him again, and she really shouldn't. He wasn't trustworthy.

But today was her last day here, and his little boat was so much fun. She scanned the horizon. The day seemed safe. The sky was blue. Only a few wispy clouds floated very high.

"Did you check the weather?" He grinned down at her and nodded. With a quick glance at her car up in the parking lot and a deep breath to give herself courage, she smiled back at him and walked toward his boat.

The day was beautiful, and as Hadley and Zane raced out onto the lake, leaving the marina behind, it once again seemed as if they were all alone in the world, at least to Hadley.

Now she understood why Zane commanded his vessel with such skill. Earl said he raced boats, that he was very good at racing boats. She admired his strong, bronze arms at the wheel, angling the low craft through a wake created by a fiberglass speedboat, tearing through the fabric of the lake.

The runabout crested man-made waves with minimal impact. As they slid down the other side of a large swell, it broke, showering them just before they escaped its range.

That's what I need this morning—a cold shower— thought Hadley, realizing how Zane's proximity and strong masculinity had been affecting her senses. How they had once again been overpowering her brain.

The long sleek boat crested another wave, then slid into a calmer area, protected by a breakwater. Hadley could tell they were near a town by the number of boats on the water and houses along the edge of the lake.

A little girl ran along the shoreline, followed by a collie, its tongue hanging out as it splashed through shallow water.

A young couple on a waverunner intersected Zane's boat, laughing and waving, the bikini-clad girl on the back clutching the waist of driver tightly.

A flock of seagulls followed the wake of a larger boat, diving daringly when they spotted fish churned up to the surface.

As their boat slowed and made its way under a busy bridge, a huge semi-truck rattled above them. They zipped out of the shadow of the structure into the bright sunlight once again and idled into a marina new to Hadley. Zane tossed out the bumpers as they coasted to a courtesy dock where an attendant tossed them a rope with which to tie up.

"This is where you live?" Zane shook his head as he killed the motor.

"Nope. But my dad is here." Zane jumped to the dock and turned to offer Hadley a hand in embarking. "Actually, we have a slip here, and the Sea Skiff is right over there."

Hadley looked around at the tidy docks, and didn't see many older or wooden boats around. Most of them were very new and very large.

The people walking around tended to be well-dressed and prosperous-looking. The restaurant attached to the dock probably served a slightly higher quality of hamburgers and chicken fingers, she speculated, and maybe even something slightly healthy, like an iceberg lettuce salad with rich creamy, fat and calorie-laden dressing.

She sucked in her stomach. Breakfasts like she'd had this morning would soon run havoc on her slim form.

But, of course, after today, she wouldn't be eating Grand Lake food anymore. She'd be back home where the cuisine was fresh and satisfying, and where she could get back into shape. Not that she had a problem yet, thankfully.

She glanced down at the way her green sweater skimmed her slim waistline. Following Zane, she wondered where his father lived—and where Zane lived.

He led her up to a lot where his truck was parked, and opened the door for her. The air conditioning was welcome, as the sun was hot, as usual. As they drove out of the marina, she saw that the town was lively with tourists.

Obviously, many of the buildings and businesses were recent, as construction equipment growled around, creating new parking lots.

The town had a beachside look to it. Signs in windows advertised colorful towels, boat equipment and trendy clothing. A much different atmosphere than that of the sleepy, shabby town near Hadley's home marina. This one looked fun.

Flashing neon signs screamed Happy Hour and Margarita Specials. Boat and car dealers competed with grocery stores. Hadley didn't remember anything like this being on Grand Lake when she had been a child.

Zane explained about his dad as he drove. Sonny had taken his wife's death hard. She'd died about a year ago. Hadley forgot about staring at the town, focusing on Zane instead.

"Your mother?" He nodded. "Oh Zane, I'm so sorry. I guess it's easy to forget when something like that happens to a person, that it happens to other people too."

"Yes it does happen to everyone." He stared straight ahead, at the road.

She studied his face. His jaw was clenched, and she knew he was trying to control the pain of that loss. Hadley felt ashamed of her own self-indulgence, yet she still needed answers about Zane and his father's involvement in Mère's death. That hadn't changed.

"When your mother contacted my father…" She could tell that what he was telling her was tearing him up inside.

She bit her lip, realizing that she was very near to finding out what had really happened. Did she really want to know?

She'd thought she'd known Mère so well. But she could not imagine what had motivated Natalie to come back here. She must have had reasons, but was her daughter ready to hear them?

Zane glanced over at her as if he suspected that what was coming would be as hard for her as it was for him. She managed an uncertain smile, encouraging him to continue even as her stomach knotted in anticipation.

"She had heard that my mother had died, somehow." He stared straight ahead. "She called from Paris."

Hadley stared out the window, no longer thinking of Zane, but of Mère, in Paris, telling Hadley of the trip she was planning, managing not to supply any details except that she was going back to Tulsa to "take care of some business."

Hadley, in the middle of planning for a show and a gem buying trip, had let her slip away without demanding more information.

"My dad's health hasn't been good ever since Mother, uh, left us." They drove in silence for a moment, both caught up in their own sorrow.

"When your mom called, he seemed really glad to hear from her. She was an old friend, he told me, and I was glad to see him interested in something again."

Zane glanced over at Hadley, sitting very still in the beige leather seat of his truck, her hands clutched in her lap. Zane didn't think he'd ever seen her so still.

"Earl and Norma told me that your dad and my mother had been friends before Mère met my dad."

Well, all that his father had to say would not come as a complete surprise to her.

"Anyway, my dad can tell you more, but when the accident happened and, and, your mom…." He gripped the steering wheel for support.

"My dad took it really badly. We have a house up north, but Doc thought Dad should stay in town for a while, so the nurses could watch him.

"It's just for a little while, I'm sure. He'll be better soon. But he's at an assisted living center here in Grove. That's where we're going. But it's just temporary."

It had better be temporary, thought Zane. His dad was all he had now that his mom was gone. Oh, he had friends, but his dad was his family, and the ranch was awfully lonely without him, even though they saw each other almost every day.

Well, his dad was about to meet Natalie's daughter. Zane sure hoped the meeting would end up being positive. He glanced over at Hadley, sitting as still as a cornered mouse. Positive for everyone. After all, she didn't have anyone left.

38 Lies and Damn Lies

The truck pulled up in front of what looked like a rambling rustic apartment building. The sign read "Lakeside Gardens - Independent Living - Retirement Community."

Hadley stole a sideways look at Zane. This was a surprise. He was biting his lip, and his expression was grim. His hand grasped the steering wheel as his head drooped, eyes shut, obviously working hard to control his emotions.

Something was hurting him badly. She waited for him to make the next move. When, after a few minutes, he raised his head and smiled at her, she thought the smile more a result of bravado than of happiness.

"Let's go in. He's waiting for us." Zane eased himself out of his side of the truck and walked around to open the passenger door for her. Butterflies fluttered in her stomach, as she climbed down from the truck. She had to know what had happened and why, but she wasn't sure she was ready.

And Zane was upset. Because he could no longer keep the truth from her? Was he afraid she of her discovering how Mère had died? Or was something else bothering him, something unrelated to her questions? Well, Hadley had the feeling she was going to find out, and soon.

The place was nice. That was a relief. Hadley had never visited any kind of home for the elderly, but she'd heard tales of them. She didn't really want to see people who were just waiting to die, to smell disinfectant and urine. That's not what she'd signed up for.

But, as they passed through the big, heavy entry doors, Hadley and Zane were greeted with fresh flowers and sunshine pouring through a skylight into a cheery lobby with a western theme.

A young woman with a blond ponytail, dressed in blue jeans and a frilly blouse greeted them with a smile. Her shiny purple badge announced that her name was Brent.

Her smile brightened noticeably when her eyes met Zane's, and she didn't bother to speak. Obviously she recognized him and was aware that he knew where he was going. No guards, it seemed.

Zane led the way to an elevator. Waiting, Hadley glanced around. At the far end of the room, glass doors led out to what seemed to be a large deck. She could see the lake peeking through the wooden rails. A man and woman stood looking out toward the horizon, their arms around each other.

Another woman, Hadley noticed, sat over to one side in a porch swing, reading a book. A big, friendly looking dog lay on the decking near her mistress's feet. The elevator dinged, the doors slid open, and Hadley followed Zane inside.

"Dad's only here for a little while. He'll be moving back home soon." Zane looked awfully determined, but she sensed that he might not be 100% sure about what he was saying. Although it was clear that he sincerely wanted it to be true.

They emerged into another sitting room on the second floor, attached to a large kitchen area, complete with a dining table. A plate of chocolate frosted cupcakes set invitingly on the table, visible through a clear plastic cover. Beside the platter was a stack of small dishes.

The navy carpet had a white dot pattern. Again, Hadley could see the lake in the distance out of a large window framed by frilly navy curtains. The furniture was leather, and several tables held bouquets of fresh flowers. Hadley was impressed.

"Hi!" A little girl in shorts ran down the hall and climbed onto one of the sofas with a smile at Hadley and Zane, then, just as quickly, jumped back off to pick up a remote control on the far side of the table.

Turning on the large screen television and finding a children's show to her liking, she climbed back onto the sofa, stretched out comfortably, and seemed to forget all about the adults.

In the upstairs hall, white paneling covered the walls from the wainscoting to the ceiling. Below was wallpaper, a country print. Photographs that looked like they'd probably been taken around the lake hung on the walls.

They depicted scenes of boats and skiers, a deserted cove with icy edges, overhung with snow-laden tree branches, and other beautiful vignettes. Zane stopped at a white door and knocked.

"Come right on in." The door slightly muffled the voice coming from the other side. Zane turned the knob, pushed the door ajar, and peeked around.

"Are you decent, Dad? You've got company!"

"Ain't never been decent, son, but bring her in anyways!"

Zane pushed the door the rest of the way open, and there stood the man in the photographs, much older than when his picture had been taken with her mother.

His face was an aged version of Zane's. His skin was darkened by many years of sun and weather. Deep ridges ran from nose to mouth, and the crinkles around his eyes, so attractive on his son, were deep wrinkles on Sonny, but not unattractive even at his age.

His hair was white. Not grey, but snowy white, and, while not as long as his son's, it still fell over his collar, full and thick, with no receding hairline.

His eyes were brown, with a sparkle that seemed to reflect a love of life and a sense of humor. But at the same time, they were sad, as if he laughed at himself. He was not quite as tall as Zane, and he leaned on a simple wooden cane.

Hadley's breath caught. She'd forgotten to bring his cane back to him, the beautifully carved one he'd left in Mère's hospital room.

Had she ever mentioned the cane to Zane? She thought not. She'd had other things on her mind.

They stood in a small living room/kitchen/dining room combination with two doors, which probably led to a bathroom and bedroom.

It was nicely furnished, and family pictures sat around on tables. She recognized one of Zane and Sonny and the other woman from the album, Zane's mother.

She glimpsed a montage of what had to be Zane's school pictures, one for each year, and wished she had time to look at it more closely, but she turned to face the older man.

"Name's Sonny. Thank you for coming to see me."

"I am very glad to meet you Mr. Bowman." She smiled politely. "I'm Hadley, Natalie's daughter."

The man wore blue jeans, new, starched blue jeans, and a red polo style shirt. On his feet, he wore a pair of comfortable slippers, rather than the cowboy boots that many men his age seemed to wear around here.

She glanced over at Zane's white deck shoes. She'd never noticed him in cowboy boots. Of course, as much time as he spent on boats, they wouldn't be practical for him.

The older man looked her over. "You look so much like her." He sighed, turning away to look out of his window at the lake, which seemed to almost surround this building.

"Won't you please have a seat? We need to talk. Would you like a coke or something? Zane, would you get Natalie, uh, Hadley a coke?"

"No, No, thank you Mr. Bowman, I'm OK. Really I am."

"Well, let's all sit down." Zane indicated that Hadley should sit on the white leather loveseat. "We came here to clear this matter up."

Hadley took a seat, but Sonny stayed at the window, looking out to the horizon. Why couldn't he face her? Hadley waited, trying not to draw conclusions. Zane looked from one to the other, and sighed.

"Dad." He walked over to the window and put his hand on his father's shoulder. "Please sit down. We have to talk. We owe it to Hadley. It'll be easier on you if you're sitting down."

The old man did not look at his son. Instead he shrugged off the hand on his shoulder. Hadley watched carefully.

Was he angry at Zane? Didn't he want to tell her the truth? Zane had said Sonny wanted to talk to her. She'd had just about enough lies from this family. She stood up.

"Listen, Mr. Bowman." Zane darted a look at her that plainly said, back off, but Hadley was through backing off. That time was past. She raised her chin into the air and steeled herself for conflict.

"Listen!" She could feel the muscles in her face tighten in anger, and she breathed deep to stay in control. She walked over to the two men, the older one with his back toward her, the younger one staring angry daggers at her.

She reached out, grasped the old man's shoulder and turned him around where she could face him. Hadley barely noticed Zane's protest, because she was staring at his father, tears running down the craggy face, mouth trembling.

"Dad?" Zane grabbed his father's elbow to stabilize him.

"I'm, I'm sorry Mr. Bowman, Zane, but I deserve to know the truth. You were there when Mère died. And you were there when she fell. I want to know the truth and I want to know it now!"

She backed off as the son led his father, no longer protesting, to his red chair and helped him sit down. Hadley noticed the cane still leaning against the window pane and took it over to where he sat.

But the old man wasn't looking at her, so she leaned it against the arm of the chair and resumed her seat on the loveseat.

Hadley watched and waited as Sonny Bowman struggled to regain control. He swallowed and breathed deeply. Zane stood behind him, not meeting her eyes, staring straight ahead as if watching a scene playing itself out inside his head.

His hand was on the high back of his father's chair, not touching him, but close enough that his father had to be aware that it was there.

Sonny looked at Hadley through reddened eyes, which held sorrow and questions, she thought, but not defiance.

"I'm listening."

Sonny nodded, but still sat there for a moment, quietly.

"I killed her," was all he said. Then he dropped his eyes to his hands folded in his lap and bit his trembling lip.

"Dad! You did not." Zane looked astonished at his father's words. "Hadley. He. Did. Not. Kill. Your. Mother!" But Hadley was on her feet, her head spinning.

"Oh, didn't he? Was it you then? Is he protecting you? Zane, why did he say he killed my mother? Mr. Bowman, did this, this, hypocrite of a son of yours try to get you to lie to me?

"Who did it? Someone must have been responsible or you wouldn't have said what you just said! What happened? Who caused Mère's accident?"

Tears ran down Hadley's cheeks now. Mr. Bowman cried silent, sorrowful tears, but tears of fury streamed from Hadley's eyes.

"Hadley, Zane wasn't even there. I, I did it. I didn't mean to, but I did it."

Hadley could barely see the old man through her blurry eyes, but her glare locked on him as she clenched her fists.

More aversion, more lies. And all they could think of was themselves. What of Mère? She was dead. Cold.

She'd lost everything and these two assholes didn't even want to tell Hadley what had happened. She whirled and ran toward the door.

"Hadley," Zane called after her, but she was gone. She ran down the hall. The elevator was too slow. This place was suffocating her.

The little girl sat on the couch and stared as Hadley flung open the door labeled "stairs" and, letting the door slam behind her, bounded down them two at a time.

The door at the bottom opened into the room where they'd entered. The blond woman with the pony tail was behind the desk. Hadley didn't want to go that way. She looked for a clear way out, and chose the deck out back.

She ran, only pausing to open the glass doors. The dog lying at its mistress' feet raised its head and uttered a half-hearted bark.

Hadley rushed to the other end of the deck where a wooden ramp offered access to a lawn stretching to the lakeside. She didn't stop running until she reached the water. Then she stopped only because she couldn't run any farther. Now it was her turn to stare out toward the horizon as she caught her breath.

"Hadley." She whirled around. She hadn't heard Zane come up behind her. When he started to put his hand on her shoulder she backed away from him, daring him with her eyes to touch her.

39 The Rotten Board

Hadley clearly didn't want him to touch her. He took a step back to give her more space. If she backed up any farther, she'd step into the water at the edge of the lake. And, he thought, that would not make her any easier to reason with.

"Hadley, listen to me, please." This woman had him begging again. No woman had ever done that before. But he was doing this for his dad.

No, he had to admit to himself, he was doing it for both of them. For Hadley and for his Dad. They had to understand each other. And for himself as well.

Hadley deserved to know the truth, and he sincerely hoped that he could tell it to her in a way she would understand.

In a way that would inspire her to say the words that would ease his father's conscience and sorrow. To say she understood. That she did not blame him for her mother's death.

The woman held her head high, and as the wind blew her hair, the intense color of the lake and of the sky outlined her petite figure. How could that tiny body hold so much that he desired? And feared right now.

"Yes?" Her arms were crossed over her chest. "What are you doing to do now, Zane? You tried to get your father to lie to me, but he couldn't.

"I don't know what happened, but I know my mother is dead. I think it's time to let the police figure out who was responsible." Her eyes were so narrowed, they were merely slits.

"No matter what you tell, me, I won't believe you now. You've lied to me over and over again. But I think your father will tell the truth to the police." She pulled out her cell phone and stood staring at it.

"Hadley, I, uh, we'll go to the police if you want, but they already know everything."

She glanced up at him sharply.

"Just listen to me for a minute, then we'll go get Dad and drive straight to the station, or call the sheriff and have him come here. Whatever you want. Just listen to me for a minute, please." Hadley crossed her arms again, glaring at him.

"Make it quick. I'm ready to get this over with." Her eyes were steely, her posture unforgiving.

"I told you that my mother passed away last year."

"Yes. Go on."

"Her dying almost killed my dad. He loved her very much. We both did. You've seen her pictures, how beautiful she was. She was everything to both of us. My dad was broken by her loss." He sighed. "But then he heard from your mother."

"Really?" Hadley's voice was scathing. "Didn't take him long to get over being broken when another beautiful woman turned up, huh?"

"It wasn't like that."

"Then tell me what it was like."

"They'd known each other before your mother met your dad."

"I know. But, so what?"

"They were very young, but he fell in love with her back then. And he thought she loved him too." He heard Hadley's intake of breath.

"I didn't know any of this until lately, either, Hadley. And it was hard for me at first, to know that my dad loved someone before my mother.

"But, anyway, my dad went to 'Nam. Your mom met your dad and married him. My dad tried to understand, and never hated her. Warren was dashing and very rich."

"Dad was wounded over there. And when he got home, he met Mom, and, they loved each other. And don't let what I'm going to tell you next make you doubt that for one minute. He loved my mom."

"Go on."

"Natalie heard about my mom's death, and called my dad."

"You told me that."

"I don't know how she heard about it, but she did...."

"Mère has...had...her ways."

Zane glanced at her sharply, then continued.

"Talking to her again after all those years seemed to revive him. I'd really begun to worry about him, and it was good to see him happy, even if I didn't really understand the reason.

"Then she came to see him, drove down from Tulsa." He looked at Hadley, wondering how she felt about the fact that he'd seen her mother after the last time her daughter had seen her alive.

"Dad wasn't sure why she was coming. Thought she was just in town and wanted to comfort him as an old friend."

He shuffled his feet, a bit embarrassed to be going into the personal life of his dad and her mom. "But it was more than that, I think."

"You think? You think! How dare you 'think' what Mère's intentions were. You don't know her. You don't know anything about her."

Sparks seemed to shoot from Hadley's eyes, or was it just the refection of the bright sun overhead? He knew he was dealing with an angry woman, but standing there with the sunshine sparkling on her hair, her jewelry, and with the water framing her, she looked like a goddess. A goddess who could kill.

"I'm sorry, Hadley. I don't, didn't know your mom, but just listen a minute, please. She came out to our house, and I met her, and left them alone. They talked for a long time, hours. Then she drove away.

"I didn't ask Dad anything about it. Just thought it was really nice for him to have a visit from an old friend. And you know how nice your mom is, uh, was. And so pretty, of course."

"Yes, I do know how nice and pretty my mother WAS. Go on."

"Well, my dad was really thoughtful and quiet, and went for a drive. I didn't see him until the next day. He was all smiles and told me that he was having dinner with Natalie that night.

"I'll admit that I was surprised, but I didn't think much of it. They met here in town for dinner and had a really nice time. (I learned a lot of this later. Dad was not giving me a blow by blow account. I want you to know that.)"

Hadley nodded her head, her eyes steady on him, now looking a little calmer, maybe curious. Well, he would be too, if someone were telling him a story like this about his dad, or his mother.

"Anyway, the next day they went for a boat ride in the Sea Skiff."

"And does your dad drive a boat like you do?" Sarcasm dripped from her soft question.

"Just, please, let me finish. I'm nearly finished. The ride went really well. They visited some old places they remembered as kids, you know, before your dad....

"They stopped at this old dock that they both remembered. It had some special meaning for them. And don't look at me that way. I don't know that story and don't want to.

"Anyway, there was this rotten board, and Dad stepped on it and his foot went through. And your mom grabbed him and they both fell. Dad almost fell into the lake, and your mom broke her leg trying to keep him from doing so."

"Sure. That's why he says he killed her."

"If she hadn't been with him. If he hadn't taken her to that dock.... He knew it was in bad shape, but he never thought about anything like that happening.

"And the police and sheriff have talked to him, by the way. He made sure that that dock will be demolished, even if he has to pay for it. But he feels so guilty.

"And I don't know what he and your mom talked about, but whatever she said had made him very happy. Had pulled him up from the depths of his sorrow. Then when she died, he was there. I wasn't.

"It almost killed him. Hadley. Sorrow for your mom and my mom is killing my dad." He couldn't stop the tear that slid down his cheek. He dropped his eyes.

"Sorrow almost killed me." Zane jumped. He hadn't seen Sonny hobbling up beside him. His dad had evidently heard the last part of the story.

"I'll never be the same again. But I ain't going to die." Sonny took another step and put his hand on his son's arm. "Cause love will keep me alive, Son." Zane looked up into his father's eyes. "Love for you."

40 Second Thoughts

Hadley pushed her hair back off her sweaty forehead and looked out across the lake, then turned back to the Zane.

"Why did you lie to me? Tell me that. Why did you show up on my boat and pretend you were a handy man? You seem to have answers to everything, so give me an answer to that!"

"I asked him to, Hadley."

"Why, if you didn't have anything to hide?"

"I had reasons, and with the shock…. Hadley, I think that if your mother had been able to choose, she would have preferred that you didn't know the story.

"That's why we didn't tell you. You knew she was injured in an accident, and we thought it best to leave it at that.

"We, I, thought Natalie would want me to let you go back home to France and just go on with your life, and not be troubled with why she came back here."

"Well, that is what I'm going to do. Tonight. But, why would knowing the story you've just told me prevent me from going back or going on with my life?"

"I don't think it will, but I think, how do I say this, your mother may have been having some second thoughts about her life."

"What?"

"Well, you know we were in love once, or I thought we were. Then she married, and I married, and we went our own ways. I felt really sorry for her when all that happened with your dad, the divorce and all.

"But it was too late then. I loved my wife, and had a son, and anyway, she took off and made her own life. I always hoped she'd figured out how to be happy."

"She did! She was extremely happy in France. What I can't understand is why she came back here. Can you tell me that?"

"I can try, but I'm not sure she had that figured out herself yet. But she was looking for something. Maybe something she'd lost along the way?

"And thought maybe, maybe…. I don't know how to say this Hadley, but you mother needed to be loved. And she came back to see if what we'd once had was still there for her."

"Let me get this straight. Are you telling me that Mère wanted to have some kind of relationship with you?"

"She hadn't been here long when all this happened, but we talked a lot when she was in the hospital. She had a lot of thinking to do.

"We weren't going to jump into anything. We'd waited a long time. We were going to take it easy. And that's why she didn't tell you, Hadley."

"She talked about that to you?"

"She wanted to figure it out for herself before she told you anything. She was afraid you'd be disappointed in her if you knew that, that, oh, I don't know. That she needed something more, that she needed somebody to grow old with, I guess. Does that make sense?"

"Frankly, no. It doesn't. Mère was a free woman. She had Paris. Why would she choose to come back to the middle of nowhere? You think that she was going to leave Paris? Are you serious?"

"Oh goodness, Hadley, we hadn't gotten that far down the road. We were just getting to know each other again.

"But she was going to fix up the boat, *Black Gold*. She wanted to work on it again. She had big plans for that boat, and she was excited about it.

"That check. She'd asked Zane to help her fix it up and made out that check. We wouldn't take it, of course. Zane had everything he needed and I contributed some materials that he didn't have. And we were going to get it back in shape for her."

"Then she was planning to move back here?"

"Well, to spend some time here, at least. Like I said, she hadn't really made many plans yet. Just fixin' up the boat."

"I still don't understand why you didn't tell me any of this before."

"I figured since nothing worked out, and, and, well, you know. From the way she'd talked, I thought she'd probably just rather you never knew about this whole thing, and just kept thinking she was perfectly happy and, well, maybe I was wrong, but I thought that's what she'd have wanted me to do."

Hadley felt as if the world had just dropped away beneath her feet. In just a few minutes, her world had certainly changed.

"Will you forgive me, Hadley?" The old man took a step toward her, looking deeply into her eyes.

"For not telling you? For asking my son not to tell you anything? For what happened to your mother?"

"No. No. Not that. I'll never forgive myself for that and don't have any right to ask your forgiveness." Tears streamed down his face as he stood there by the lake, and Hadley didn't know what to do. Was she really supposed to forgive this man? She needed to think.

"You probably need some time to ponder about all I just told you." The old man tried to smile through his tears." "But could I treat you to lunch tomorrow? I have more to tell ya. I want you to know more about your mother."

The two men stood silently, giving her time. She had a late flight booked, to get out of this place forever. Did she want to stay one more day? She'd lose her flight. Could she get one on the fifth? Did she want to? Zane cleared his throat.

"Tomorrow's the Fourth of July." She glanced at him, standing there with a slight smile on his face, his eyebrows raised in question.

"How about it, Hadley? How long has it been since you've celebrated that holiday? You know, fireworks, beer, hot dogs. Everyone in the world will be out. The lake will be one big party."

His handsome face looked so wistful, with that expectant, puppy-dog expression. She could tell he was willing her to say yes. He was just so cute, damn him. And she wasn't really angry any more, just sad and confused. She still had questions she wanted to ask, and his father was right. She needed to think.

She picked up a flat rock at her feet, examined it for a minute, stretched back her arm, flicked her wrist and let fly, counting the times it skipped across the water. Plop. Plop.

Plop. Plop. Plop. Plop. It finally sank beneath the blue ripples.

Zane whistled in appreciation. "Don't see many girls who can skip a rock like that!"

Sonny laughed, then turned and started slowly back up the incline to the deck. "Natalie teach you that?"

He looked back over his shoulder at them. "You shoulda seen that girl skip a rock, Zane. Never could teach your mom, God rest her soul."

"OK," Hadley called after him. "I'll come tomorrow. I want to hear more about her back then."

He gave her a sad, wrinkled smile. "Thank you, girl. I'll look forward to it. Take care. Zane, you comin' to dinner tonight?"

"Yes, Dad, I'll be here."

But, thought Hadley. I'm changing my ticket to the 5th of July. No more delays. I'm going home.

41 The Perfect Silhouette

Zane skidded the truck to a stop at the dock where he'd left the boat, keeping an eye on the sky where a few dark clouds were starting to build. Hadley stared at her hands, folded in her lap. She seemed to be lost in thought after her meeting with his father. Had she even noticed the incoming storm?

"We can drive back in the truck the long way if you want. We don't have to take a boat, but I think we'd make it safely in the Sea Skiff. It's here. But only if you want to." He draped his arm over the steering wheel, waiting for her answer.

Hadley shook her head as if waking up from a dream. Her eyes widened as she peered through the windshield at the clouds racing above them, then bit her lip, as she peeked at Zane from under her bangs.

"Do you really think that we could make it, before the storm hits?" She unbuckled her seatbelt.

"I can't promise, Hadley, but I'm pretty sure we can get to my shop safely. We can take the other truck from there. That way we won't have to drive all the way around the lake to get you home."

Hadley took a deep breath and smiled bravely. "OK. Let's do it."

"You sure?" Her anger from the last time he'd taken her out in a storm loomed in his memory. He didn't want to anger her again, or to scare her either. "I don't mind driving us."

She showed a hint of dimple. "I know you can handle that boat in a storm, Zane, and I feel like taking a chance today. I feel brave."

"Well, if you're sure." Zane hopped down from the truck. Hadley jumped down on her side before he could make it around to open her door. They raced to the dock.

Zane jumped aboard the boat, and fired up both motors. Hadley untied the ropes, making sure the boat did not swing against the dock until it began to move out of the slip; then she jumped aboard and started pulling in the bumpers. Zane thrust the throttle forward for more speed. As they headed out, he was pushing the maximum speed for a no-wake zone, but Hadley didn't complain.

Perching herself on the dinette table, high enough to see out of the windshield, Hadley noticed that most boats were coming in rather than going out. The sky was darkening. Although the wind had not yet increased much, a light breeze roughened the surface of the water.

Once out where speed was legal, the old boat soared over the main body of the lake, racing ahead of the storm. This time Hadley was neither afraid nor angry.

The combination of their speed and the rising wind whipped her hair about her face and into her eyes and mouth. Zane adjusted the steering wheel and motors just enough to enhance the old boat's ability to do what it was built to do.

Hadley watched the intensity, the aliveness of his face. This man's love of boats defined him. Speeding across the water in a craft he understood completely, he was in his element.

Raindrops plopped onto the windshield as the wooden boat rounded the headland near the Bowman shop and coasted into its slip at the small dock.

So much like last time, but so different. The drops gathered force as Hadley and Zane jumped onto the dock, battled wet ropes together to tie up the boat, and ran for shelter.

Today, however, Hadley laughed as she ran, and darted inside without a doubt of Zane's intentions. In fact, she had a few intentions of her own. Her heart was pounding. Speed and danger had pumped adrenaline through her body.

Inside, she let herself fall back against the sheet metal wall as Zane hit the lights. Her breath came in gasps. So did his as he turned to face her, the excitement of the race against nature sparkling in his golden eyes.

Hadley giggled. "Seems I'm destined to end up dripping wet almost every time we get on a boat together."

Her giggle caught in her throat. Zane was not laughing. His eyes, locked on hers, smoldered. Their flames burned into hers and down through her body, reigniting the fire she'd woken up to that morning, and taking away her breath once again.

"Hadley?" He took a step closer. They were almost touching. He hovered over her, his hand reaching for her face. Her lips parted as she waited for his touch. The world narrowed to the space between them, charged with desire. The storm forgotten, she stretched up on her tiptoes, and he leaned down toward her.

When the building shook as a gust of wind slammed shut the door they had just entered, Hadley screamed and threw herself against Zane's chest, burrowing her face in his damp shirt. His arms encircled her, crushing her against his strong chest.

Another door flew open against the opposite wall, sucked inward by the air pressure changes. She clung to him, breathing in his warmth. As he held her close, she looked upward into his eyes, staring over her shoulder, fixed on the back door that had just blown open.

She followed his gaze to the soft light pouring through it, outlining a woman's figure. A perfectly still silhouette. Zane disengaged himself from Hadley, turned and quickly strode across the shop to close the door.

"What was that?" Hadley was a few steps behind him.

"Nothing." Zane laughed easily, taking her arm and leading her toward a wooden stand in the shadows near the back of the shop. Reaching up and pulling back the dark canvas, he uncovered the skeleton of a wooden runabout similar to the one she loved so much. "Let me show you the boat I'm building."

Hadley glanced back toward the closed door, making a mental note to ask Sonny about that room tomorrow at lunch. Zane casually encircled her shoulder with his arm as he showed her the tools that he used to shape wood to his bidding. She let her body mold into his.

Another wooden boat, paint peeling, was propped on a larger frame nearby. It looked like the Sea Skiff, only smaller. Missing planks in the hull made it appear naked and wounded. As he explained how he planned to restore it, she watched the expressions playing on his face, and knew that he would make that boat beautiful again.

Turning to her, Zane cupped her chin with his strong hand. Her body buzzed, every inch of it, as his lips neared hers.

At that first touch, a Mère brush, a shared breath, time stilled. They stood, eyes closed, as their lips met again, just touching for a long moment.

Then his lips moved, and touching wasn't enough any longer. Hadley's mouth opened, welcoming his intrusion, tasting him, his tongue, his passion. She lost herself in his domination of her mouth, the way he took and gave and controlled.

He lifted her up, one hand slipping under her thigh. She wrapped her arms around his neck, their lips now inches apart. She could feel him hard against her as she crushed her body tightly to his, her legs encircling him.

42 Insured by Smith and Wesson

The storm outside raged as their passion rose together. Hadley closed her eyes as his hand, holding her body tight to his, moved, cradling her, then slowly inching between her legs, and under the light elastic of her lacy panties.

She arched her back as Zane buried his face in the breasts that had teased him so ruthlessly at breakfast, determined to take Hadley past the brink before he tumbled them both into the sawdust that covered the floor of his shop.

He would finally possess this woman who had driven him mad since the day he'd met her. The tattoo of the rain drumming on the metal roof drove him on. She gasped.

The flash and the boom of lightning hitting close and hard brought a cry from Hadley, but not the one he had hoped to hear. They both froze, locked in their embrace. As the smell of smoke wafted in, they both stared at the closed door at the entrance to the shop.

Shit fire. Zane set Hadley firmly back down on her feet. For just a second, he saw her push down her skirt, which had been hiked up around her waist, before he sprinted for the door.

The rain was pelleting down, but Zane plowed out into it, as Hadley watched from inside. The fire was around the corner of the shop. Fire and wood were not a good combination, but a quick glance told the story.

The lightning had hit a pile of rotted wood, piled safely away from anything else flammable. He turned and was back and inside the door before he had time to become completely drenched. He wiped his eyes and shrugged.

"Hit a pile of rotted wood. Started a fire, but it's pretty much already out. I kicked it to make sure the rain could get everything wet. It'll be OK."

He grinned at her, raising his eyebrows in that way he had. She laughed. They both knew that if the lightning hadn't struck, they'd be on the floor right now.

"I'm sorry about that." Zane took both her hands in his as he looked down at her. "I mean, I'm sorry about the fire. The lightning." He hugged her. "I'm not sorry about the other. Sorry, but I'm not."

Through the door, behind Zane, Hadley saw that the rain had let up.

With a sigh, she gently disentangled herself from him. He let her go with a sad smile. The moment had passed.

"I guess I'd better be getting home." Hadley looked out of the door toward his truck, gauging the distance and how wet she'd get. *Damn.* Well there was always tomorrow. One more day before she left Grand Lake forever.

She was going home. Finally. So why did her throat feel tight? Why did she almost feel like crying when she thought of watching Oklahoma disappear from the airplane window?

She forced herself to smile as she glanced quickly around Zane's shop, then took a deep breath and ran for the truck.

"Wouldn't mind a cold drink, would you?" Zane nodded toward a convenience store across the intersection. The rain had stopped and the sun was out. They were stopped, waiting for a traffic light to turn green.

"Actually, I'm starved. How long has it been since breakfast, anyway?" Today had been a long day, a long day of anger, grief, excitement and lust. No wonder she was hungry.

"Yeah, well, so am I, now that you mention it." The light turned green and Zane made a sudden right hand turn, causing the driver of the car behind them to lean on his horn.

"Opps. Sorry. Didn't have on my turn signal." Zane looked at Hadley sheepishly. "But there's a place to eat right down this road."

"I forgive you. Just feed me." Hadley looked into the mirror on the back of her sun visor and grimaced. She looked like a drowned rat. Again. Zane, watching her expression, laughed.

"Don't worry. You look great. Really. But this place is a drive-in. No one will notice us."

They ate foot-long hotdogs topped with chili and cheese, trying not to make a mess in the truck, and shared a helping of tater tots.

Zane and Hadley discussed their parents, and what she'd learned today. She did not tell him that she still could not imagine Mère with his father!

She liked Sonny, and she believed what he'd told her, but she just couldn't picture those two together in her mind, even though she'd seen the photo of him with his arm around Natalie.

"I'm so glad that your dad was there, that day. Heaven knows, I wasn't." She stared out the window, but what she saw was not the small town in Oklahoma. She saw Mère. Her mother was just not the kind of woman to look up an old flame. But she had. And that changed everything Hadley thought she knew about her mother.

Zane was sexy and fun, yes, and obviously not a bad person. She admitted to herself that she liked him a lot. More than she should.

And it had been sweet and romantic of his dad to visit her mom and lend her his cane, which she had to get back to them tomorrow! That still didn't mean….

A big black truck pulled into the empty spot beside Zane. It sported a window sticker that read, "Cowgirls Kick Ass!"

The tinted window rolled down and a gorgeous over-made-up face framed by long blonde hair emerged.

"Zane! Coming to the party tonight?" Hadley recognized the girl from the day they'd had lunch on the dock, the day she'd met Norma and Earl.

Oh yes. She needed to call them when she got back to the boat. To explain.

Zane smiled at the girl, but shook his head. "Won't make it tonight, Dixie. Having dinner with my dad."

The blonde girl pouted. "Well, I'm sure I'll see you around tomorrow. Gotta go!" She rolled up her tinted window and screeched backward, exiting the drive-in way too fast for safety. Hadley noticed her bumper sticker, "Insured by Smith and Wesson."

Hadley finished her hot dog and licked the chili off her fingers. Huh. Zane wouldn't be missing her when she left. That girl was more his type, anyway.

On the Dock: A Tale of Grand Lake

Hadley was not a jealous woman, but the thought of Zane with that girl upset her stomach. She threw her last tater tot out the window, no longer hungry.

43 The Setting Sun

Zane steered his truck across the grand old dam. *It was Grand. A grand old dam on Grand Lake.* His home. He directed a quick glance at Hadley, who was sitting so quietly. She would be going back to Paris soon. She'd made no secret of her plans.

They'd have tomorrow, and he planned to make the Fourth of July special, but one day wasn't enough. He shifted uncomfortably in the truck seat as his mind wandered back to the scene in his shop. And she had been as hot for him and he had been for her.

How had she gotten under his skin so quickly? He'd never doubted Hadley's hotness since the day he'd met her, but actually having his arms around her, his mouth on hers, touching her like that…. How could he let her go?

Hadley gasped, snapping Zane out of his reverie just in time to jam the brake to the floor to avoid hitting a mother deer, her spotted baby close behind her, as they dashed across the road in front of the truck.

Hadley screamed as the truck slid sideways, and grabbed hold of the dash as two wheels momentarily left the pavement.

"Sonofabitch!" Zane's arms hardened, the muscles cording and popping as he manhandled the truck back into his control and onto the right side of the road.

Two motorcycles screamed around the curve in front of them and flashed down the hill behind. Hadley and Zane shared a look of terror at what might have happened.

Hadley looked like she'd almost had a heart attack.

"*Merde*! I'm not sure I'm going to make it out of here alive." As the words escaped her, Zane met her eyes. He could tell what had just popped into her mind. Her mother had not escaped this place alive.

Should she be angry at his recklessness or thankful that he'd saved her life? She just didn't know. She seemed to get into trouble a lot around Zane, but he always saved the day. Was he irresponsible or a hero? Probably some of both.

Whatever he was, she was going to miss him, even if he didn't miss her. But she'd be able to get him out of her system.

Like her mother had gotten Sonny out of hers? Would she still think of him years down the road, when he was happily married to Dixie?

He'd forget her and go on with his life, of course. And never think of her in Paris. Or would he? After all, she was a Barrington woman, and no matter how sexy these Grand Lake women who seemed to congregate around Zane were, they were not Barringtons.

As Zane turned into the road leading to the marina, they met Meg & Adam, headed toward town. Hadley wondered if they'd be back in time for a talk tonight. She hoped so. Might be her last chance.

She'd never expected to make friends here. When she'd arrived, no one could have convinced her that she'd leave part of her heart behind when she returned home.

She gave Zane a sad smile, wondering if she might be able to convince him to come to Paris for a visit. She'd love to show him Paris.

At the marina, she quickly hopped down from the truck. Zane started to climb out, but Hadley protested, rounding the truck to stand at his open window.

"No, No, Zane. Don't get out. Really. I have loads to do and we'll see each other in the morning." She jumped up onto the running board, and gave him a quick peck on the lips, and jumped back down to the ground. He looked sad, and she wondered what he was thinking.

"I'm looking forward to lunch with your dad. And fireworks."

The way he looked at her made her wonder if he had a special kind of fireworks planned for the next day. She waved and started down to the marina with a chuckle. Nothing she couldn't handle.

That afternoon was a blur. She had so many things to do. She made new reservations to fly back to Paris, and emailed her assistant her itinerary.

Hardest of all, she hauled all of her mother's things down to the boat and decided what to ship back home. Looking at Natalie's clothes was like losing her all over again. Many of them they had bought together, and shared.

Hadley pulled a blue dress out of the suitcase and held it up. What was it doing there? It was one of her favorites and she hadn't realized it was missing.

Natalie had obviously "borrowed" it for this trip. Had Mère worn it when she'd had dinner with Sonny? She'd try to remember to ask tomorrow.

Mère had definitely worn it sometime. It smelled like her. Hadley buried her face in the dress.

She dragged herself into the galley and poured a glass of wine. Outside, she settled into a chair, looking out over the water. The sun would be setting soon. The breeze felt cool on her skin. At least cool for Oklahoma. A flock of gulls flew low over the water, diving for the occasional unlucky snack. Hadley checked her phone for the temperature in Paris. Considerably cooler. No surprise.

"Hey Hadley!" She looked around to see who was calling to her. From down on her boat, Margo grinned up at her. "I just made Salad Niçoise, too much for me. And I have some wine chilled. Come on over."

"I'll be right there!" Hadley climbed down the ladder and walked to Margo's houseboat. As she sipped chilled Chardonnay and nibbled at a piece of boiled egg from her salad, Margo told Hadley a little about her life and how she'd come to be the cougar on the dock.

44 Choices

"I met Max when I was just a girl. I grew up in the hills of Eastern Oklahoma, not so far from here. Near Tenkiller Lake, not Grand.

A lot of people out in those hills are really poor, like a lot of people on the backside of this lake. I was working in a store after school, and he was working on a case out there. He was an attorney."

"How old were you then?"

"Seventeen." Margo chuckled. "So young. Max was handsome and rich and so very nice. He'd come in there and eat dinner back in the deli where I worked. I know he could've eaten in some pretty fancy places. Well as fancy as we had out there, which wasn't very, but more than the deli."

"So he came there just to see you?"

"Yeah, and by the time he'd won his case, he'd won me too."

"How old was he?"

"Max was almost fifty. Divorced. No kids. Handsome. Smart."

"And so you married him?"

"Yes. A big church wedding. He paid for it all. My family didn't have the money for anything like that. I hadn't even graduated from high school. It was the summer before my senior year."

"But you did graduate, right?"

"Oh yes. I finished high school and even went to college. Max made sure of that. And it wasn't easy graduating from a Tulsa high school after the back hills schools I'd attended before that.

"Max really helped me, and I had a tutor. I mean, I was smart, I think, but I was just really behind the other girls in my class. And it was pretty weird being married and going to high school, you know?"

"That's difficult for me to imagine." Hadley studied Margo. The woman was still beautiful, probably in her fifties now, she guessed.

"I'll probably never marry. I don't believe two people can love each other forever. Most marriages are disasters. What happened to yours? Who left whom?"

"Max left me, but he didn't want to." A tear slipped down Margo's tan cheek.

"You mean?" Hadley did the math in her head and realized how old Max would be today. "Oh."

"We had a good marriage, Hadley. A very good marriage. He taught me everything. And gave me everything. I must be one of the luckiest women alive to have been married to Max."

"I'm really sorry, Margo. When, how long have you been alone? Do you think you'll marry again? I guess you believe in true love?"

"Max died ten years ago. Neither of us had any children, so he left everything to me, and, and he told me 'Margo, you've made me happy. You've been exactly the wife I needed. And I know it must have been hard for you sometimes because you were so young and I was so old.'

"It wasn't hard at all, but he thought it was. So he told me to go have fun. He said, 'Don't let anyone tell you what to do. Do it all. Try everything.' He said I gave him my youth and now it was time for me to just have fun. What do you think of that?"

"I agree with you, Margo. You're very lucky. My mom was a lot like you in many ways, but she never had what you had with Max. Her marriage wasn't like that at all. I'm not sure she would have even wanted a marriage like that. Before this week, I would have said definitely no. But now I wonder."

Just then Connie and Meg strolled into view, boat drinks in their hands.

"Hey, ladies, come join us. We're having a girl talk." Margo rose to pull a couple more chairs up to the table. As Connie and Meg approached, Hadley picked up the empty dishes and silverware and carried them over to the tiki Bar, stacking them neatly out of sight.

"So tell us what Zane and his dad told you! Did you get to the bottom of the mystery? Is he a good guy or a bad guy?"

Connie and Meg waited for the story, and Hadley repeated the conversation by the lake to them. Margo didn't know as much of the background story as the other two, so they had to fill her in on the details.

"What I don't understand though," Hadley looked at the three women. Maybe they could help her comprehend her mother's actions.

"I don't understand why Mère didn't want me to know about Sonny, and why she was coming back here at all. I wish she'd told me. I wish I could ask her so many questions right now. You know, I thought I knew my mother and now I don't know if I knew her at all. Why did she do that to me?"

"Because she wanted to figure out what she really wanted, or needed, before she explained it, I think." Margo reached out and took Hadley's hand. "It sounds like your mother was doing a lot of soul-searching. I met her, you know. I told you."

"They came out to the boat together."

"Yes, she and Sonny. Hadley, I didn't know any of this, that you didn't know, or I'd have told you a lot earlier. Would probably have saved you some trouble.

"I mean, I didn't know any of the past stuff, really, but she and Sonny looked happy together. I don't know if I should tell you, but I saw them kiss. They didn't know I saw. It looked like a sweet kiss, nothing needy. Kind of timid, as if they were just trying it out. Made me smile."

"What did Mère say when you met her?"

"Nothing really. Didn't even tell me the boat was hers. I knew Sonny a little. I'd met him though Zane. Don't look at me like that Hadley. I know your guy from around the lake. Nothing personal."

He was not her guy. But Hadley didn't say anything. She wanted to hear the rest of Margo's story. She was leaving him and this lake for good. After tomorrow.

"Sonny introduced me to her. I thought maybe she was thinking of buying the boat. Didn't know she owned it. But now that I've heard the story, I can tell you that they were really cute together. I think they were friends. You should be happy to know she had that time with him, I think."

"But she was always so strong. She didn't want any man to be in charge. And she really wasn't interested in men her own age. Just like you. What could have happened?" Margo smiled and shrugged, as if to say Hadley had to figure that one out on her own.

"I would have liked to have met your mom." Meg took a last drink and looked sadly at her empty glass. "Don't have any vodka, do you, Margo?"

"Oh course she has vodka. Do you mind?" Connie looked at Margo, who nodded toward the tiki Bar, then picked up her own glass and Meg's.

From the bar, she called back over to see if Margo and Hadley wanted a refill from the wine chilling in an ice bucket, then proceeded to play bartender for everyone.

"Hadley, when someone you love dies, I think most people end up being angry with that person at some stage of their grief. It's natural. I was angry with Max for quite a while. I mean, what was he thinking about, dying on me? Leaving me to figure out how to live without him? Damn man!"

Margo laughed, but it was a soft laugh, wistful. Connie and Meg laughed too, and Hadley made a feeble attempt to join in.

Then they all sat quietly a minute, sipping their drinks. Everyone had losses. Everyone at this table had lost someone they cared about. Zane had lost his mother. Norma Halloway had lost hers. It was part of being human, maybe the hardest part of being human.

"Don't blame her for following her heart, Hadley." Connie's eyes were red. Yes, she'd lost someone too. Maybe her mother. Hadley suddenly hoped Gordon lived a long, long time to be there for her friend.

"You've told me that the French believe in fate, that you can't really plan your life." Connie swirled her drink. "I know, I know, that's one reason you don't believe in marriage, but look at the other side of fate.

"Your mother may have found herself wanting something she'd never planned. Maybe she'd been feeling the need for someone to love for a long time, but wouldn't admit it to herself. Or to you. Maybe when she heard about Sonny's wife dying, it just hit her like a bolt of lightning.

"But whatever happened. She had to figure it out, sounds like. She had to figure out what she really wanted, what fate had in store for her." Connie set down her glass.

"But, I need to get going. We're getting up and out on the water early tomorrow, before all the good spots are taken. Are you going to stay to watch the fireworks, Hadley?" The woman pushed back her chair and stood.

"Yes, I am." Hadley and Meg both stood. "It's supposed to be a beautiful day!"

"I'd better get back too." Meg looked down toward her boat. "Looks like we have company. I should probably get to bed early, but I won't. I never do."

She tossed a smile over her shoulder at her friends before she took off down the dock with Connie. "If either one of you gets lonely, come on down. We'll be partying!"

Hadley said her goodbyes to Margo, thanking her for the story of Mère and Sonny. She wasn't really sure what to think about what Margo had seen, but she was glad she knew about it. One more tiny part of the puzzle that might help her make sense of Mère's decisions.

Hadley stood in the shadow of her boat, watching Connie and Gordon making their area neat, sharing a drink, petting their dog. Gordon sneaked a kiss before they closed the door of their boat to the world.

She watched as Margo fixed herself a drink and walked out to the back of her houseboat, and leaned over the rail, seemingly deep in thought. Was she thinking about her husband and her choices?

45 In Her Footsteps

Hadley smiled at the ruckus going on down at Meg and Adam's boat. Quite a crowd had gathered. The music was a little loud. Everybody seemed to be enjoying themselves.

Someone walked down the dock toward her from shore and she waited to see who it was. Probably a late arrival to Meg and Adam's party. But Paula, from Norma and Earl's party, walked out of the night instead.

"Hi Paula." Hadley stepped out of the shadows, startling the redhead. But the girl had come looking for her. She wanted to talk, so Hadley invited her up to the boat and offered her friend a glass of wine.

They sat outside on the deck as Paula poured her heart out, telling Hadley how much she loved Kip and asking her if she knew anything about him.

"I haven't seen him since the party. I've called and left messages on his phone. I don't know what's wrong. You know his grandparents, Hadley. Have you seen him or talked to him?"

Well, Hadley had put herself into the middle of this mess, so it wouldn't be honest, or kind, not to follow through with the other side of the relationship. Why hadn't Kip called her or something? Coward.

"Yes, Paula, I saw him. I was visiting his grandparents the other day, and Kip was getting ready to leave for the Middle East, I think."

"What?" The long-legged girl stood up abruptly, her eyes sparking anger. Hadley stood as well, and put her arm around the girl's shoulders.

"I think, uh, his granddad wanted him to do some kind of emersion course in Arabic so he could take an engineering course next year.

"And Kip finally saw that he should do it. Instead of spending the whole summer playing at the lake. That makes sense, doesn't it?"

"But why didn't he tell me?" Paula shrugged herself away from Hadley, her anger melting into tears. "He doesn't love me, does he?"

"Do you think he loves you?" Hadley picked up Paula's wine glass and followed her to the rail.

"I love him." Paula sobbed, looking out over the water.

"And you'd be happy living in big cities and traveling all over the world and always having to be the corporate wifey-poo?" Hadley handed Paula her glass.

"Paula, I know we haven't seen each other for more than half our lives, but I remember you as being a free spirit. In fact, we were a lot alike in that way. I wouldn't want that life. I want to make my own rules, be creative, be free. Don't you?"

"I'd be anything if I could be with Kip. Without him, I just don't care what happens to me." Paula gulped down her wine, and Hadley led her indoors where they could refill their glasses.

"I wish I could take you to Paris with me." She sat her friend down in one of the stained blue chairs in the boat salon.

"I learned so much growing up there. At first it was hard. So different. School was much harder than in Tulsa. I struggled.

"And, Paula, there's really no concept of popularity there. Everyone's just determined to learn to be themselves, unique, well-read, opinionated, well-dressed." She laughed.

"And it's OK to be single. Every woman doesn't have to have a man. Oh you have men friends. Good friends. And lovers. And French men are the best lovers in the world.

"Paula, think before you get all wrapped up in Kip or anyone else. You need to learn to be yourself first. Enough yourself that you don't need anyone to make you happy. My mom was that way…."

Or had she been? At least she'd known herself well enough that if she'd decided…. But Hadley wasn't ready to go down that road. It was her turn to gulp down her drink.

"Paula, I want you to come visit me in Paris. I mean it. I do. We'll make plans. You've spent too much of your time in the middle of nowhere. I'm going to introduce you to French men!"

Even though tear drops sparkled on Paula's eyelashes, Hadley could tell that she was perking up. She needed time and she needed to meet other men. She'd be much better off with someone different than Kip. Someday she'd understand that.

"Hey, let's go down to Adam and Meg's boat. They're having a party. What do you say? Do you know them?" Hadley forced a smile on her tired face.

"I don't think so."

"Well, come on. Let's go. There's the bathroom, right there. Wash your face."

Hadley was ready for bed, but she thought a party would do Paula good. They strolled down the dock, and when the crowd saw them coming, the two beautiful women were engulfed in a welcoming warmth. Hadley was thrilled when she was able to manipulate Paula into sitting next to Ryan.

Hadley relaxed quietly in a comfortable chair, out of the limelight, listening to everyone's plans for the Fourth of July for a while. Then she quietly slipped away, back toward her boat. Paula, deep in conversation with Ryan, never noticed her leaving.

Hadley sat outside on the deck, away from the noise down the dock, listening to the water slosh and the old deck creak. She had learned so much, but that knowledge only intensified her need to know more.

Mère had chosen freedom. She'd fled Grand Lake and Oklahoma, had chosen to live life to its fullest, not to be trapped in a backwater like this. Had she really had regrets?

She had come back for some reason, and had searched out an old love. Why had she rejected Sonny all those years ago and chosen to marry the man she did? What had changed? What had she learned?

Hadley wanted to get to the bottom of it all, but she was afraid. She would probably never know what had been going through Mère's mind during the last few months. How could she?

She just wished she knew why Mère had chosen to hide what she was thinking from her. That's what hurt most. But whatever had happened, Mère had chosen her own path, as always.

Hadley looked at the old pictures of her mother and Zane's father. Well, Sonny had really been pretty hot in his day. Hadley laughed at herself. But, then, so had her Dad. And both of them had loved Mère. Once. Mère had had that.

She picked up the family portrait from where it lay by her feet on the deck and compared the two men. Yes, Sonny had been a good time, a summer love, just like Zane, but had Mère ever taken him seriously back then?

Or had she only come back to see what he was like today, to see if he still loved her? What had been her intentions?

Sonny seemed to have taken her looking him up when she was back here seriously, but he really didn't know her mother. He knew nothing about her lifestyle in Paris, and didn't realize that he was just another of her conquests.

How would Zane and Sonny react if they realized that Natalie had been a highly skilled cougar?

Well, Hadley didn't see any reason to tell them. Let Sonny remember Mère as she'd been when he'd first met her, innocent and full of potential.

Time for her to get out of here and back to real life. Just like her mom had. Sonny had been a pleasant diversion for Mère at one time and Zane had been fun for Hadley get to know.

One more day, the Fourth of July. She'd find out more from Sonny, and she was sure Zane was plotting something. Well. She hoped so. It was about time.

He was an unusual and special man, and he tempted her like no man had tempted her before. But, like Mère, she would not be trapped. She would not make a mistake. She would follow in Mère's footsteps. As she always had.

46 The Whole Story

Her last day in Oklahoma. Her last day on the boat. Hadley stretched. Why wasn't she happy and excited? What was nagging at her and keeping her down?

She'd accomplished most of what she'd come here to do. She was free to leave. She could leave the boat with the Bowmans and Connie. It would be well cared for.

Life was waiting for her in Paris. She would be home soon. She dragged herself out of bed and stood looking at herself in the mirror, sighing. What's wrong with you, she asked herself. It's the life you want. The life Mère taught you to live. The life she wanted for you.

She peeked out the door. Time to get this day rolling. It might be fun. She was ready when Zane arrived to pick her up.

She had dressed for the day in a filmy dark blue asymmetrical skirt she'd found in Mère's luggage, and a short cropped red and white striped sleeveless top. Her soft blue flats were studded with shiny silver stars.

Zane stood there looking at her when she opened the door, bag in hand, ready for the day. His face held a peculiar expression. His eyes were soft and heavy, as if he were remembering yesterday, but his mouth had a determined twist.

She almost wondered if he would reach out and pull her to him or touch her. Her body responded as if it felt his touch,

271

as if he really had cupped her breast or pulled her body close. She took a deep breath to steady herself and dropped her eyes from his hypnotic gaze.

She watched as he slowly reached toward her and took her hand, turning it over and bending down to kiss her wrist. Tendrils of sensation snaked up her arm and throughout her body. Where was he going to kiss her next?

"You look wonderful, as usual, Hadley." He smiled, then turned and started for the dock, her hand held firmly in his.

"He'd brought the Sea Skiff. He helped her board and settled her into a comfortable white padded folding chair on the back deck, where she could watch the show of boats and other watercraft streaming out of the bay. And it seemed that everyone was out today.

She saw Adam and Meg backing out of their slip, deck overflowing with friends. Someone waved frantically, and Hadley smiled as she recognized Paula's long red hair. Connie and Gordon were already gone. Margo and a handsome young man Hadley had never seen looked as if they were getting ready to launch off. Personal water craft zipped everywhere, with riders young and old, and the air was full of laughter and music.

A small airplane chugged overhead trailing a banner advertising a local strip club. A strange boat that looked somewhat like an old-fashioned river paddleboat, but on closer examination was just an old houseboat with some kind of fake paddle stuck on it, was being towed out by a much smaller skiff. The 'paddle boat' was crowded with guys with long hair and girls in cutoffs and bikini tops. Rock music blasted from it.

Another boat, much larger and moving of its own accord, but equally crowded by beer-drinking passengers, flew a gigantic red and white flag with the logo of the University of Oklahoma.

The lake was crawling with people and boats. Hadley leaned back and enjoyed the show as Zane skillfully navigated the congested waterway.

Out on the main body of the lake, the waves were choppy, churned up by so many boats in a hurry, but Zane's skillful control minimized the effects.

The sun was hot, however, so Hadley moved into the cabin, perching on the table so she could see where they were headed. They didn't talk, but the physical tension between them spoke louder than words.

Finally, after about a half hour of travel, they approached the marina near Zane's father's temporary home. They jumped into the truck, parked nearby, and drove to Lakeside Gardens.

"I hope you like the restaurant we're going to. It's Dad's favorite. If you want to wait here in the truck, I'll get Dad. I'm sure he's waiting right inside."

Zane climbed out of the truck and Hadley scooted to the middle of the seat to make room for Sonny. Sure enough, father and son were back in fewer than five minutes. Zane helped his father up into the truck, Sonny grumbling that he could make it without any help.

The truck door closed, crowding the older man against Hadley.

"Good grief, girl, you smell as good as you look." The older man eyed her appreciatively, then looked away as Zane crowded in from the other side. Hadley felt Sonny's shoulders shake slightly and glanced over at him. What was wrong? A tear was trailing down his wrinkled face.

"Sonny? Are you OK?" She put her hand on his, and he smiled at her through his tears.

"Your mother wore that skirt when I first saw her after all those years. She looked like an angel that day."

"Oh. I'm sorry. I never thought…. We kind of always borrowed each other's clothes and I found this in her baggage and it seemed to work for today. I just never thought."

"That's OK, girl. I'm sure your mother would want you to wear that skirt. I'm sure no other woman in the world could make it look as good as you do, except Natalie, of course."

"Thank you, Sonny. I wish I'd known, though." She squeezed his hand just as Zane pulled the truck into a parking place at a log cabin restaurant that proclaimed itself the Backyard Bar and Grill. A huge plastic banner announced, '4th of July Lake-Side Barbeque.'

Country music filled the air as they rounded the building, following a cobblestone walk. At the back of the restaurant were a huge deck and a lawn that sloped down to the water.

Picnic tables were scattered around everywhere. On the deck stood a long buffet table. A man in a stained apron manned a massive grill, carefully turning hot dogs, hamburger patties and chicken thighs as they browned and crisped and emitted a heavenly aroma.

After Zane paid, all three stood in line, then piled meat and salad and beans and fresh vegetables onto their plates.

Zane led them to an empty table a little way from the crowd, down under a spreading oak tree near the lake. He snagged three ice-cold bottles of beer from a barrel of ice, opened them and sat one by each plate.

Then the three sat there, looking at each other. Or at least Hadley and Sonny did. Sonny had promised information and Hadley was waiting to hear the whole story about him and Mère.

Zane busied himself with his food, taking a giant bite of hamburger and chewing noisily to make the point that the first move belonged to one of the others, certainly not to him.

47 Before it was too Late

"So." Hadley poked at her chicken thigh, then looked up at Sonny, who just sat there, seeming to forget his food. His mind was clearly elsewhere.

"Uh, how did you meet my mother?" Sonny focused on her for a minute as if being brought back from somewhere far away in space or time. He smiled a weathered, wrinkled smile.

"I rescued her. She took a rowboat to see some friends whose parents stayed at another marina. It wasn't a bad row, but a storm came up, real sudden like, and she was being tossed around pretty bad.

"Lost one of her oars. I almost hit her tiny boat. Couldn't see a thing out there. The rain was bad. But all at once, there was this rowboat with this girl in it and she was hanging on like crazy and was wet through and scared, and I, of course, I hooked on to her boat and got her out and tied her boat to mine.

"She was shiverin' and all wet and crying and, well, I just got a jacket on her, and we had to wait out the storm a bit, so we ducked into a cove and sat there waiting. She calmed down and we just sat under a tree and talked.

"Then I took her home, but we'd see each other off and on after that. I was in love. I guess she wasn't, or I guessed she wasn't back then. Now I'm not completely sure."

Hadley looked up at him sharply. Surely, after all this time, and as old as he was, he knew that he had just been a passing fancy for Mère? But what did it matter now? If it made him feel better....

"Anyhow, there was a time we kind of dated, but your grandparents didn't approve, so we kept it pretty low-key. Then I got drafted and she said she'd wait for me. Go to school, then come back here and wait until I got home.

"We wrote. I have the letters. We wrote for over a year, then, well, it happened to a lot of guys. Out of sight, out of mind. I don't blame her either.

"She was so busy at school and meetin' new people, and I was so far away and, and, I might of gotten kilt. And it was easier to pull away before that happened.

"Happened to a lot of my buddies too. We talked about it. Tried not to get mad. Those girls were smart to do that. The ones that stayed true got hurt too bad when their men got kilt."

Hadley didn't know what to say. She took a bite of chicken, but she'd lost her appetite, so she took a drink of her beer.

"Gonna get another beer," announced Zane, the only one who had been eating and drinking. "You guys want one? Dad? Hadley?" They both shook their heads and he strode away.

"And when you got back from the war, Sonny?"

"Oh, when I got back, I already knew. She'd got married to your dad. I met Zane's mother, Ivana. Me and Natalie went our own ways.

"Life got pretty busy. I was happy. But I heard about her troubles with your dad, and about when you were born, but wasn't my business any more.

"I had a wonderful wife, the best, and Zane. I never looked back, Hadley. Really I didn't. But I felt bad about some things I heard, and I always hoped she'd end up happy." Hadley reached over and patted Sonny's hand.

"I guess it all turned out then, because she was happy, Sonny. You can rest easy about that. She had a wonderful life.

"She lived in one of the most beautiful places on Earth. She traveled, had great friends, lived life her own way, just the way she wanted to. She was happy."

"Was she?" Sonny took a slug of his beer. "Did she ever find love again, Hadley?" He took another sip of his beer and looked across the table at her.

"Love is an illusion. And not necessary for happiness."

"Where did you learn that, girl?"

"From my mother, Sonny."

"Hmmm." He took a bite of his beans and chewed for a few minutes. He took another sip of his beer. Then he locked his wrinkled eyes on Hadley.

"You ever been in love?" He waited for her answer. She laughed self-consciously.

"No. I've never been in love. But I'm happy. Or I usually am. I mean, I'm not happy that my mother is dead. That's going to take some getting used to.

"But I'll be happy again. I just have to get home. And get used to living alone. And get used to Mère being gone, and, well, you know. But I am a happy person, Sonny. I like my life. And Mère was happy. Really."

Sonny put down his fork. "I wonder." He put his elbow on the wooden picnic table and rested his chin in his hand. "Why did she come back here then?"

"I don't know why she came back here, Sonny." It was Hadley's turn to lay down her fork and stare at the older man. Zane came back with another cold one. He looked from his father to Hadley, arched an eyebrow, and picked up his plate.

"Goin' to get dessert. That apple pie over there looks good. It's included in the price of lunch, you know."

Neither Sonny nor Hadley acknowledged him. "Anybody want me to bring them pie?" He sighed and escaped.

"Hadley, I don't know how to tell you this, but your mom told me she came back to see if, if she could love again."

"Mère said that? Sonny, she may have used that word, but I don't really think you knew Natalie very well. Wait, I know you knew her a long time ago, but she changed. She wasn't still that girl."

"I know that."

"Sonny, I don't know what to say. Love meant different things to her than it means to you."

"Think so, girl?" Sonny took a bite of his hamburger, not looking at her.

"You know Margo? You know, Margo with the houseboat?"

"I know Margo. Fine woman."

"Well, my mom, Natalie, was kind of like Margo. Do you understand what I'm saying, Sonny?"

"Both fine women. Margo's really luckier. She was married to a man she loved."

Sonny looked straight into Hadley's eyes. "Natalie told me all that, Hadley. We talked a lot. She wasn't sure but what she'd missed out on something really important in life. That's what she came back to find out."

"Is that why you thought you had a right to keep what happened to her a secret from me, Sonny?"

Hadley was confused and angry. "Because you knew what she wanted more than I did? You thought you had a right to lie to her daughter?

"Do you really think, if she did decide she needed some 'love,' she'd choose you when she could have had men much younger, much richer, and a hell of a lot smarter?"

She threw down her fork, and started untangling her skirt and her legs from the picnic table.

"She didn't want you to know yet, Hadley." Sonny's voice was low. She glanced back at him. "She didn't know what she really wanted, and until she knew what she wanted, she didn't want to upset what you believe, what she'd taught you.

"But she thought she wanted to try to love again, before, just once more…." Tears ran down Sonny's face. "Before it was too late." He dropped his face into his hands.

48 Kissed by the Sun

"Where's Dad?" Zane had his hands full, juggling three paper plates of apple pie, which had looked so good that he'd picked up one for everybody, though they hadn't asked for it. Depositing the desserts on the table, he scooted in beside Hadley, just as his cell phone rang. It was Sonny.

"Hey Dad! Where are you? Oh, I see." He glanced over at Hadley. She sat there quietly, staring at her food, but not touching it.

"Well, yes, OK. Are you sure? Um.... I'll see you tomorrow." As Hadley looked up at him, clearly listening to his end of the conversation, he clicked his phone off and stuck it back in his pocket.

"Where is Sonny?" Hadley asked quietly.

"Found a ride home. He's sorry he upset you."

"I'm sorry I got upset. But, Zane, what he told me is hard to believe. And, I don't want to hurt your dad's feelings, but I don't really believe Mère came back to really, to see...because she needed a man to love. You and your dad don't, didn't really know my mother very well."

"I don't totally get it either, Hadley." He probably should have stuck around longer to have listened to their conversation, but he had figured it needed to be between Hadley and his dad. He may have been wrong.

"But I know she wanted me to fix up the boat, and she planned to spend time here and figure things out. I guess she didn't really know, herself, but it seems she was searching for something. Does that make sense?"

"Searching? Mère was open to experience, to what the future might bring, to fate. But I have a hard time imagining her searching or pursuing something to fulfill her life, Zane. It just doesn't sound like her."

"Hey, take a taste of this pie, Hadley. It's the best I ever tasted, except my mom's." She shook her head. "Really. Just a bite. Please. For me?"

A small, tentative smile touched her lips and Hadley picked up her fork.

"Just one bite. For you." But when she tasted the very small forkful, the sweet, flakey crust, the tangy sweet and sour apple, her smile widened to a grin. "*Ouah!* That's good!"

She scooped up a bigger bite this time, and closed her eyes. Zane sat in silence, watching her eat the rest of her pie in silence, enjoying the show. Hadley just might find that there was more to life than she knew, more that she hadn't quite figured out yet.

"I'm ready for a nap." She yawned as she pushed away the empty plate. "Too much emotion and too much food, I guess." She propped her elbow on the table and leaned her cheek into it, eyes closed, and sighed.

Zane gathered up the discarded paper ware and cold food from the table and hauled them to a nearby trash can. When he returned, Hadley was standing by the table, waiting for him.

"What do we do next?" She looked up into his eyes as he grasped her hand is his and led her through the crowd, pausing here and there to acknowledge acquaintances.

Back in the truck, he sat grasping the wheel as she buckled herself in. His senses prickled with awareness of every sensation surrounding him.

The smell of the plastic of the dash, heated up by the sun shining through the windshield. The hot leather scent of the seats. Hadley's light perfume. He felt so alive, like something was beginning.

Because he planned to do everything within his power today to have her, at least one time, but maybe…. One step at a time, he warned himself.

He smiled over at her and turned on the key. As he revved up the truck engine, his own internal engine was revving at full torque as well.

"Let's get back out on the lake, Hadley. We're missing all the action. Did you bring your bathing suit, I hope?"

Why hadn't he asked her earlier? But he'd been so wowed when he'd first seen her this morning that all practical thoughts had fled.

"Of course I did. She opened her small purse and pulled out two very small pieces of fabric. He gulped.

"Well, we'll stop down at the marina and change then. I, I think we'll both be more comfortable in fewer clothes."

Had he really said that? Right now his body would be more comfortable with no clothes between Hadley and himself.

He shifted in his seat to ease the pressure, gripped the steering wheel a little tighter and gunned the motor, zipping past a red convertible and pulling back in in front of it, way too close.

He whipped through a yellow light as the driver of the convertible honked angrily, but he didn't slow down until he reached the parking lot by the marina.

Squealing to a stop, he glanced over at his passenger, who smiled up at him, displaying her dimple. Damn, but it was hot in this truck, even with the air conditioner on high.

Hadley wiggled into her bikini inside the marina bathroom. The bathing suit didn't cover much, but her skin needed to be kissed by the sun today. And, she thought, surveying herself in the full-length mirror, kissed by Zane.

Oh yes. Today was the day. Her skin tingled at the memory of his lips on her wrist that morning. She wanted him to do it again, then kiss on up her arm to the inside of her elbow, then on up until....

Well that was never going to happen if she kept standing in here daydreaming. She rolled her skirt and top neatly and placed them into a plastic bag, took a deep breath, opened the door and walked out almost into Zane's arms, as he stood there waiting for her.

Her eyes wandered over his muscled, tan chest, and before she even realized it, she had reached out to touch the amber pendant hanging there.

"Does it have a story?" she asked, looking up into his eyes. He smiled down at her with a nod, then put his arm around her shoulders, hugging her close to him as they turned to walk down to the boat. "I'll tell you about it sometime. Maybe even today."

On the boat, as they worked in unison and cast off. The sun flashed off the water. Birds circled above the accelerating boat. A cooling spray mingled with the wind to drench the couple. They rounded a corner and headed toward open water, then Zane suddenly turned the boat toward a cliff.

"Where are we going?"

"See that boat over there, bobbing around?"

"Yes. I see it. Do you know those people? Are they friends?"

"Not sure, but they may be in trouble. I think we need to make sure they're alright. This shouldn't take long."

As they eased nearer the boat, a girl started waving at them and shouting. Zane slowed, letting the momentum of the Sea Skiff drift them closer. A man came up behind the girl and held up a marine radio.

Zane rummaged in his bag and pulled out his own, dialing it to channel 16, the distress channel, so he could talk to the man. After a brief conversation, he explained the situation to Hadley.

"I was afraid of that. They've lost their motor. Tow boat is on the way, but a big enough wake could send them right into that cliff. We've got to get closer to them, close enough to throw a line and tow them out a bit.

Zane threw out the rubber bumpers on the side of his boat nearest the other craft, to prevent a collision. The other man did the same thing. He pulled a Styrofoam ring off a hook at the side of the boat and tied the end of the rope attached to it to the railing.

"Here, this ring should throw better than just a rope. I'll get us closer and you see if you can throw this life ring over there."

He handed it to her. "When I tell you, throw it as hard as you can. Try to get it over their rail, so they can grab it." His eyes sparkled at her. "Throw it like you'd skip a pebble. Underhanded. Like that."

"This thing is a whole lot bigger than a pebble, Zane, but I'll try," she called after him as he headed back inside to back the sea skiff up and take a run past the other boat.

Hadley stood there, tense, sure she wouldn't be able to do it right. Zane got them pretty close and she threw the ring as hard as she could. It bounced off the other boat's rail and would have fallen into the water, but the girl leaned out over the rail, catching it on the bounce. The man grabbed her to make sure she didn't go head first into the water.

Then the man slowly pulled the rope to bring the boats closer, but not touching, and tied it off so Zane could slowly tow them out of danger.

Away from the cliff, down the shore a way, both boats floated, still attached, for about ten minutes, bobbing in the water. Occasionally Zane would goose the Sea Skiff a little to keep both boats from being swept onto the rocks. Although they were too far away to hold a conversation, the stranded couple managed to clearly express their thanks for the rescue.

"Where are we going when the tow boat gets here, Zane?" Hadley called from the back deck.

"Not far, really. In that bay up there. See where all those boats are headed?" She squinted her eyes to see through the glare of the early afternoon sun.

"It looks like every boat on the lake is headed there. At least half anyway."

"Yeah, we're late. Won't get a very good spot, but I figured we'd stop by for a while. It's part of the tradition of being on the lake on the Fourth."

"So I guess someone puts on fireworks, and there's music?"

"Well, all of the above, but mostly just people. You'll see."

Finally the tow boat rounded the headland. After handing the stranded couple off to the white bearded captain, Zane popped open two beers from a cooler under the table and handed one to Hadley.

"Well, that was our good deed for the day." He took a long swig and settled himself into the captain's seat. "Ready to party, Hadley?"

49 Jello Shots and Fireworks

As they approached Dripping Springs, what Zane had meant when he'd said "mostly people" became apparent. The bay was full of boats, tied up so closely together that people were walking from boat deck to boat deck, swarming like ants on a pile of picnic leftovers.

In the few spots of water left open by the boats, giant brightly colored squares of rubber called Lilly Pads stretched out, parts of them floating and parts slightly submerged. Little kids crawled around on them, some with life jackets and others without.

People dived off the sides of boats or floated in the water drinking beer. Jet Skis and Sea Doos prowled where they could, although the crush of boats and people limited their range.

Zane threaded the Sea Skiff through an almost invisible channel, then could finally advance no more. They tied up to one of Zane's friend's ski boat.

Holding Zane's hand and following his lead, Hadley jumped from the deck of one boat to another. They climbed a ladder up to the top of that boat and managed to jump and pull themselves up to the deck of a large yacht.

As they continued their progress through the crowded vessels, Hadley wasn't surprised that Zane knew almost everyone.

"Hey Dude, you're late. Where ya been?"

"Who's the pretty lady, Zane? Have you met Darla and John? Guys, meet Zane."

"Wanta cold one? Plenty here. Take one."

"Zane! We got jello shots. Pick your poison, margarita or car bomb flavor?"

Hadley met about a hundred people, and both she and Zane accepted a few of the beers and jello shots offered them. The bands playing from several boats, along with all the shouting, laughing and splashing, created a cheerful cacophony.

Up on top of a nearby boat, a blond girl ripped off her bikini top and started dancing. A couple of other girls joined her, ripping off their tops as well.

When Hadley glanced at Zane to see if he was enjoying the show, he was laughing. Turning to her, he explained that on the Fourth of July at Dripping Springs, common wisdom had it that there were usually about two girls to every bikini top, although most of that kind of thing happened later in the evening.

"Ready to get wet?" Zane took her hand and led her over to the side of the boat. They stood in line behind two other couples who joined hands and dropped into the water below. Diving was impossible in that small space, but there was just enough clear water to drop straight down.

After the couple in front of them bobbed back to the surface, Zane and Hadley took their turn, laughing as they plunged down below the water, and bobbed back to the surface, still holding hands. They swam slowly between the boats, stopping to talk to a few babies and mothers on lily pads.

They saw Margo's, boat and climbed on board to meet her newest boyfriend and all of his pals. After a couple hours of swimming and drinking and laughing, Zane pulled Hadley aside.

"Well, this is Dripping Springs. Can't do the Fourth on Grand Lake without coming here. What do you think?"

"Fun. Kind of reminds me of Saint-Tropez, except with jello shots instead of champagne." She shook the water out of her hair. She'd just crawled back on board from a dive. "And will we watch the fireworks from here as well?"

"We could. Some do. But I have a better idea." Zane reached out and lightly ran his finger down her wet arm.

Their eyes locked. They might have been the only people there, standing in the sun among hundreds. The heat and the alcohol and Zane's nearness sent Hadley's head spinning.

"I happen to know the very best place on this lake to watch the fireworks." He moved closer to her until their bodies were almost touching.

"Wanta let me show it to you?" He smiled a slow, lazy smile, and she wanted nothing more than to go wherever he wanted to take her. Tomorrow was reality and Paris. Today was fun. And Zane.

They made their way across decks and rails to the Sea Skiff and managed to convince all the partiers who'd converged on their back deck to go elsewhere.

"Are you sure you can get out of here?" Hadley scanned the jumble of boats. The channel though which they'd entered had closed.

"I'll get us out." With a determined scowl, Zane started the motors and eased forward. Surprisingly, a boat moved and allowed them through. Then another opening appeared, and then another. Slowly, slowly, they made their way out of the crush and back into the lake.

"Want to drive?" he asked her, but she shook her head sleepily, willing to let him do all the work while she just enjoyed the breeze and the deep blue surrounding them.

After about a half hour of companionable silence, she realized that she recognized where they were. It was Zane's workshop. Her face heated, remembering what had gone on there the day before. She glanced up at him.

"We'll take the Gator up to the house. No better place to watch a sunset, or the fireworks, than our deck." He pointed up to the top of a cliff overlooking the river.

"That's our house up there." He jumped out of the boat and tied it up. "Come on. I'll show you."

"At least it's not raining this time." She let him help her out of the boat. And they walked up the dock toward the shop.

"Wait here just a minute. I'll get the Gator." He unlocked his shop and switched on the light. She followed him in, quickly glancing at the door in the back that had swung open yesterday, but it was firmly closed today.

She watched him open a wide interior door, exposing a green John Deere all-terrain vehicle with huge tires and two seats.

He climbed in and started the motor, motioning her to the other seat, then he slowly advanced through the shop and out the door.

He jumped off to lock up behind them, then crawled back on, shifted gears, and headed toward a narrow trail that twisted through the woods up toward the house on the cliff. When they emerged from the trees up by the house, he paused to let her look around. Hadley gasped.

"What a view, Zane. And you live here. And this is where Sonny really lives?"

"Yep."

"Wow. What it must be like in all the seasons, this view!" She just sat there, taking it all in.

All the boats and even the far shore were so tiny. They were so high up that she was looking down on birds flying. She could see the dam off to the left. Zane pointed toward it.

"That's where the fireworks will be. Told you this was the best place on the lake to watch!" He looked as proud as a kid with a new toy, thought Hadley.

A dog barked not far away, and she turned toward the sound. Across the yard came a black and white mother shepherd, followed by a row of fat puppies colored just like her. Zane laughed.

"Look at that. First time they've gotten this far from the deck that I've seen." He jumped off the Gator and strode toward the dogs. Bending down, he scooped up a puppy, brought it over to Hadley and put it into her arms.

"Sorry. Smells like a puppy." She held it up to her face and it licked her nose. She couldn't help laughing and hugging the fuzzy little creature, enjoying the puppy smell.

"Come on up. We'll just leave the Gator here. I'll move it later." Hadley climbed down onto the ground and set the squirming puppy down so it could run back to its brothers and sisters, falling and rolling over as it reached them.

The puppies were a squirming mass of black and white fur, but they regained their feet and followed as Zane led Hadley up the path the rest of the way to the house.

After they'd both quickly showered, and Hadley had changed back into her skirt and top, Zane gave her a tour of the house.

Everywhere, she saw touches of his mother's personality. Pictures of Zane as a little boy, and of the whole family, remnants of their life.

She wondered how Natalie had felt visiting this house. Mère had been here. She might have sat in that chair or walked down these steps.

Hadley stood, trying to feel Mère's spirit. What had she been thinking? Had she really considered coming back here and living with Sonny?

Hadley shook her head slowly. If she had, Mère had harbored needs and dreams that her daughter had never suspected. Mère had known what love was after all. She'd experienced it. Unlike her daughter.

Hadley followed Zane back outside to the deck and settled into a cushioned chair, a glass of wine in her hand, relaxed and comfortable. Zane walked around to the back of her chair and put his big hands on her shoulders, then slowly bent down until his lips were almost touching her ear. She shivered at his closeness.

"Hungry?" he asked in a whisper. She jerked in surprise, then sunk back down, laughing. Yeah, she was hungry, and for more than food.

"What are you serving?" He'd walked back around to stand in front of her. She smiled up at him.

"Well…" He seemed to consider. "I just happen to have a salad in the refrigerator."

"Come on. I need more than salad." She grinned at him and he shrugged.

"I told you I'd take you to see the fireworks. Did you think I'd let you go hungry? I am prepared to cook you dinner."

He shooed a puppy off the deck. "They can come up after we've eaten. Not now."

Zane started up the charcoal grill, then disappeared into the kitchen, returning with a tray of fish filets and onions and peppers, which he placed on a special rack to cook.

"Caught this fish this morning. It's really fresh."

"This morning?" You were up early, Zane Bowman."

"Couldn't sleep last night. Had something on my mind."

"Really? I slept like a baby." Hadley crossed her legs and held out her wine glass for a refill.

He brought out plates and silverware to set the table, and a chilled salad, and they ate, watching the sunset deepen.

"When do the fireworks start?" Hadley savored her last bite of fish. Just at that moment, they saw a single streak explode in the sky by the dam. Grabbing her hand, he pulled her over to a deep cushioned double lounge.

"You have to watch the fireworks from down here. The angle is just right."

He took her wine glass out of her hand and set it with his on a nearby table, then pulled her against his shoulder. With a sigh, she cuddled closer.

Another blast streaked high into the sky and exploded in a rainbow of colors. She knew the dam was far away, but the fireworks flew so high that they seemed to burst directly overhead.

Somehow Hadley fit perfectly into the curve of Zane's arms. She inhaled the sunshine smell of his golden tanned skin. He smelled like summer. And not a Paris summer, but an Oklahoma lake summer.

As his smell engulfed her, so did a wave of desire, languid, then so hot and intense, so primal, that she caught her breath. He must have felt it too, for he turned and brushed her lips with his, a butterfly touch, but she felt her body respond, her nipples harden.

She turned in his arms and saw his eyes darken with desire. The muscles in his arm around her shoulders tensed as he drew her closer, until they were breathing the same air.

She sighed as she sought out his neck, and licked instinctively, tracing the contours of it, just a tiny lick, then a nibble. She raised her head as he shuddered and captured, her mouth.

No longer satisfied with just a touch, she welcomed him in a dance of tongues and lips so intense that she didn't even realize when she fell back on the lounge, pinned by Zane's chest.

She wrapped her arms around him, running her hands over the strong warm muscles of has back, pulling him to her, on top of her. He pulled back from the embrace, leaving her panting for more.

Zane looked down at her in wonder. Did Hadley really want him as badly as he wanted her right now? Her striped top was pushed up to partly reveal a perfect breast. She didn't bother to pull it down.

Her full lips slightly parted in a pant as she closed her eyes. God, he hoped she wanted him, because he didn't think he could stop the inevitable.

He nuzzled his mouth to her neck. She caught her breath and wrapped a leg around his. Oh yes. His tongue danced down her neck and lower.

He pushed back the fabric and ravaged that budding breast which seemed to strain to fill his mouth. Just perfect, so sweet and taunt.

Not the buxom almost overblown lushness of the Grand Lake girls he had known before, but the delicate promise of a rose bud, waiting to be opened. Sleek, with the precise curves of a wooden sculpture.

As she reclaimed his mouth, demanding what he was so ready to give her, she breeched the barrier of his shorts, her desire insistent and demanding.

They were one with the night, and the explosions that shook the sky above them were no more powerful than those of their lovemaking as she invited him in and they explored each other's passions.

As the fireworks died from the sky. They slept in each other's arms under the stars, unaware of the puppies that snuggled beside them.

50 The Amber Pendant

She'd didn't see him build the fire in the fire pit on the deck and feed the amber to the flames, but she vaguely remembered him lifting her sometime during the night and carrying her up the log staircase to his room.

She awoke naked beside him on clean white sheets. The window was open and a cool breeze blew over their bodies. With a shiver, she snuggled closer for warmth.

His arm snaked around her and pulled her close. He didn't open his eyes, but his lips touched hers and she melted into him.

"Oh Zane. I really have to get going." Hadley's eyes opened wide this time. The sun shinned in the window. The day was heating up. She jumped out of bed and reached for her clothes.

"I could make you breakfast." Zane stood and stretched.

"Oh." She turned to him, smiling, then stood on her tiptoes and kissed him. "Zane, I can't. I'm sorry, but can you take me back to my boat? I have so much to do."

She stood there a minute taking him in. He was a beautiful creature and she wanted to remember every inch, every kiss, every whisper.

But she had a plane to catch and she was running late. She grabbed her shoes and ran down the stairs, calling back, "Please hurry Zane. I'm have to go. I'm so sorry."

The Gator had never been moved the night before, and they jumped aboard and headed down the trail. Zane knew the cows were hungry, but mentally promised them he's be back as quickly as he could. They stood by the fence staring at him with big, hungry docile eyes as he drove off.

Zane stashed the Gator in the shop and they jumped into the Sea Skiff and headed out across the lake. It was a beautiful morning. And he just had to ask.

"Ever thought about living anywhere but Paris, Hadley?" he asked.

"No." She laughed lightly. "Paris is my home. It's where my business is." She peeked over at him.

"Ever think about living anywhere but Grand Lake, Zane?" It was his turn to advert his gaze.

"I love Grand Lake and this is where I live, and where I plan to keep living."

"I see."

"I mean, I have traveled a bit. I do race boats, you know, and I've placed in some races abroad. Their small talk turned sad. Zane was having a hard time just letting her walk away.

"Do you think you might come back to visit some time?"

She looked at him for a while, seeming to consider. "We'll see, Zane. We'll see." Her answer did not sound promising.

"And you, Zane, you could visit me in Paris."

"I just might do that, Hadley." And he might, he thought, but once she got back into her own world, would he really be welcome? How would he know?

So he took her to her boat. He offered to help her get her things together, but she insisted that everything was already packed into her car. Well, that sounded final.

He kissed her goodbye. As on that first day, she stood there watching him leave, but this time, he motored away slowly, looking back several times and waving.

She could feel tears start to flow down her cheeks. She stood there until he disappeared out of sight, then hurried back to shower, pack her last bags and lug them to the car.

She had lied to him. If he had stayed to help, she wasn't sure she'd have been able to leave. She laid the cane out where Zane would find it. She'd never remembered to give it back.

She looked up at the hummingbird nest. The little ones were visible now moving around up there. The mama zipped over Hadley's head toward them.

"Well, little brown mama, your babies will fly away soon." As she watched the tiny family, she realized that she had just been pushed out of her nest. She was flying alone now. All alone.

Her future had always been so clear. She'd always known what she wanted. Like Mère. But what if Mère hadn't? What if, having experienced love, she hadn't really been able to let it go? Hadley slid closed the door to her boat, deep in thought.

Hadley actually arrived in Tulsa early. Then, when she checked her flight, it had been delayed. It wouldn't leave for hours, but she was glad to be away from the lake, from Zane. Yes she was glad. She was.

She hadn't felt like eating that morning, so after she texted Violette her new itinerary, Hadley stopped in a small shopping center that had an attractive sandwich shop.

She ordered a vegetarian sandwich on whole wheat and coffee. Sitting in a booth near the front of the shop, she noticed an art gallery across the parking lot from her. She had time to kill. Just as well stroll through it and see what native Oklahoman artists were producing, she decided.

After finishing her sandwich, she crossed the parking lot and peeked into the window of the gallery. Beautiful pieces. A special exhibition featured carved wood. She opened the door and went inside to examine the work more closely. The wood was so smooth, she wanted to run her finger down the grain. The artist was truly talented.

Zane finished up taking care of the cows and stepped into the shower, letting hot water run through his hair and down his body. He hurt all over.

The fact that she had walked out of his life was crushing him. And he had let her. But what could he do? What would stop her from leaving?

He'd thought maybe last night…. But she didn't believe in love. He needed more time, but time was what he didn't have.

So she had walked away, was leaving forever. And there was nothing he could do. He stood there letting the hot water mix with his tears.

Or might there be a way? He stepped out of the shower, grabbed a towel and rubbed hard as the gears of his mind started to turn. She wasn't ready to make a drastic change in her lifestyle. She didn't believe in love.

But he did. He loved Hadley. So he had to be the one. He had to show her what it was like to be loved, he had to do something, and he knew what that was. There was a way, and he was ready.

Zane stepped into his bedroom and pulled on his clothes, then rummaged in the pocket of his dirty shorts for his phone. He looked up Hadley's number and paused, his thumb on the dial button.

"Would you like a brochure of our featured artist?" An attractive, dark-haired, impeccably dressed woman approached from a back room and handed her a slick folded brochure. Hadley accepted it graciously, and slid it into her purse. Maybe she'd look through it on the plane.

As she left the gallery her phone rang. She pulled it out of her purse and saw Zane's name displayed. She considered not answering it.

That would be easiest, but could she live the rest of her life not knowing what he might have said to her? She touched the answer button.

"Hadley!"

"Zane?"

"You're still here!"

"Yes. I'm in Tulsa. Is something wrong? Is Sonny alright?"

"Oh, yes. I guess so. I haven't seen him today. Listen, when does your flight leave? Are you at the airport?" She paused, considering if telling the truth was the right thing to do.

"Well, no. My flight was delayed."

"Good!"

"Well, really not so good. I won't get home until late tomorrow."

"Let's have dinner."

"Oh Zane. Is that really a good idea?" She was tempted. So tempted. "We've said goodbye. Is there really anything else to say?"

"Yes, I mean, yes. Hadley, say you'll see me. Here, I'll give you the address. I won't be there for a while, but why don't you turn in your rental car and take a taxi and I'll get you back to the airport in plenty of time.

"By the time you do that and have a glass of wine, I'll be there. I'm already on my way. I'm in the truck. Please, Hadley."

She shook her head, listening to him. But she had hours until her plane left. That was the excuse she used to convince herself. It wasn't that she couldn't leave without seeing Zane again. Not at all.

"OK, Zane, what's the address of the restaurant?"

When she arrived, the staff was expecting her. Zane had called ahead and arranged a table, and for them to bring out a bottle of the same wine they'd drunk the night before. Thoughtful. She smiled, thinking of last night under the fireworks and stars.

He wouldn't be here for a few minutes yet. She sipped her wine and enjoyed the view of the Tulsa skyline out the window. The background music was soft jazz.

Good time to look at the brochure she'd crammed into her purse. She dug it out and opened it up. Zane looked out at her from the inside page. She almost choked on her wine.

She looked more closely, holding the brochure to the light of the candle at her table to be sure. It was him.

"Hi there." She looked up, and there he was, standing at the table in person. She looked from the brochure to the man and back again. He slid in beside her, and noticed the brochure in her hand.

He took it from her and opened it up spreading it on the table.

"I don't know where you got this, but it will make things easier." He smiled at her gently.

"I saw the gallery and went in there to see the art. I didn't even look at the brochure until a minute ago, and I almost choked on my wine." She watched him carefully. What was he up to? "So, you're an artist, Zane?" Well that explained the woman's figure she'd seen through the open door of his shop, still as a statue.

He continued to smooth the brochure out on the table, nodding slowly.

A waiter approached. Zane nodded for his wine to be poured, but set the menus aside, and turned to face her.

"Hadley, I've been running from a lot of things. I've been running from my mother's heritage, from anything that wasn't all-American, from a part of myself."

He told her all about his mother then, about the amber about the way he'd felt about her being different when he was a boy, about just how different, and special she was. About the way he'd felt about Hadley when he'd met her.

He fingered the amber pendant hanging around his neck. "They brought this back for me, from Latvia. Dad took her there after the iron curtain fell. They wanted me to go, but I wouldn't. I wish I had."

And he told her about his sculpture, how he had come to it from his work on boats, how wood just seemed to become art when he worked with it. How his agent, the girl at the gallery, wanted to show his work in Paris, and how he'd refused. Because he didn't want to leave Oklahoma.

"But I'm going to do it Hadley." He looked her in the eyes. "I'm going to take my show to Paris." I have to work things out with my dad, make sure the ranch is taken care of, but I'm coming over there. Will you want to see me when I come?"

She nodded her head. Yes, she wanted to see him. She wanted to see him standing in front of the window in her bedroom in the Paris apartment, rumpled after a night in bed with her.

She wanted to cook breakfast for him and sit at the counter and plan their day. Suddenly, Paris, the apartment, life without Mère, seemed possible again.

And suddenly she began to understand why Mère had come back to find Sonny. Sonny. She smiled. Had she really thought she'd never see that old man again? And the rest of the Grand Lake gang? She wasn't sure how this was all going to work out, but suddenly she knew it was.

"To us." She raised her glass. Zane looked her steadily in the eye as he raised his glass to the toast.

"To us."

Epilogue

Hadley pressed her shoulder against Zane's, trying to stay dry under the single large umbrella they shared. She loved Paris in the rain as much as she loved Grand Lake in the sunshine, and felt lucky that she had a lifestyle that allowed her to enjoy both.

They stopped under a marquee to peek inside the double stroller to make sure the girls were dry. As she lifted the bubble that protected them, they gurgled at her happily.

She smiled up at Zane, then her eyes darted to a man standing behind him. Zane turned to see who she was looking at. There stood Sonny, a big grin on his face. Zane and Hadley both rushed to embrace him.

"How was your trip, Dad?" Zane checked out his father carefully, anxious about his emotional and physical well-being after the trip to his deceased wife's country.

"Let's find a place to grab a cup of coffee, and I'll tell you all about it." Zane led the way to a nearby café and the family settled into a warm corner to talk.

Hadley lifted her daughters, Natalie and Ivana out and plopped one on each of the men's laps, first checking to make sure their diapers were still dry.

So, How was Latvia, Sonny?"

"Ah, it is the most beautiful place on earth. Next to Grand Lake Oklahoma, of course."

"More beautiful than Paris?"

"More beautiful than Paris, but not more beautiful than you, my dear." He leaned over and gave her a peck on the cheek, balancing himself on his carved wooden cane.

"And your two daughters. I brought all of my beautiful girls a present." Handing Natalie back to her mother, he dug a sack out of the bag he was carrying. Turning it over on the table, he dumped out two tiny amber teething necklaces.

"I think your grandmother Ivana would want her girls to have these." As he dangled them in front of the girls' eyes, they smiled up at him, showing their dimples, and reached for their new treasures.

Then Sonny pulled a box from his pocket and opened it in front of Hadley. Inside was an exquisite necklace with a carved amber pendant."

She smiled at her husband as she took the necklace from his father. "Now, I have one too."

"Let's get back to the apartment," suggested Zane. "How long are you staying this time Dad?"

"I'm flying to Oklahoma tomorrow." Sonny took the last sip of his coffee. The new building should be finished by now. I hope you both like your workshops."

They both assure him that they were sure they would. And that being able to work in them would make their long stays back in Oklahoma much easier.

"I'll spend more time in Paris next winter, too. When will you guys be able to get away and bring these girls to the lake?"

"Pretty soon. We still have a few lose ends to tie up here. You're probably going to get tired of all of us being loud in your quiet house, but we'll be spending some time on the boat too."

"Don't worry about that. It's just..." He looked at the girls sadly. The corners of his mouth turned down. Zane & Hadley exchanged a look "What is it, Dad. What's wrong?"

"It's just that I'm going to have to wait at least a couple years, I think, to start teaching these little chickens how to skip rocks." He made a face at the babies.

THE END

ABOUT THE AUTHOR

Susan Vineyard is a former university instructor and current technical writer who grew up in Oklahoma but now resides in Brisbane Australia with her husband, Daniel Brown and her three dogs. She has been a writer, in one form or another, since she was a teenager. As the owner of a vintage wooden boat, she is proud to present this fictional story set on Grand Lake, Oklahoma with its unique wooden boat culture.

On the Dock: A Tale of Grand Lake

Susan Vineyard